De
tha...
you work. I
sincerely hope you
enjoy this story
Best,
David

IN
WELLS'
TIME

DAVID NASH

For information contact:
Unsolicited Press
Portland, Oregon
www.unsolicitedpress.com
orders@unsolicitedpress.com
619-354-8005

Cover Design: Kathryn Gerhardt
Editor: S.R. Stewart

ISBN: 978-1-963115-01-7

IN WELLS' TIME

PROLOGUE—LYONIZATION

He walked through the historic neighborhood of Norfolk, Virginia. November had finally arrived. The sticky, oppressive summer had given way to dried, rattling leaves that tumbled off the treetops with each swirling gale. Fall and spring seemed to last forever in Norfolk. The result was a short winter. He appreciated that about the Mid-Atlantic. Most autumn days were pleasant in every way possible. Today, however, was the rare exception. It was gray, cold, and wet. Bone chilling. This man was raised in the frigid winters of the north and would have gladly traded dry and sub-zero for the soggy, wintry air of the Chesapeake Bay, unless he was surfing, of course. Sadly, he was not surfing. He was merely killing time, and what he needed now was a hot cup of coffee.

He had parked his car near an upscale wine bar, leaving himself a bit of a walk through the old neighborhood. He strolled up the road and away from the shining windows of the bustling medical school, a striking contrast to the nearby tired-looking hospital complex. The man looked to be somewhere between twenty or thirty years old but wore an expression of someone with more life experience than his appearance suggested.

On his right, he passed a gastropub, windows dark, trash cans filled with the scraps of high-end versions of a McDonald's menu, brioche buns, and chicken bones. About forty-five seconds later, he walked by the tall stone and stained-glass edifice of a Lutheran church standing proudly and much longer than both the opposing Starbucks and the Chipotle further up the block. Through a speaker mounted high above the street, a bell counted the morning's hours. He liked communities with working clock towers. He thought everyone deserved an interruption to remind them time was passing.

Jumping over a puddle on Baldwin Avenue, he caught the scent of freshly roasted coffee and his mouth watered. His stomach gave a longing groan. He was hungry. It had been fifteen hours since his last meal. He walked up the wooden steps, counting each stair as he went, and entered the toasty home that used to raise a family, but now served as a temporary refuge from the chaos of life.

This is the locals' coffee shop. Here, he will savor a scone, feed his caffeine addiction, and finish the last chapter of Bob Dylan's memoir before starting a new book of poetry.

Can memories like Dylan's, which have been given so much poetic license, be considered a memoir? he thought to himself as he stepped up to the counter. *I guess that's half the fun of Dylan: The timelines don't always meet up. He keeps you guessing.*

The man placed his order and left the change on the counter. He turned to find the chair that had served as his morning refuge the previous week and would continue to do so for a few more days until the hurricane hit. He hung his jacket on the back of the chair.

"Large dark roast and scone for Wells," said the barista with a sincere smile. She had worn that smile since the man's first visit, but now there was a hint of recognition behind it, an unspoken acknowledgment indicating the man, Wells, had moved closer to becoming a "regular."

Everything takes time, he thought.

Wells thanked her and headed back to his unoccupied corner. He set aside his bookmark, a worn polaroid of a red-haired girl looking directly into the camera with a thoughtful stare as if she was asking him right then and there what his next move would be. After a few minutes and five pages of Dylan, he felt a familiar, warm pressure curling around his calf. Wells looked down to see the shop-owner's cat tiptoeing its back hip into his leg, tail raised high as if flagging down a taxi.

"Hey there, Zeeba."

He reached down and ran his hand over the sleek, soft fur. The cat looked up and answered with a gentle meow. She was mostly black but speckled with several large patches of orange and white on her face and body. She is the first calico the man has known, but he has been considering these particular felines' genetics for a while now.

The colored patches of fur are decided by the random inactivation of each skin cell's extra copy of the X chromosome, where there is not only information related to the sex of the animal, but also hair color. If Zeeba were a male with only one X chromosome, this inactivation wouldn't need to occur. Zeeba's cells would be left to express the only sex chromosomes available, just like Wells.

Wells sipped his cappuccino and thought of this genetic minutiae as he scratched the cat behind his ears. His thoughts drifted from his own genetic history and the traits that have skipped down his maternal family tree. He'd been mulling over a question for some time and decided to test it out on the cat.

"Zeeba," Wells said.

The cat had begun to walk toward the next customer but stopped to look back at Wells. The cat's expression implied neither interest nor annoyance but something close to the girl's expression in the photograph.

"If Adam came before Eve, where did his X chromosome come from?"

The cat flicked its tail and walked away without a second thought of the man, his genetics, or his question.

CHAPTER 1: THE FUNERAL

"Thank you, everyone, for being here today."

Charles Monasmith was wearing a black suit that hung loosely from his bony shoulders. The edges of the cuffs were worn-through. He reached into his blazer and pulled out a piece of paper, unfolded it, and smoothed it on the lectern. His hands shook as he fumbled with a pair of cheap reading glasses and balanced them on the tip of his nose. He looked around the room and locked eyes with his wife who gave him a smile and the courage he needed to continue. He had imagined this day many times over the years, but now that it was here, no amount of practice could have prepared him for the task at hand. The sanctuary was big enough to hold nearly four hundred people. Today, it held closer to thirty.

A tall wooden cross hung behind Mr. Monasmith. It was illuminated by the soft golden light peeking through the windows high above the balcony. According to his watch, it was only a little after four o'clock P.M., but the winter sun was already retreating toward the horizon. *The days certainly don't feel like they're getting longer,* he thought. But in spite of everything, they were. It was usually about every two weeks after the equinox that Mr. Monasmith could convince himself there was more sunlight. He caught himself on the verge of a daydream and brought his attention back to his notes, took a deep breath, and continued.

"Wells was our little boy. But he was also a man who lived his own life and had his own stories to tell. I feel truly lucky to have known many of them. You may not know this, but

Margaret and I spoke with him a couple times a week this last year. We had a weekly standing date for coffee at his apartment. And believe it or not, he did tell me what he wanted his funeral to be like if we ever found ourselves in this situation." Mr. Monasmith paused for effect. "He said he wanted us to sneak into the Xcel Energy Center, drill a hole at center ice, and pour his ashes into the rink."

Some smiles lit up the faces in the pews. Monica Monasmith, the oldest of the Monasmith children, looked up from reading an email on her phone and gave an unintentionally disapproving chuckle that said "Of course he did." Her cheeks went pink, and she quickly stifled her laughter when no one else made a sound. Her father continued, not noticing his daughter's reaction.

"I told him there was no way I'd risk getting arrested and breaking a hip just so he could be run over by a Zamboni every day while the Wild crafted another losing season."

The smiles turned to laughter. The sound fueled the amber sunlight and the room seemed to warm up.

"Among other things, he and I did talk a lot about time." Mr. Monasmith paused and swallowed hard as if battling with the next sentence. His eyes began to tear, and he decided to abandon the rest of the speech. "I love you, Wells. Thank you for being my son," he said in a shaky voice.

Mr. Monasmith took off his readers and wiped his eyes with the back of his hand. He steadied himself on the lectern then went to sit by his wife. She put her arm around him while he cried.

The pastor patted Mr. Monasmith's shoulder as he walked up to the front of the sanctuary. He had kind eyes and a permanently amicable expression, one that said "All are welcome here." He spoke using his comforting tone reserved for messages of hope and encouragement as well as loss. The pastor thanked everyone for coming. He spoke to the brevity of life, speaking of time on Earth as a mist that evaporates into the ether only to condense to rejoin the Lord where one day is a millennium and a millennium is one day. He shared that life on Earth is a gift from God, and he was sure Wells was able to enjoy the wonders of God's creation in his own unique way, and, of course, the lives he touched were better because he had been a part of them.

The attendees sang a song. The pastor said a prayer, and, finally, he announced that there was a private family reception to follow at the Monasmith home. The organist played "Amazing Grace" as Mr. and Mrs. Monasmith walked out of the sanctuary and into the foyer, where they hugged and thanked each of the guests.

"That was nice, Dad," Heather said.

"Thanks, sweetie."

The tall, brown-haired woman looked strikingly like her mother, Margaret Monasmith. The Monasmiths had three daughters in addition to their son. Monica was the oldest, then Heather, and after Wells, the youngest was Leslie. Heather straightened out her black cardigan and hugged her father. Behind her stood a man with dark eyes and a warm smile. He shook Charles' hand and gave him a one-armed hug.

"Hey there, Christian," said Mr. Monasmith.

"Nice job, Charles," Christian replied and squeezed his father-in-law's arm.

"Love you, Mom," Heather said, embracing her mother. They held each other for several seconds before letting go.

11

Hugs continued to be exchanged between the mourners until the pastor looked at his watch a third time and told Mr. and Mrs. Monasmith he would help bring the flowers out to the car.

"Do you want them all in your trunk, or would you like to leave a few here for this Sunday's service?" he asked.

"Oh, that sounds nice. Keep a vase or two here. And thank you, Pastor, but you don't have to carry them out; we can do that," Mrs. Monasmith said.

"Hey, Leslie," Monica's voice cut through the crowd toward her sister. Monica was putting on a coat and stuffing her phone into her purse. "Do you have a minute to grab some beer on the way to Mom and Dad's? I forgot to pick some up, and I've got the kids, so, you know." Monica said this as if there wasn't a single thing she could accomplish when the kids were in tow.

Leslie walked over to her oldest sister.

"Sure, no problem. We're probably fine, though. Don't you think?" Leslie said.

"Can you just pick some up, please? I don't want Mom to have to worry about something as silly as having enough beer." The irritation rose close to Monica's surface. Leslie noticed but kept quiet. This was hard on everyone, after all.

"Gotcha. Not a problem. Light beer okay? Or IPA? What does Jack like?"

"I don't care. Sure. IPA is fine. Thanks." Monica took her phone back out of her purse and the screen lit up. "Shit," she murmured. "Four-thirty-five already?"

"It was a pretty quick service," said Leslie.

"Yeah. Not too bad." Monica didn't look up as she spoke and let out a sigh.

Heather walked over from her parents who were now milling about with a few neighbors. "Are you both going straight over?" she asked.

"Yeah, but I just need to grab some beer," said Leslie. She put her arm around Heather and smiled at Christian who was standing to the side. "Christian, you like IPAs, right?"

"Sure do," he said.

"Hey," said Leslie, looking at Heather and pulling her close. "Do you want to ride with me?"

Heather wiped her nose with a tissue. Her lids were puffy and her eyes red. She tried her best to manage a grin.

"No. No. Thanks though," Heather said. "I'll meet you there." Heather looked at Christian. "You ready?"

"Yeah," he said. "I've got the kids in the car. I'll pull it around." He kissed her on the cheek and walked outside.

"How long do you plan on staying?" Monica asked as she looked out the glass doors to the parking lot of the church and saw Jack, her husband, pulling up in a white SUV.

"As long as Mom wants us to, I guess. I don't have any plans. Do you have something else going on?" Leslie asked.

"No. Just some hospital stuff. It can wait. I was just curious." Monica walked over and hugged her parents before walking out of the church, leaving Leslie and Heather behind.

"I can't believe her. 'How long do you plan on staying?' Are you kidding me? Our brother just died for Christ's sake." Heather wiped her nose again, this time trembling from anger instead of sorrow.

"Shh. I know. I know," Leslie said in a comforting tone pulling Heather by the arm. She moved them away from the small cluster of mingling people. "She's always like that. You know how crazy her work is. It must be super stressful. Plus, I think she is probably just processing this differently."

"You mean by not giving a shit?"

"It sure looks that way, doesn't it? Hey, let's just go and support Mom and Dad." Leslie squeezed her sister's shoulder and slid her hand down to rub her back. Heather nodded. "This is just going to be a tough week for everybody. We should be prepared for that. I have a feeling we all are going to need a little grace. And booze."

"Okay. Yeah. I'm sure you're right." Heather chuckled and rubbed her nose again with the tissue. "Ope. Christian is here with the kids. I'll see you over there."

"Sounds good," said Leslie. She waved hello to Christian who was pulling the pale blue minivan up to the door and turned to find her mother who was across the foyer wearing her coat and putting several vases of flowers into a cardboard box. Margaret was just about to slide the overfilled box off the table and into her arms.

"Hey, Mom, let me get that." Leslie trotted over to her mother and lifted the box easily. She still had the athletic build of a college track athlete even though her time spent running had been replaced these days by shifts at a small bookshop and pondering graduate school duties. Margaret, on the other hand, wore her sixty years like eighty. Her mind was sharp, but Leslie could see that the last summer really aged her. But who wouldn't look weary after their son's funeral?

"Thank you, sweetie," said Margaret. "Would you mind putting these in the trunk of your dad's car?"

"Sure. Monica asked me to stop and pick up some beer, but then I'll be right over." Leslie looked at her mother who carried her exhaustion like a heavy winter jacket. "It'll be good to spend some time together this week, Mom."

"I know it will. Thanks for all your help with the service. Your dad and I really appreciate it." Mrs. Monasmith smiled at her and pulled a stray silver hair off the shoulder of her youngest daughter's coat. Leslie didn't notice.

"Of course, Mom. I'll put these in Dad's car and see you back home, okay? Gosh, it's hot in here." Leslie's cheeks were flushed. "Can you just unzip the top of my coat a bit, Mom?"

"Sure. Is that better?"

"Yes, perfect. Thanks." She blew a strand of hair out of her eyes and heaved the box upward. The vases clinked like the handbells used on Sunday morning services. "Okay, see you there."

"Alright. Drive safe." Margaret watched her youngest daughter turn around and back out through the church doors, moving into the fading light of the winter evening. Against her better judgment, she held onto the moment a little longer and slowed the glow of an icy sky surrounding her daughter for just a few seconds. She sighed, took a picture with her mind, and released Leslie into the night.

CHAPTER 2: THE FAMILY

Monica Monasmith and Jack Beha

Monica walked around the front of the white SUV to the driver's side. Jack opened the door, jumped out, and walked around the back of the vehicle to hop in the front passenger seat. Jack fastened his seatbelt and looked back at the kids. The two sisters sat buckled up with faces turned down and illuminated by their tablets. They both wore large brightly colored headphones.

"You girls set to go?" He asked.

Neither girl looked up.

"Helloooo? Everybody ready back there?" Jack snapped his fingers and waved a hand in front of the tablets. The girls batted him away like a mosquito.

"Uh-huh."

"Yes, daddy."

Michelle, the older of the two children, didn't look up. She tapped at the screen of her device, her dark Monasmith hair pushed back behind her ears. Sam's hair was blonde, like her father's, and she had it tied up in a ponytail with a large bow clipped to the crown of her head.

Jack rolled his eyes, shook his head, and turned around.

"I'm not so sure about those tablets. I know school says they're educational, but all they seem to do is turn the kids into zombies." None of the three girls in the car immediately responded to this. It seemed as though he was talking to himself.

"What?" Monica replied ten seconds later without looking up from her phone. Her response was disinterested at best. "I wish they could just function for one day on their own." She shook her head from side to side as she scrolled through her messages.

"Never mind," said Jack. "You just want me to drive?"

"Oh, no. I've got it." She moved the shift lever at her side to the "D" position and pulled out, still reading her email. Jack looked out the passenger window and waved to Charles and the pastor who were chatting in the cold parking lot.

"I hadn't realized how close your parents had gotten to Wells. I mean, I didn't realize they talked to him every week. Sometimes I think you and I barely talk that much."

Monica crinkled her nose and sighed. "Yeah, I guess I didn't realize that either." Jack wasn't sure if she was envious of this tidbit or distracted. He thought of Monica as the most independent of the Monasmith children but also knew her relationship with her parents leaned more toward formality than friendship. Her feelings toward Wells were tense at best.

"When was the last time you talked to Wells?" Jack asked. "He stopped over a week or so ago to see the girls, but you were at the hospital."

"Hmm. Must have been Christmas, right? At Mom and Dad's?"

"No. It was just your sisters there. Wells was feeling under the weather, I think. Right?"

"Well, then I'm not sure when it was." Monica paused. "Oh, I know. It was last summer. We saw him around July fourth. I remember because he'd been back in town for a few months, and Mom and Dad really wanted us to all be together for lunch." Jack heard the annoyance in her voice and remembered where the story was going. "Remember? It dragged on so long, by the time we'd gotten back to Madison, we'd missed the introduction to the medical foundation banquet. We had a sitter lined up for that for weeks."

"We'll make it this year, I'm sure."

"We better." There was a short clip in her voice.

Monica left that summer lunch with her brother livid and was in a tirade the entire ride to the gala after speeding away from her parents. Jack listened as she ranted, listing complaint after complaint about how she was supposed to drop everything in her life any time her delinquent brother, who could barely hold a respectable job and likely had a drug problem, strolled back into town. Monica's words were laced with resentment. Jack knew he was collateral damage in this hell storm and took the stray bullets willingly.

"Everything is just so easy for him. And it's always been that way. He loafed through school and got straight As. He practically missed his SATs by sleeping in and still pulled off an insanely good score, and then he doesn't even finish college when the rest of us are cruising around, working our asses off…" This went on and on. Jack cracked the window to lessen the blow of the anger.

Ironically, Jack had thought the lunch at Monica's parents had gone pretty well. He admitted Wells had a habit of being a bit aloof over the years, and sure, some things came easy to him. But over this last year, Wells really seemed to have changed from the picture-taking surfer he'd known in the past. More recently, Jack was impressed by how present Wells was in each conversation. He was quickly becoming his favorite of the Monasmith children, besides Monica, of course.

The car jolted and the kids bobbled as Monica bumped a curb.

"Hey!" the girls said in unison.

"My bad," Monica said, lifting her eyes from her phone.

"Really, honey. Can't you just put that down for one second?"

"Don't even start, Jack." Monica's tone went from irritated to furious in a fraction of a second. "When you begin making all the money for this family, and are responsible for the education of half of the residents in the hospital, *and* have your own set of patients on the verge of dying, then you can ask me to 'put that down.'"

"Hey. I'm sorry. Just, can you at least try not to answer emails and drive when the kids are in the car? It'll be a lot harder to take care of those residents and your patients *and* your children if we careen off the road."

Monica didn't respond. She turned the car into her parents' neighborhood. The streetlights were now on, and a light snow was falling softly beneath the glow covering up the gray sidewalks.

Heather and Christian Belsfield

"Hey. Are you gonna be okay? You want me to take you home for a bit before heading over? You could just come when you're ready."

Christian leaned across the center console of the minivan and put his arm around Heather. The moment she sat in the passenger seat, she began to cry again. Christian held her and rocked slowly. She hated when she got emotional, but loved that he was always quick to comfort her.

Her emotions had always been a guide for her actions. If she needed to laugh, she called her best friend Rosie on the phone who was quick to tell a dirty joke. If she needed to cry, she watched the clip of Anne Hathaway singing "I Dreamed a Dream." If she needed to feel loved, she leaned into Christian or laid on her kids' beds when they were sleeping. They still were young enough that they rolled into her as opposed to pushing her away. Today, she just needed to be sad. Sad for her brother. Sad for her parents. Sad for her family as this loss tested the strength of their connections by highlighting their differences.

"It's okay, Mommy," said Mary from the middle row of the van. Even though she had just turned six years old, her awareness of others' feelings, especially her mother's, was second to none. Heather cherished this about her oldest daughter and imagined it could be something that binds them throughout their lives.

"Do you want my juice, Mama?" asked Adrienne. The four-year-old reached her hand forward, offering the magenta sippy cup.

"Oh, that's sweet, baby, but I'll be fine." Heather tried to look happy. "Mommy's just a little sad, but I'll be okay." The juice offering had cheered her up enough to keep her going for now. *Sometimes that's all you need*, she thought. *An offering of juice to a four-year-old was akin to a year's worth of mortgage forgiveness from the bank.*

Maya, the almost two-year-old, was already unconscious in the rear-facing car seat. Heather turned to Christian who was now holding her hand.

"No. I'll be okay. Let's go. The girls will want to play with Sam and Michelle, and I want to be there for Mom."

"Okay. If you're sure." Jack straightened up, brushed his wife's hair out of her face, and put the car in drive. Heather shoved the used Kleenex in her coat pocket and pulled out a fresh one to dry her nose. She turned over her phone to check the time and saw the photo of the girls and Wells playing on the living room floor, taken just two weeks ago. She liked the shot so much she set it as her background. It was so nice to see him, even if it was for such a short visit.

Seeing her younger brother was always such a relief. To Heather, he was like a son she never had. Always running away. Always consumed with his own projects and adventures. She knew family wasn't his highest priority. Or, at least, he didn't hold his family as close as she tried to. He definitely didn't intentionally carve out time for them, at least not until recently. He was younger though, and seeking adventure. She could understand that even though it hurt when he didn't always come back for holidays. Still, when he returned, her mothering love for him absolved him of his preference for distance from the family. Losing him so young made it all the worse, especially when it seemed like he finally might be changing. But now it was too late.

"Your mom seems to be doing alright, don't you think? It's your dad who might need more support."

"I know. She's always been the collected one. I sure didn't inherit that," Heather joked.

"Did it surprise you to hear your dad say they talked to Wells a couple times a week?"

"I mean, I knew they talked every now and then and even went over there a bit. But, yeah, I didn't think it was that often. Wells has always been so hard to get in touch with."

"Yeah, not as much as the last couple months, though. He's been, I mean, he was great at visiting the girls. But yeah, he doesn't... didn't call or text much."

"I miss Uncle Wells, Mommy," said Mary, reminding her parents the kids were always listening.

"Is he going to be at Grandma's?" asked Adrienne.

"He's with God, Adrienne, remember?" Mary said with an assuredness only children have when speaking about religion.

"No, sweetie, Uncle Wells won't be at Grandma's," Christian said as he looked at Heather. She had turned to the passenger window, hands held to her face. "I miss him, too, girls. Maybe we can tell funny stories about Uncle Wells when we get there, okay?"

"Like his stinky farts?" giggled Mary.

"Yay! Stinky farts!" shouted Adrienne.

"Yes, that is a perfect story to tell at Grandma's," said Christian. He heard his wife laugh and cry as the girls chanted "Stinky farts! Stinky farts!" all the way to Grandma's house.

Leslie Monasmith

Leslie Monasmith started the ignition of her faded, blue Toyota Corolla. The ignition turned over and gave its familiar whine.

"Thatta' girl." Leslie patted the dash and then buckled her seatbelt. She clapped her mittens together a few times to warm her fingers. The temperature gauge in her car read eighteen degrees for a split second before falling to seventeen. She always thought falling temperatures were the pessimistic ones, feeling about ten degrees colder than they read. But the cold had its silver linings, too, and she wasn't about to curse the cold for being what it was meant to be.

She turned out of the church parking lot onto Main Street and made her way to the river road that led to her parents' house. At the stoplight, she pressed play on the cd player and saw the words "track three" flash on the screen. A half second in and the piano began to play. Full. Soothing. A single chord. A half second more and Regina Spektor's voice rang as smooth and jarring as vanilla-infused Russian vodka. It was a song about a woman who loved a man with demigod strength and the love that could have been had his hair not been cut.

She sighed. Wells had always given music recommendations to Leslie. He'd send text messages or emails. Once or twice she'd even woken up to a CD on her doorstep.

"Leslie, check out so-and-so. I think you'll really like them. Listen to track seven first, then start at the beginning. Love, Wells."

He was almost always right, too. His music choices resonated with her, calling out like a lone voice in a tunnel. And if she didn't connect to the music right away, she often found herself circling back and finding the recommendations grew on her over time. As a matter of fact, this CD was from over a decade ago when she was in grade school. She didn't start to like it until last summer when she finished college and was trying to decide whether to go to grad school or just keep working at the bookstore. She still hadn't listened to his most recent gift. He had just stopped by to drop off the album of an up-and-coming Twin Cities musician called Humbird. Leslie liked that name for the way it sounded similar to a noise she made when she felt particularly comfortable. That day, he handed it to her on her doorstep, and she took a selfie with her brother.

That was the last time she saw him. It felt longer than just two weeks. That duality of him feeling closer than he was at any point in time was always true. Even though he was her older brother and their lives never seemed to run at the same pace, she felt a connection to Wells that, even now, lingered after his sudden passing.

Leslie kept driving further south, and Regina's vocals emptied into the car through the speakers. Her mind slipped into the song's story.

"Oh crap," she laughed as she said it. She had almost forgotten the beer. She switched lanes and turned away from her parents' neighborhood. There was a liquor store not too far down the highway that crossed the river and led back into Wisconsin. Any sign of daylight was quickly fading in the southeast to wake in someone else's sky.

Leslie pulled into the liquor store parking lot and put the car in park. She turned the volume up and rolled the window down, feeling the swirling, mixing air currents of the warm car and the biting night, now only fifteen degrees. She leaned her head out of the window and exhaled, blowing plumes of smoke that vanished into the darkness.

"Mist," she said, recalling the pastor's message. She wasn't sure how she felt about religion. Her parents raised her in that very church, but these days, any conversations about God left her with more unanswered than answered questions. She trusted the weather. She trusted the taste of a glass of wine. She even trusted in the inherent good in most people. She didn't think she could trust a text that had layers of outdated cultural context which often seemed to go so against her morals and instincts. At least, not yet.

The next song began with a baseline that brought her back from the ether to a solid state, and she remembered the beer. She rolled up the window, shut off the engine, and headed inside.

Leslie was filling up a green basket with an assortment of beer she thought would satisfy Monica when she felt a tap on her shoulder.

"Leslie? I thought that was you."

Leslie turned to the tapping hand and saw a familiar face with strawberry cheeks and chocolate hair sneaking out of a floppy stocking cap.

"Oh my gosh, no way!" Leslie leaned in and hugged her old high school friend. "Sara, how are you?" At one time, Sara Hannon had been one of Leslie's best friends. During the summer between eighth and ninth grade, they had twelve consecutive sleepovers. Records for both of their families. They became experts at making bracelets, playing "would you rather," and sneaking out at night to ride bikes down the deserted, lamplit streets of their hometown.

"Oh, good, you know. How about you? I almost didn't recognize you with your hair. It looks great."

Leslie brushed back some of her silver-streaked dark hair. "Oh, thanks. I can't stop the gray, I guess, so I'm just letting it fly." Leslie stared at Sara who looked back at her the way old friends do, but the glance didn't linger that fraction of a second that indicates there might be something more. Those moments always left Leslie feeling alone in her small hometown, but she had become accustomed to shaking them off in a heartbeat.

"It's natural? Wow. Well, it looks great. I was so sorry to hear about your brother," Sara said.

"Oh, thanks. That's actually why I'm here. At the liquor store, I mean. I'm picking up some stuff for the family." She lifted up the basket to show her haul.

"Well, I'm really sorry. He was so young."

"Yeah. Thank you, Sara."

"Where are you living these days? Weren't you up in the cities?"

"Yeah. Still am. I'm trying to figure things out, I guess. I'm just working at a bookstore for now. I thought about more school for a bit, but I don't really know what I'd do with it. I kinda just want to work for a bit, you know? I'm in no rush."

"Ugh. Yeah, I hear you. I bet the cities are fun though." Sara had a longing in her voice that Leslie wished was directed at her and not the destination.

Ten minutes later and fully caught up on the recent Hannon family history, Leslie walked out of the liquor store and put four six packs of India Pale Ale into the back seat of her car and drove toward her mother and father's house, listening to the song "20 Years of Snow" while flurries danced around streetlights like moths.

The depth of the blue in the sky and the darkness enclosing the town was so numbing it was almost warm. Leslie drove the long way home to swing by her old grade school. She passed the outdoor ice rink where she spent evenings with other teens playing boot hockey. Tonight, a lone figure was skating hard up and down the ice, taking shots into an empty chain link net.

She slowed the car to a stop and put it in park to watch as the skater raised their hands after scoring on a breakaway. The empty lot around the rink might as well have been filled with thousands of fans and television crews. Her grin widened at the goal as she imagined the roaring crowd and the goalie slumped on the ice in defeat.

Leslie reached to the back seat and pulled out a can, cracked it open, and took a long sip of the sweet, hoppy beer. She watched the snow sprinkle down on the rink. The player turned sharply around at center ice, pumped toward the net, and scored with another impressive move. Leslie swallowed another mouthful, rolled down the window, and shouted into the night sky.

"Woooo! Nice shot!"

The player looked up, startled. By the shrug of the skater's shoulders, Leslie could tell they were a little embarrassed, but they raised an arm in salute anyway. She squinted her eyes and watched the skater's speed slow to a crawl, moving at a turtle's pace, impossibly slow, arm frozen in the air. She absorbed the scene just as a sponge soaks up water. Leslie lifted her beer and the skater sped up again. She drained the can in a few long gulps, stashed the empty under the front seat, and shifted the gear to drive, knowing she should get a move on. Monica was likely going nuts about the delayed beverage delivery.

Margaret and Charles Monasmith

Margaret and Charles Monasmith drove out of the church parking lot. Neither spoke. The crystal flower vases in the back of the Subaru clinked together as the car clipped the curb.

"Ope, sorry." Charles glanced into the rear-view mirror at the white lilies packed tightly in the boxes and thought of his youngest daughter and the few streaks of gray in her hair. Minnesota Public Radio played in the background. The announcer was recapping news from across the world. News that seemed so distant from the funeral they had just attended.

"The World Health Organization states extra measures and precautions need to be taken in Wuhan Province where cases of the novel coronavirus have reached four thousand five hundred and fifty-four deaths." Charles pressed the search button and it turned to the classical station where Vivaldi's "The Four Seasons" danced on the airwaves. He cleared his throat and looked over to his side where Margaret sat staring out the window. He couldn't have known it, but except for the silvery hair, she looked almost exactly like their middle daughter, Heather, in this moment.

"You did it again, didn't you? When Leslie was walking out the door?"

Margaret let out a sigh but didn't turn. "Yes."

"I know I can't stop you. But please, could you just…?" He pulled back, choosing not to finish the question. It was no use asking her, once again, to stop. It clearly had never worked before. He knew he was being selfish, but for Pete's sake, she was his wife. He wanted her to be with him as long as possible. "Was it worth it?"

"It was, but I *am* sorry." She tilted her head as she said it wearing an expression somewhere between apology and happiness. "Did you see her hair?"

"I did. She's been doing it, too, I suppose." Charles turned the car down their street in the little town. "Do you think she knows?"

28

"Maybe, but I don't think so. At least, I don't think she's put a name to it."

"We have to tell them… the kids," Charles said. "We should have told them a long time ago."

"Yes." Margaret turned to look back out the window. She felt tired. She felt guilty and ashamed. But what were they to do in a situation like this? She had meant to talk to the rest of their kids long ago, definitely before the grandchildren came along. But how do you start that conversation? One so unbelievable. So unprovable.

When Heather got married and Monica got engaged shortly thereafter, she tried to sit down with all of the girls before her oldest started having children of her own. Margaret wanted to give them the opportunity to make the most informed decision about having kids. There were other options of course, adoption or fostering. Margaret had never regretted having children, but she didn't really understand the implications of everything about her family history until well after all of hers were born. And besides, Wells was not around very much until more recently. She wanted him to be there when she told his sisters. Margaret told herself he was the only one who could really help answer all of the questions. The other children might not even believe her unless he showed them how it worked. But he was hard to nail down and get to commit to anything. He was traveling the country and would only touch base with a phone call every few months. And Leslie was still so young. There were certainly many readily available excuses to choose from.

In hindsight, she realized one thing was for certain, the longer she waited to have hard conversations, the harder it was to start them and the weaker the excuses needed to be to keep those conversations at bay.

Chapter 3: The Reveal—Leslie

Leslie parked in front of her parents' house. It looked cozy, like a candlelit lantern sitting on the snow-covered lawn. The windows blazed with a warm, yellow glow, and she could see the girls in the living room jumping on the couches. Heather carried a glass of wine to Monica. Jack and Christian were moving toward the kitchen with her father. Leslie walked to the mailbox and brushed the fresh layer of snow off the top with the sleeve of her coat. She grabbed the mail, a few bills and one heavy manilla envelope addressed to her parents, stuffed it in the brown paper bag that carried the beer, and walked into the house.

"Beer here! Get you ice cold beer here!" Leslie shouted as she kicked off her shoes. From the living room at her right, Monica furrowed her brow in annoyance which Leslie interpreted as her sister's way of saying "Took you long enough."

Jack came over and took the bag from her. "Right now, you're my favorite Monasmith."

"Aw, thanks, Jack," Leslie said. "I bet you say that to all the Monasmith women."

"Just the important ones." He nudged her with his elbow and gave her a wink as he walked to the kitchen.

She hung up her coat and followed Jack to the kitchen. Her mind felt fuzzy from the beer at the ice rink. She felt as warm as the house looked. If she hadn't just been to her brother's funeral, Leslie would have thought she was coming home for Christmas. The buzz wrapped her up like a soft blanket and she couldn't help but grin. Yes, it is sad to lose a family member, but glancing around, seeing the children playing, Heather sitting at the table trying to get Maya to eat pulled pork, the dads talking in the kitchen, she felt fortunate that she had family who were able to even be in the same room together on a day like today. Oftentimes, it was tragic events like these that tore families apart.

"Oh, this smells amazing, Mom." Leslie peered over Margaret's shoulder who was turning over the meat.

"Hey. We thought we'd lost you. You didn't need to stop and get beer. We were fine," said Margaret.

"Sorry. I ran into Sara Hannon at the store, and we caught up."

"Oh. How is she doing? You two were so close growing up." Margaret handed an empty paper plate to Leslie.

"She's good. Mmm. Yes, please." Leslie filled the plate with smoky-sweet pulled pork, baked beans, and iceberg lettuce salad and walked to the table where Heather and Maya sat. "Oh, Mom, I grabbed the mail for you. It's in the bag with the beer. Did you want one, Heather?"

"Oh no, I've got water, thanks." Heather was losing the battle at keeping her daughter's hands clean as Maya was more interested in painting the table with the barbecue sauce than eating it. "Two-year-olds and barbecue. We should be eating in the bathtub."

Leslie watched her sister try to re-fasten the bib on Maya. Heather had always been so caring. She was the one who consoled Monica when she broke up with her high school boyfriend at the end of senior year. And it was Heather who vouched for Leslie's innocence when she wrecked her parents' car. And it was *also* Heather who spent the most time watching

Wells when a babysitter was needed. Monica may have been the oldest and typical first child in terms of achievements, but it was Heather who mothered them all. And now, Leslie saw how that love of caring for others had been directed toward her children.

A few drops of wine splashed onto the table, and the honeysuckle notes of the pinot grigio danced around Leslie's nose as Monica plopped heavily down in the chair and huffed.

"Sorry," Monica said absentmindedly, wiping the small spill up with a napkin. She brought the glass to her lips and took a long sip. Leslie thought she noticed her spit some of the wine back into the glass.

Must not live up to her standards, Leslie thought.

"How's work been?" Heather asked.

Monica was always high-strung, but things had been pretty tense even before their brother's passing. Leslie watched Heather and noted how she was always good at getting straight to a person's stressor in a way that didn't presume anything, but prompted the person to open up in an unrestricted way.

"Ugh. Crazy. I'm up to my ears in shit... Oh, stuff. Sorry," Monica said, looking at baby Maya before continuing, barely missing a beat. Leslie saw Heather wince, but didn't think Monica caught it. "The residents are such whiny little..." Monica caught herself this time, looking at her niece, "...babies. They are magnets for drama. Half of them run around hooking up with each other, and then I'm the one who hears about it when it inevitably ends in disaster and causes issues at midnight while on call. Not to mention, I literally have their parents writing me emails vying for awards or better hours. You name it."

"That sounds draining," Heather said. "I don't know how you do it."

Sam, Monica's younger daughter, walked up to the table and handed a tablet to her mother. "Mommy, help," she whined. "It isn't working."

Leslie watched Monica grab the device from her daughter, tap the screen, and press a button on the side. A low battery symbol flashed on the black surface. "Sorry, kiddo. It's dead. Go watch your sister's."

"Okay," Sam said in a little whimpering voice that she paired with a quivering lip. Leslie thought it was cute and likely mostly for show. Sam's eyes sure didn't look like the tears were starting to well. Sam turned back to the living room, but not before slapping a half-eaten pickle on the table. "Here, mommy. I don't want this." She ran off to find her sister.

"I know you like the responsibility you've gained at work, but is it really worth all the stress? You sound unhappy," Leslie said. Leslie didn't feel there was much need to beat around the bush when talking to her oldest sister.

A sour expression spread across Monica's face, and she closed her eyes. "Excuse me." She stood up and rushed from the table, leaving Heather and Leslie there.

"What? I thought that was a fair question." Leslie was taken aback.

"You know how she is, Leslie." Heather looked at her younger sister reproachingly. "Maybe just give it a rest right now, okay?"

"I didn't mean to piss her off. I just don't know what you gain when you're so stressed all the time."

"I know. I know." Heather stood up. "Can you watch Maya for a sec?"

"Sure thing." Leslie watched as Heather followed Monica down the hall toward the bathroom. She heard Heather knock on the door.

"Your mother has always been the one to try and take care of us, Maya. Did you know that?" Maya looked at Leslie and puffed out her cheeks, her face slathered with barbecue sauce.

CHAPTER 4: THE REVEAL—MONICA

"Fuck. Fuck. Fuck." Monica cupped some water from the faucet. She put her hands to her mouth, swished the water around, and spat. Some foods were easy to identify after throwing them up. Pulled pork sandwiches was not one of them. She scooped what she could out of the sink and flung it in the toilet, and then pushed the rest down the drain with her fingers.

"Fuck," she spat again and glared at her reflection. Beads of sweat glistened on her forehead. Her pale northern winter complexion was all the more ashen. The nausea had passed, but she still felt like shit.

There was a soft knock on the door, followed by a gentle voice from the hallway.

"Hey," said Heather. "Are you okay in there?" Heather was using her concerned mothering voice. Monica clenched her jaw. She was the oldest, not Heather.

"Um. Yeah, I'm fine. I'll be out in a second," Monica said.

There were about fifteen seconds of pregnant silence that followed before Heather spoke again.

"You know," Heather's voice paused. Monica could tell she was deciding whether or not to proceed. "Leslie didn't mean to upset you. You know how she is. She just says what's on her mind. We all see how hard you work. Everything you do is amazing."

At first, Monica wasn't sure what her sister was talking about. Then it occurred to her. Heather thought she had stormed away, pissed off at Leslie's question. She thought her feelings were hurt, but Monica had been barely listening to the conversation at the table. Her mind didn't have room for much more today.

When Monica Monasmith woke up this morning, her first thought was of the funeral and that her only brother was dead. She was sad her brother had died, even if she felt she hadn't known him that well. He had stopped by more in the last few months to see Michelle and Sam, which was nice. But other than that, he mostly came up in text messages from her parents. "Wells is in town again," or "We talked to Wells last night. He says hello."

Say hello yourself, jackass, Monica had thought to herself when reading that last text. But of course it was still sad, losing a family member. Twenty-eight is so young, after all. The saddest part was acknowledging that she really didn't know who Wells was anymore. They just weren't that close. When they were little, they giggled, wrestled, and imagined entire new worlds together, but by the time she was in high school, and then college, and then medical school followed by residency, they were totally different people and the gap between them had grown into a canyon. Not to mention she had always been irritated by his nonchalant way of getting through life. He could procrastinate until the very last minute and still seem to pull off decent grades, land a cool job as a photographer, and travel the country as a bachelor without children dragging him down. Maybe her irritation stemmed from jealousy. Maybe her career success came with regrets. She preferred not to follow this train of thought too deeply.

Her ruminations continued swerving from her life choices to focusing on how, as the older sister, she could have reached

out more, but there were the kids and Jack and work and…
That's when the second line of thought entered her mind this
morning. It started with a familiar sensation. A feeling you
never forget once you've felt it. Like a cocktail mixed with one
part deja vu and one part premonition. She lay in bed and felt
the dial in her senses begin to turn up. Her eyes were closed,
but she could tell the light was on in the bathroom by the foot
of their bed. She could smell Jack's cologne that hadn't
completely washed off in his shower last night. She felt her body
begin to tingle. The sheets were cold, and her breasts felt sore.
She'd had this feeling two times before. She opened her eyes.
The house was quiet, and she was pregnant.

"Fuck," she whispered into the early morning stillness.

"I'm gonna go check on Maya, but I can come back and
check on you if you want." Heather was still at the door. Her
voice pulled Monica back from the reverie and into the
bathroom.

"No. I'm fine. Thank you." Monica rolled her eyes at her
sister behind the door. She came to the bathroom to puke in
peace. If she wanted company, she would have thrown up on
the kitchen table.

"Okay. I think we are all going to chat in the living room,
so just come and join us when you're ready."

Monica heard Heather's footsteps fading away. She
inspected her face in the mirror. Her color was returning to her
cheeks. She felt stupid. *I am a fucking doctor, and I still can't keep
track of my cycle. Why didn't we get Jack fixed like we talked about?*
In that bathroom, a litany of conversations ensued in her head.
*Should I tell Jack? Of course. Unless we don't end up keeping it.
No. I have to tell him. We will keep it.* She felt sure of that last
thought. They'd discussed getting rid of pregnancies before, but

in the past had decided it wasn't the choice for them. It was far too late for the morning-after pill. *When was my last period? Shit. It doesn't matter.*

She couldn't help resenting Jack. This would be so easy for him. He wouldn't be sick, rushing for garbage cans in offices, bathrooms in hallways, and coffee mugs in the car. His feet wouldn't swell and his back wouldn't ache. He wouldn't have to feel this growing child's body lengthen, pushing his diaphragm into his lungs so he couldn't breathe and down on his bladder so he had to pee every thirty-five minutes. She could kiss drinking goodbye till Christmas. She'd need to start carrying spare underwear again for any time she accidentally sneezed too hard.

Yeah, this will be great, she thought.

And then there was work. Everything would be harder. Everything. With Michelle, she had plans to breastfeed and pump for a year. *Nope. Try two months. I can't pump in the hospital. For one, they're designed by men, so there is no convenient place to do it, and two, I barely eat and drink enough on call as it is, let alone enough to sustain a healthy supply.* Also, she hated carrying around the pump, not to mention sitting in one place, plugged into the thing while she could be rounding or seeing patients. When she had Sam, she didn't even try. *What's the use?* Most people didn't seem to care, but every once in a while it came up that her infant was drinking formula, and Monica saw the looks. It was bullshit, but when you're a mother, you always notice judging eyes. And you always care, even when you don't.

Monica pushed herself away from the sink and blew out a long breath that frustratingly brought her back to her first Lamaze class, but the breath was long enough to let her shoulders relax and be certain her stomach had settled. Her mind was easing up on the gas now. *Three kids. We're gonna have three kids. We can do this. I can do this. Michelle and Sam are great, and this kid will be, too. I won't have to cut back at work.* She hated missing the kids growing up, but she had worked too hard to go part-time now. *Maybe we can hire a nanny. Or Jack could stay home. We can do this. I can do this.*

She brushed back her hair and touched the outside corner of both her eyes with the pads of her ring fingers. She turned and unlocked the door, thinking she would tell Jack later this week after this whole mess with Wells had settled. She opened the door and walked toward the living room where everyone sat sharing a drink.

God, I could use one of those right about now, Monica thought.

CHAPTER 5: THE REVEAL—MARGARET

"Oh, this smells amazing, Mom."

Margaret felt Leslie lean over her shoulder. She tilted her head toward her youngest daughter.

"Hey. We thought we'd lost you. You didn't need to stop and get beer. We were fine," she said.

"Sorry. I ran into Sara Hannon at the store, and we caught up," said Leslie.

Margaret thought she saw her rosy cheeks blush, but it could have also been the cold or the beer she smelled on her daughter's breath.

"Oh. How is she doing? You two were so close growing up." Margaret had often thought Leslie and Sara would have been cute together. She grabbed a paper plate and offered it to her youngest child.

"She's good. Mmm. Yes, please. Oh, and I grabbed the mail for you. It's in the bag with the beer."

"Thanks, sweetie," Margaret said. After Leslie was done serving herself, Margaret put the cover back on the crock pot and set the spoon on a plate. She took a sip of her water and felt the cool liquid rush down her neck and into her belly. She walked out of the kitchen and into the dining room where Jack and Christian were sharing a laugh and drinking the beer Leslie brought. Margaret liked seeing how her family had grown. Both of those boys were nice additions to their circle. They loved her daughters and would stick with them no matter what lay ahead. She knew that.

"Hey, rowdy boys, would you mind gathering everyone in a few minutes so we can chat in the living room?"

"Sure thing, Margaret," said Christian. "Jack and I will round up the kiddos and put something on the babysitter."

"The what?" asked Jack.

"He means the TV, Jack," answered Margaret. "Even I know that," she added with a wink.

She circled into the living room where Sam, Michelle, Adrienne, and Mary sat playing on phones and tablets, neglecting their food.

"Hey, mine stopped working. Can you help me, please?" Sam thrust the tablet into her sister's lap.

"Don't! Go ask mom."

Sam stood up, pickle in one hand and tablet in the other, and walked toward the kitchen. Margaret's heart fluttered at the sight of the kids on the floor. She was so thankful to have granddaughters. Boys would have been much more complicated. But then again, she would have definitely talked to her children about all of this madness by now. Partly, she had feared her daughters might not have had kids at all had they known about the family's condition, and Margaret couldn't imagine not having these little girls in her life. Her granddaughters softened the sting of her guilt from not telling her daughters about the condition.

"Hey girls, what would you say about some cake and a movie?" All three heads jerked up.

"Cake? I want some!" shouted Mary, and Adrienne's hand shot high into the sky.

"What movie?" asked Michelle who was being drawn back into her phone. Sam had returned from the kitchen with a dead tablet and was just sitting down at Michelle's side to investigate her sister's screen.

"Let's see what your daddies can find for you. Hey, Jack? Christian, would you mind getting these little monkeys some cake?"

"Hey! We are not monkeys," said Sam sounding affronted, but the toothy smile betrayed her.

Margaret leaned down to Michelle's ear who had barely looked up from the screen. "Yes, you are a bunch of little monkeys," she whispered. "Go get some cake, kiddo."

"O-kaaay." Michelle followed Mary and the line of girls through the kitchen. Margaret corralled them past Heather who was returning to the table where Leslie was using the barbecue sauce to finger paint with Maya. She saw Charles opening the mail. He caught her eye. The benefit of being with him for over forty years was that, with only a glance, Margaret could have an entire conversation with him. With the concerned look Charles gave Margaret, she had a strange feeling one of the letters had something to do with her son.

"I just need to talk to your father for a second," Margaret said to Heather and Leslie. "You two head to the living room, and we'll be right there. And don't worry about the girls. Jack and Christian are turning on a show."

"Sure thing, Mom," said Leslie.

Margaret approached Charles who was holding a thick envelope. It was addressed to them in handwriting similar to her husband's. She recognized it immediately.

"He must have sent it just before. What is it?" she asked. Whatever was inside, she had a feeling she knew what it might say. For some time now, Wells had alluded to the importance of telling his sisters about the family secret. He thought it should come from his parents, but admitted it would be helpful for him to be involved considering everything that he had done. He even hinted that he was working on something to help explain it all, but had wanted to keep it a surprise until he was finished.

Charles pulled out a single sheet of paper and unfolded it.

Mom and Dad,

I have a feeling I won't be there when you tell them. I'm sorry if that's the case. I'm hoping these will help.

Love,

Wells

Charles took a deep breath and reached back into the envelope where he found a thick stack of papers. The stack was divided into four packets of double-sided, single-spaced print. They were bound by three staples running down the left edge. Paper clipped to the front page of each booklet was a polaroid photograph. The photo on the top packet was of Leslie standing on her doorstep, looking as if she was just about to speak. Her lips were slightly parted, dimples showing, and eyebrows raised. An expression of pleasant surprise.

The second was a picture of Heather in her living room, looking down toward the three girls. Mary was holding Maya who was in the middle of one of her big belly giggles as if being tickled. Mary and Adrienne were laughing and looking off to their side at an empty space on the floor.

The third picture was of Sam throwing snow high in the air while Michelle squeezed her eyes shut tight. The flakes were just starting to touch her cheeks. The photographs had the soft, tinted glow characteristic of polaroids, giving the impression they could have been taken thirty years prior, but, at the same time, felt tangible and present.

The last stack of papers had the words "For Mom and Dad" written in pencil in lieu of a photograph.

Margaret read the first few lines of the document. She made eye contact with Charles and took a deep breath.

"Okay, can you help me do this?"

"Of course," he said. He hugged his wife. She felt an urge to hold the hug for hours, but resisted. Instead, she squeezed him back and entered the living room where Monica was just sitting down with her glass of wine, the glass still nearly full. Margaret and Charles squeezed together on the piano bench. The packet of papers rested in Margaret's lap.

"How are you holding up, mom?" asked Heather.

"We're fine, thank you, dear. And thank you all for staying. I know you all have things to get back to, so it means a lot that you spent the extra time here tonight."

"Obviously, mom. We'll stay as long as you need us," Leslie said. She looked around the room in affirmation. She didn't catch Monica giving an eye roll while checking the clock on her phone.

"Margaret," said Christian, "do you need any help with Wells' apartment? We could help with boxing and sorting if you like."

To be honest, Margaret hadn't thought of Wells' apartment since his death. It was just five days ago when she and Charles found him. They had plans to meet for coffee at Wells' apartment as they had done almost weekly since he returned.

His apartment was a small efficiency. It was all he needed. The location was close to downtown which he said he liked because he could feel the energy of the little city, and he could walk or bike to most places including his new job at a local café.

Earlier that week, Margaret and Charles drove across the river into Wisconsin and walked up to Wells' apartment. When no one answered the door, they tried the handle and found it unlocked. Wells was sitting in the chair. A shoebox of photographs rested on the coffee table to his left. His eyes were closed, and his head hung to the side as if he'd fallen asleep watching a late-night movie. Charles was more shaken than Margaret. He sobbed and hugged his son until the ambulance arrived. Margaret, however, knew this day was coming. She had sensed it from the moment he said he'd be moving back. She figured Wells knew, too. Now, the letter in the package confirmed her suspicions.

It was cliche to say, but he did look peaceful when they found him. It was almost identical to the way she found her younger brother, Owen, who died just before her wedding. Just like Wells, she had sensed Owen's death before it happened.

Margaret's innocence to the death of a loved one was lost even before she found Owen. Her older brother, Stanley, had died when she was only a teenager. That was harder to process. Margaret had adored her older brother. He rode a motorcycle, wore a leather jacket, held a cigarette in his hand so casually you'd have thought he didn't know it existed, and had long shaggy hair that curled just enough to give a sense of boyish innocence. He was just over twenty when he killed himself.

It was Margaret's mother who talked to her after Stanley's death. She sat down with Margaret and Owen and did her best to explain the perplexing history of their family and what she referred to as their "condition."

And now it was Margaret's turn to tell her children. She cursed herself for waiting so long. It would have been so much easier with Wells here. She knew she had missed a bullet, given there were no grandsons at this point, but she wasn't sure how long that would last. She could hope, couldn't she? Maybe it would skip a generation or simply fade away.

An idea suddenly occurred to Margaret. They'd need time to process the secret she was about to reveal. This heirloom that had been passed down through the generations was only the beginning of the story.

"Christian, you know, that is a good idea. If you're able, it'd be great for you all to come to Wells' place. Maybe in a few days? Monica," she said, knowing her oldest had created a life that was already over-scheduled, "I completely understand if you can't make it back, but it would mean so much if you could."

"Thank you, Mom. I mean, I'd love to. But, honestly, I…"

"It's fine," Margaret interrupted. "The invitation is open if you find it works for you." *Unconditional love and forgiveness, that's what parents give*, thought Margaret. *Hopefully, you'll forgive me in return for holding onto Wells' story for so long.* She took a deep breath and fiddled with the papers in her lap.

"Do you all remember that I had two brothers?" Margaret looked around to see nods of recognition.

"Owen and Stanley, wasn't it?" Leslie asked. She stood up and grabbed a black and white photograph sitting on a shelf near the piano. In the picture were three kids lined up by height, standing in front of a modest, shuttered home with a cocker spaniel at their feet. The tallest boy was squinting at the camera, short, dark hair dangling in front of his face. On the other end was the shortest of the children, a freckled-faced boy in bare feet and overalls. In the middle, wearing a flowered dress and pigtails, was a brightly smiling girl with eyes that were unmistakable as the matriarch of the Monasmith family.

"Oh, I forgot about them," said Heather. "How'd they die? I mean, what happened to them?"

"Well, Stanley died in a car crash." *The fact that it wasn't an accident isn't important right now.* "And Owen died of a heart attack just before our wedding."

"A heart attack?" Monica sat up a little straighter. "What was he, twenty-something?"

"Nineteen, yes." Margaret could feel where this was going. *No sense in hiding*, she reassured herself.

"So," continued Monica in the serious tone of a medical sleuth from a television show, "Wells has a stroke at thirty, and your younger brother has a heart attack at nineteen? That can't be a coincidence. Do we need to be worried about familial hyperlipidemia? High cholesterol, sorry. Or maybe another predisposition for vascular disease?"

"No, we do not think any of you are at any risk for things like that." Charles jumped in, trying to keep things from spiraling prematurely. He could see everyone's anxiety creeping up as if feeding off Monica's probing of their medical history.

"You know, there are, literally, hundreds of genes that might be worth looking into even if you think there is a *potential* link. I could make a call to someone in my department." Monica picked up her phone as if she'd contact someone this evening if given the word. Involving a group of doctors was the last thing Margaret wanted right now, but she had to keep pushing forward.

"You are all safe, because you aren't boys," said Margaret. "Wells and my brothers do have a genetic condition, or at least, I think that's what it is. It gets passed down by the women, but only the men seem to be fully affected by it."

"So you know about it? What's it called?" asked Jack. His tone was more interested than concerned.

"It doesn't really have a name. You see, the condition is just really hard on their bodies, and the more they use it, the more of a toll it seems to take." Margaret rubbed her hands together and looked down at the papers from her son.

"Use it? What does that mean?" asked Heather.

"Yeah, Mom," said Monica, "this sounds a lot like something we *do* need to worry about."

"No. No. It's not what you think. It sounds so strange to say it out loud. You see, Wells, my brothers, they could..." Margaret had everyone's attention. All eyes were on her. The room was still. *This is the moment all of my children will remember as the day their mother lost her mind. Here we go.*

"Wells could stop time."

The living room was silent except for an aged oak clock ticking away on the wall. Laughter came from the other room where the children sat watching television. Monica was the first to speak.

"Stop time?" Monica sounded skeptical and irritated. "I don't understand. Is that a metaphor or something?" Margaret felt like a patient who's doctors didn't believe her symptoms. Margaret heard "I don't have time for this shit" in Monica's inflection.

"No. It isn't a metaphor, honey," Margaret said patiently. Really, she felt the desire to apologize for keeping this from them for so long. If she had told them when they were kids, they might have just accepted it like she did. On the other hand, maybe she was currently causing more trouble and should have let them live in their ignorance. Margaret continued despite the conflicting internal dialogue. "The men in my family have always been able to do it. And sometimes," Margaret looked at Leslie who was picking her fingernails, "sometimes the women can do it, too. Not as well, but to a degree."

"Margaret, I'm not quite sure I understand." Christian stood at Heather's side with his hand on her shoulder. His tone was slightly patronizing and Margaret interpreted it as if he, indeed, thought she might be crazy. "First of all," he continued, "that kind of sounds made up. I mean, it does, doesn't it?" He glanced around to see if anyone would nod in agreement. "Second of all, how would that lead to a heart attack or stroke? And third, it really sounds made up." He chuckled at the last point, trying to ease the growing tension with a light-hearted joke.

"I know how it sounds, but it isn't made up. My brothers and Wells, their bodies aged faster. Or at least that's how the doctors put it when they saw Wells last March after his little spell. I can do it, too, but not to the extent Wells can, or could, rather. I think it's why my hair has turned so gray in the last few years. I'm only a little over sixty, and I look like I could be your mother for goodness sake." She looked at Charles with this comment who batted his eyes lovingly back at her. "I've tried not to use it, but sometimes I can't help it." She made an expression somewhere between a smile and a grimace and scanned her audience. "I know this is hard to believe. I should have told you a long time ago."

"I believe it." Leslie looked around the room, all eyes on her now. The expressions meeting her were filled with doubt. "I mean, I think I do. I've never really known what to call it, but sometimes I just want to hold onto a moment and things seem to sort of slow down." She brushed back her hair, silver strands highlighting her temples like the fresh dusting of snow beneath the streetlight outside.

"Wells went to the doctor? For this?" Monica asked. Her cheeks were flushed with frustration. The muscles in her jaw rippled. "Okay, you know what? I'm sorry. This is crazy. I can't handle this right now." She stood up abruptly. "I think it's just getting late, and we just lost our brother, and you lost your son, and everyone's a little stressed. Maybe we should call it a night and talk about this later." She turned to face her husband. "Jack, we really should be on the road."

Christian leaned down and whispered to Heather. She stood up as well, wearing a look that Margaret registered as sympathy.

"Yes, you're right. It's late," Margaret agreed. "And I do know how this sounds. Here." She handed out the stacks of paper with the photos on them. "This came in the mail today. It's from Wells. I don't know how, exactly, but he thought it would help you understand." The girls took the papers. They looked at the photos and then around the room, comparing the pictures.

"If you can make it to Wells' place on Wednesday, we can talk more about it then. Otherwise, feel free to give me a call whenever." Margaret turned to Monica. "You should get on the road and get the girls to bed. Your dad and I can clean up."

"Mom," Heather said, but Margaret interrupted.

"I'm fine, honestly. Please just read this if you can. I wanted to tell you all about this a long time ago, but I didn't. For that, I'm very sorry. But it's all true, no matter how crazy it sounds. Your brother. My brothers. They could stop time." Margaret took a deep breath and clapped her hands. The snap broke through the awkward fog that had settled through the living room, startling everyone. "Okay, time to pack up. Kids!" She walked out of the living room to go find the grandchildren.

The adults in the room exchanged worried looks, but no one said a word. There was nothing else to do but gather the coats, wrangle the children, and pack up. After some hugs and stuffing of pockets with cookies for the little ones, Margaret and Charles leaned out the open door and waved to everyone as they packed into the chilly cars.

"See you Wednesday, Mom," said Heather.

"Sounds good," Margaret waved.

"I'll call you later, Mom. Okay?" said Leslie as she hopped in her car and drove away.

Jack smiled and waved at Charles and Margaret as he got in the passenger seat of the SUV. Monica waved through the window as they drove away.

"Well," said Margaret to her husband as they walked inside, "they think I'm insane."

"Yeah. Yeah, they do." Charles kissed his wife on the forehead. "Hopefully this will help." He picked up the stack of papers from Wells. "Let's look at this tomorrow, okay?"

"Sounds good, honey."

Margaret and Charles closed the door and turned to the duties of putting their home to sleep.

CHAPTER 6: CHARLES MONASMITH

In the dim light of the now eerily quiet home, Charles Monasmith methodically rinsed, washed, and dried his way through the stack of dishes, silverware, and wine glasses while Margaret filled Tupperware with leftovers. The voice of Gordon Lightfoot floated through the kitchen, recalling the fate of the crew on a doomed voyage.

Charles's mind had floated to that middle place where an activity like washing dishes takes you adrift and allows you to ruminate freely. Overall, he thought his daughters took the news well. Considering the weight of the claim was as heavy as a ship's anchor, he was amazed at how quickly the children were able to depart. He supposed denial may indeed be a formidable floatation device in this situation.

Obviously, Monica was the most skeptical, but at least Leslie seemed somewhat onboard. Monica had been indoctrinated in the medical world of evidence-based decision making. The story was simply too hard to fathom, and without any documented case study to compare this to, how could she buy into something so far-fetched?

As expected, Charles noticed Heather's mothering nature shining through. She appeared to perceive Margaret's words as a suggestion that she was in shock or possibly denial. He figured Heather would also take some convincing to believe.

And to be fair, it had taken Charles a long time to wrap his mind around it, and he had even known Owen. Now that Wells had died, his concern for Margaret and Leslie grew exponentially. His son's death made his wife and daughter's mortality all the more real.

Charles began drying the glasses with the towel hanging over his shoulder. After each had been dried, he placed them back in the cabinet holding the assortment of family crystal and glassware. The collections from his and Margaret's parents and grandparents were all beautiful, but rarely saw the light of day. It was a shame, in a way, to use the crappy plastic cups all the time when something so special sat unused, but it lasted longer living on the shelf. That was for sure.

Deep down, he wanted to urge Margaret and Leslie to avoid any temptation to use their gift, but this could never be about what *he* wanted. He had no idea what it would be like to carry this burden in his genetics. For now, the least he could hope for was that his children read Wells' words with an open mind and showed up on Wednesday. If not, he hoped they might accept that a combination of stress and brandy was enough to drive Margaret from her lucidity. After all, who could blame her for a moment of insanity after the death of her only son?

Putting away the last of the dried dishes, he said a prayer that Margaret wouldn't need to stop the clock to prove it was all true. Above all, he didn't want anything to shorten the time he had left with the one person who made his soul complete.

CHAPTER 7: HEATHER

"Christian, should we be worried about Mom? In my entire life, I've never thought of her as someone with poor judgment or who would believe in bizarre conspiracy theories. But that was ... that was just weird."

The girls were tucked tightly into their car seats as Christian backed out of the driveway. Heather noticed his hesitation before he spoke, as if he thought he should tread carefully so as not to offend her with his thoughts on the subject.

"Yeah. I don't really know what to say about it, honestly. She is getting older, I guess."

"I'll call her tomorrow morning. Maybe Monica was right, and she just needs to rest."

"Will you go to Wells' place on Wednesday?"

"Oh, of course." Heather looked back at the girls. The minivan was their own traveling movie theater. The screen that flipped down from the ceiling was a terrible obstruction for the driver, but it was magical in its ability to turn car rides with three little children from extremely painful experiences into, honestly, pretty relaxing outings. Except when the movie needed to be changed. Then it became a ticking time-bomb for the spoiled little gremlins. Looking at the glazed-over faces of the girls reminded her of something. She looked down at her feet and picked up the stack of papers and the polaroid photograph that lay on the floor mat.

She inspected the picture first. It had a softened quality to the exposure that made it look like it was from another era. Her own childhood, maybe? Definitely not a style of photograph she was used to seeing with her own kids. The aged quality was deceiving, given she recognized the scene from her living room just over one week ago. She saw herself smiling down on her children who laughed and wrestled on the carpet. Heather felt drawn into the picture. Something she couldn't remember feeling before in any of the other photos of her family. But hell, it must have been well over ten years since she had gotten an actual roll of film developed as opposed to the thousands of shots on her phone. The fact that it was a polaroid only added to the vivid nostalgia of the moment.

Wells had stopped by for an impromptu visit, and he stayed for a half hour that Saturday.

"I just wanted to see the girls and say hi," he said. It was a touching sentiment that Heather hadn't heard from her brother until only recently. In the past, he was rarely the one to initiate a family get-together.

Heather watched her brother play with the girls on the living room floor. Silly faces turned into tickle-monster games, and, too soon, he had to leave. Heather looked at the photo and thought of her brother. She loved him. They had grown distant, but she felt like the bond between Wells and the family was starting to strengthen again now that he was back home.

When was this photo taken? she thought. She didn't remember him taking a picture during his visit. She didn't even recall him carrying a camera, let alone a boxy, antique polaroid. Heather thought he was wearing a backpack when he walked into their house. *Was a camera tied to it? Either way, I definitely don't remember him taking this picture.*

Later that night, after she was certain all the children were finally sleeping soundly, Heather sat in bed holding the gift from Wells. Christian snored beside her. She set the photo on the bedside table and began scanning the first few lines of the top page of the manuscript. Something about the picture had nudged her to at least consider entertaining the fantasy that was being sold to the family. For just tonight, she would be willing to listen to what her brother had to say.

Heather decided she would stay up as long as it took to finish reading his words. With her luck, she would likely finish just as her children began to stir with the rising sun. Her eyes began to scan the top page and about halfway down, she paused at the pitter-patter of little feet dashing through the house, confirming her suspicions that this would indeed be a long night.

CHAPTER 8: LESLIE

The outdoor rink was now empty, so Leslie pulled into the parking lot. It looked like a stage lit up for the gods of ice and snow. From November through February, she always kept a pair of skates in her car. She had a couple hours' drive before she would get back home in the Twin Cities, but she was never good at passing up a chance to skate on an open rink. Stepping onto an outdoor ice rink was like jumping off a cliff and taking flight. Reaching into her coat pocket, she pulled out one of the beers she had stashed away and cracked it. She took a swig and set the can at the base of the boards so it would be out of sight if any cops made their nightly rounds.

Thirty minutes later, her forehead glistened with sweat, and she laid on her back at center ice, gazing up into the sky where a few stars peeked through the parting clouds. She felt her heart pumping, carrying oxygen to her thighs, brain, and lungs. She slid her hands into her pockets to warm her fingertips and felt the sharp corner of something stiff dig into her left palm. Leslie pulled out the white-trimmed photo of herself that had been attached to Wells' story. She was pretty sure she knew the exact moment it was taken, but couldn't quite figure out how her brother could have snapped a polaroid of her without her knowing it. In the picture, she could see the excited greeting of "Hey!" just about to escape her lips.

Looking at the image was like looking at a mirror and a window at the same time. She felt like she could walk through the picture and find her brother again. If she could, she'd ask him what the fuck was going on. And if he was able to stop time, why didn't he stop time to spend more of it with her, if it even worked like that? If she could only just speak to him one more time. He was always good at giving advice. It was like he had lived through every scenario possible.

Turning the photograph over, she saw familiar handwriting. It looked like hers but must have been her mother's. They looked so much alike after all. It read *"When you're ready, think of Wells, and imagine yourself doing backflips underwater."* She furrowed her brow at the words, rubbed her forehead, and reminded herself to ask her mom about it later this week.

The cold of the ice was now invading Leslie's clothes and hitting her body. A shiver rose up from the small of her back, shooting past her shoulder blades and skirting her neck. She slid the picture back into her pocket and rolled onto her knees. Bringing her skates beneath her, she stood up, skated to the boards, and sat on the base of the gate where her shoes were waiting for her.

Leslie unlaced her skates and ditched the empty beer in the rusty, metal barrel by the dark warming house. She hopped in her car and restarted Regina Spektor's album. Leslie turned her car north toward home, looking forward to getting a few hours of sleep. Tomorrow, she only had one thing on her agenda: read her brother's story.

CHAPTER 9: 1/3/20 THE GIFT

There was a moment last fall when I realized I might be running out of time sooner than I imagined. I was sitting in a sterile hospital bed listening to an overtired doctor try and figure out what drugs I'd been taking. He assumed it was the most likely reason my arteries and veins were like, as he put it, "the calcified pipes of a ninety-year-old chain smoker." The thought conjured images of Burgess Meredith in his late years, living off bacon and cigarettes. Maybe that's how my insides looked, but trust me, I felt just fine.

Still, it was the first time I was really faced with the reality of what this gift, or rather, this ability, had been doing to me over the last ten years or so. And even since then, I've had a few "spells" that give me the feeling that somewhere deep inside my body, a clock is ticking, and its gears are starting to catch and stutter.

I realize I've always been pretty distant from the family. Life gets busy for all of us. We walk our own roads, and oftentimes, that leads us away from each other. In the last few months, I've been talking a lot with Mom and Dad, and I came to realize I would need to share my story with all of you at some point. I've never been much of a writer, but I felt like, with what time I have left, if I could try and write this all down for you, maybe we might understand each other a little better. Maybe it might help you understand your own children if they ever have to deal with this someday.

Do you remember when we were kids, and Mom and Dad rented that cabin up near Hayward for Christmas? Leslie, I think you were only a couple months old, so you wouldn't, but I bet you've seen the pictures. Anyway, that was the first time I can recall doing it. It was a complete accident, and it was only years later that I realized what had happened. The cabin was warm from the cast iron stove. We were all packed into the bunk beds off the main room, and Mom, Dad, and Leslie were sleeping in the other bedroom off the kitchen.

I remember waking up to go to the bathroom and seeing the small spruce tree we had cut down the day before decorated with strings of popcorn and cranberries. When we all finally fell asleep that night, the tree stood alone in the corner filling the room with that sweet conifer smell, but in the dim light of the living room which also served as a kitchen and dining room, I could see a pile of neatly stacked Christmas presents covered in red and green paper topped with gaudy, shining bows. It was a spectacular sight. I ran to the tree and began running my fingers over every smooth package, completely forgetting my full bladder. I think that is where the story starts, with me about to rip open every present under the tree like nothing else in the world mattered.

"And just what do you think you are doing under that tree?" Charles Monasmith walked into the dim living room where his mischievous son was poised to expose all of the Christmas surprises he and Margaret had planned. It was endearing, really. Seven-year-old Wells hopped to his feet, startled by his dad's voice.

"You scared me!" Wells balled up his fists and stamped his foot on the old wooden floor which creaked like a tree under the weight of the snow. For a moment, Wells thought he was going to celebrate Christmas all by himself. In fact, he had completely forgotten his family existed as he sat on his knees, hovering over the small mountain of treasures glistening in the dim cabin.

"Shhh." Charles winced and looked toward the bedrooms holding a finger to his lips. The last thing he needed was the rest of the kids waking up and digging at the presents beneath the tree, too.

"I didn't mean to scare you." Seeing Wells pinching his crotch, Charles asked the obvious question. "Do you have to pee?"

"Dad, I think Santa came." Wells ignored the urgent plea from his bladder. His voice was filled with excitement, but his gaze was hard and intense. His belief in Santa was as solid as the roof above them and the snow falling on the windowsill.

"You're right, he did, but we have to wait until tomorrow when everyone wakes up, okay?"

"Can I just open one?"

"No, I'm sorry, buddy. Even if we wrapped it back up, I think the girls would find out and be pretty jealous. Especially your mother. She's too smart for that. How about you just go potty, and I'll see you in the morning."

Wells groaned and started to walk away.

"Fine," he said as he closed the bathroom door. His mind spun considering what treasures might be resting under the tree. A remote-control car? Chocolate? A slingshot? More chocolate? A *Nintendo*? He felt anger swirling in his tummy. If I could just open one single gift, it would be the best Christmas ever. It was absolutely worth asking one more time.

He finished peeing, wiped the seat, and flushed the toilet. He skipped the hand washing. No one would know. When he got to the tree, his dad had gone back to bed. The room was empty. The presents were stacked like the building blocks of a haphazard city. He could hear the ticking cuckoo clock on the wall, an old German relic that scared all of his sisters when it called out in the middle of the night. His mom had spent all day admiring it. Wells thought if only his dad came back, he would shove all of his desire into one final plea. He balled his fists and shook his head to try and make it happen. With his eyes squeezed shut tight he could hear the heavy wind beating against the side of the cabin.

Wells loosened his fists and opened his eyes. The room was silent. The clock had stopped ticking. *It must need winding*, Wells thought, but then it occurred to him that if it wasn't ticking, it wouldn't chime. The only ticking he could hear was his heart counting off the seconds. The cabin was lost in hibernation. Even the gusts swirling around the corners of the little log building had settled down. He decided to chance it. Just one present. He needed so badly to see beneath the wrapping paper.

Wells cautiously approached the tree, pushing through the glow of the night to a medium-sized, square package with his name written in swirling letters. *Santa's elves have the best handwriting*, he thought. He carefully peeled the tape away and lifted the paper to see a small box set of Topps baseball cards, a picture of Miguel Cabrera staring back from the chrome packaging. Wells' excitement took control of his hands and got the best of him. Before he knew it, he tore through every single present, fueling his pleasure with a stick of Rolos that was stuffed into a pair of fleece socks. As he chewed on the chocolatey caramels, his eyes got heavy. The piles of crumpled paper covered his flannel pajamas and his chin nodded to his chest. As his mind slipped away into a dark river of sleep, his subconscious noted the clock beginning to tick again, and the chime rang once. The girls stirred at the sound but didn't wake.

Charles had only just walked back to his bedroom to lie down when he heard Wells flush the toilet. He had to pee now, too. His nightly ritual since his late thirties. He smiled to himself, loving the classic memory his son had just created. A young child waking up to a tower of presents beneath the tree. This was exactly the type of core memory he and Margaret had wanted their kids to have when they rented the cabin. Magic moments seasoned with sights, aromas, and emotions that could be recalled throughout a lifetime.

Charles turned back around and moved toward the bedroom door. He clicked the indiglo button on his watch and saw 12:59:52.

As Charles walked into the living room, the old clock on the wall announced one A.M. His eyes widened at the scene and his heart stopped. This was a Christmas memory Charles Monasmith would certainly never forget. Unfortunately, this was a memory he hoped would never be made. Wells sat asleep with candy in his hand and nearly all of the presents had been unwrapped. There must have been twenty-five gifts spread around him. All of the girls' presents. A necklace for Margaret. A new pair of mittens for Charles. It must have happened sometime in the last ten seconds.

The father crumpled into a recliner near his son and cried into his hands. He now knew his time with his son was on a shorter string. When his tears did their job of temporarily lifting the weight that he now carried, he picked up his little boy and walked toward the bunk beds. Wells laid his head on Charles' shoulder as he walked and then stayed asleep the rest of the night. Charles returned to the tree and re-wrapped the presents

63

the best he could. He decided not to tell Margaret until the morning. The night would seem a lot longer if she had to process what he now knew for certain.

Chapter 10: 1/4/20 A Boy on a Roof

It's funny. It's January 4th, and even as I write this, I don't quite know what is most helpful for you to hear. And even if I knew what to share next, I'm not sure I'd be able to write it in the most effective way. Why didn't I pay more attention during that junior year creative writing class?

Wells lingered on the memory of college which seemed so long ago and looked around his apartment. It was simple and tidy. His favorite poem by Charles Bukowski was framed on the wall next to a few photos. At his side was a stack of polaroids. Dates and names were scribbled in pencil on the bottom borders. Wells resumed writing.

At some point, I read that the Greeks had two concepts of time. Maybe they had more, but there are two that I remember. First, there is chronos. That is the word for chronological time, or how it moves along on a straight line. It is a form of measurement. It is a frame of reference. It is a value. As such, we measure our achievements with chronos: how many years we've put in at a job, the number of days left in a school year, wedding anniversaries, or time left until the pizza is done. And, of course, even though the units of time stay pretty consistent (seconds, minutes, hours, years, etc.), they often carry different weights. It's that "a watched pot never boils" thing.

Then there is kairos. Kairos is more abstract. It is qualitative. I kind of think of it as a location or position relative to the world around you. For instance, there is a time to settle down, a time to choose what to do on Friday night, or the right moment to tell someone you love them.

As I write this, the sun is at its peak in the sky. I've been typing for a little over two hours, and it is time to tell you about the night an angsty, brooding teenager discovered he could stop the world around him at his whim.

———————

"Get out!"

A door slammed, cutting off Monica's piercing voice. Downstairs, Margaret sipped her cup of coffee and rolled her eyes up to the shouts above her. The bickering was the staple of summer. And no matter how much Margaret tried to separate Wells and Monica, they always found their way back into one another's spaces. It was almost as if they needed the confrontation or possibly found satisfaction somewhere between the screams and reprimands. And it wasn't as if it was simply a case of the younger sibling needling the older. Monica also frequently made a point to go out of her way to irritate Wells.

"Give it back!" Wells' voice carried down the stairs along with the pounding of his fist on his oldest sister's door. Margaret heard the rattling as her son tried the locked doorknob.

The retort was muffled, but Margaret was pretty sure this time it was about a CD, or a Discman, or something of that nature. Monica must have taken back what she thought was rightfully hers. It's amazing what goes missing while you are off to college and your siblings have free reign over your unguarded belongings. It's also amazing how quickly you forget the thing you were borrowing does not actually belong to you.

"You guys, stop, please. Wells, here. You can borrow my headphones." Heather's voice had found its way between her brother and the door. Just as much as Wells and Monica felt compelled to torture one another, Heather saw it as her duty to rescue her siblings from total annihilation. Sometimes she'd be drawn to tears by how strongly she felt they all needed to get along.

Margaret picked up a slice of toast and took a bite. She'd let the drama unfold a little longer, giving her children a chance to solve the battles on their own. It was times like these she often remembered something her mother would say to her when she fought with her own brothers.

"Maggie, my job as your mother is to love, support, and guide my children, not to rescue them. I leave that responsibility to God and that brave little voice deep inside each of you."

As much as she hated it at the time, for she could remember just as many slammed doors during her childhood, she had grown to emulate her own mother's style of parenting and decided this was a moment to keep it alive.

"They fight a lot." Leslie sat at the table next to Margaret and swallowed another spoonful of oatmeal.

"Yes, sweetie, they do. But they also love each other."

"Mmmm… This is delicious."

Margaret smiled at her youngest daughter.

"What do you think? Should I go up there and put a stop to all this shouting?"

"I dunno. Do you want a bite of my oatmeal?" Leslie held up a spoon of the mushy breakfast.

"I'm okay, dear. You can have it."

Leslie made the scoop disappear as the thuds of a fifteen-year-old boy clunked down the steps. Wells burst into the kitchen with a cloud of irritation wrapped around him like a blanket. Margaret's imagination conjured images of Pigpen from the Charles Schulz cartoons.

Wells moved through the kitchen, preparing a bowl of cereal. Each motion was exaggerated with the grumpy harrumph. He sloshed the milk into the bowl and plopped down next to Leslie.

"Why does she even have to live with us?" The words escaped through a mouthful of sugary corn flakes.

"Well, soon, I expect she won't."

"But she's almost twenty. I mean, come on. It's so lame." By twenty, Wells imagined himself... Honestly, he had no idea what his life would look like because he didn't personally know any other twenty-year-olds, but he was absolutely certain he wouldn't be living at home. He'd probably have a cool fast car and be in a big cool city where cool things happened all the time. He wasn't sure what those things would be, but they would be cool. Very cool.

"We've been through this. She is saving her money to help pay for school. Hospital volunteers don't get paid very much, you know? My guess is next summer she'll have a fancy job in the cities, and you won't have to put up with her. Plus, it's only one more week, and then she's back to her classes. And besides, the rest of you start school tomorrow, so you'll barely be around each other."

"I want a fancy job. It sounds fun." Leslie seemed unfazed by the negative energy following her brother like a storm.

"Doesn't it?" Margaret smiled at her bright ray of sunshine. She was pretty sure she saw Wells smirk, too. He always had a soft spot for his little sister. "And I can't believe you are starting second grade tomorrow! Wow."

Leslie sat up straight with pride as her two sisters came down the stairs. Monica walked in first and glared at her brother.

"Mom, I need your help finding a few more boxes. I think I'll need all my books with me this semester."

"Haven't you already read them? What do you even need them for?" Wells' words were heavy with snotty distaste for his sister.

"The MCAT, Wells. Do you even know what that is?"

"Yeah, of course I do." Wells had no idea what it was, but he wasn't about to let his sister know. Monica eyed her brother and called his bluff.

"It's the Medical College Admissions Test, and it is probably the most important test I'll ever take. You see, some of us have goals and plans, Wells. Not all of us just float through life playing with cameras, kicking soccer balls, screwing around with silly friends, and letting the clock tick, tick, tick away."

Wells glared at his sister. He stuffed his empty bowl and spoon in the dishwasher and walked out of the kitchen.

"Mom, I'll be at Derek's." He slammed the door without looking back.

"Good riddance."

"Monica, that's enough." Margaret now wondered if she let it go too far. "You're going to be late to the hospital. I know you two don't see eye to eye, but I'd like you to try and be kind for one more week."

"I've tried, Mom. He's always in my space. Everything he does, or more like doesn't do, annoys every fiber in my body."

Margaret let out a long sigh and chose not to engage. "Alright, Leslie, we've got to get you to the pool. There's supposed to be thunderstorms this evening, so now is our shot. Not many days of swimming left, I'm afraid. Heather, do you want to join us?"

"Yeah, that sounds good. Ashley and Carolyn might be there, too."

Margaret turned to Monica who was putting on her volunteer badge for the local hospital. Monica was inspecting her reflection in the mirror near the door to the garage. She was careful to make sure her badge was smudge-free and perfectly positioned above her heart.

"You look great, honey. We're really proud of how hard you work. All of our kids, you each have such special talents." Seeing her daughter's eyebrows raise with skepticism, Margaret continued. "Yes, even Wells has his gifts. Sometimes it just takes a little longer for each of us to find them."

"Whatever you say, Mom. Love you." Monica grabbed her bike helmet and walked out the door to the garage leaving the happier of the Monasmiths to themselves. Margaret left a note on the counter for Wells and corralled Leslie and Heather to the garage to set off for the swimming pool.

Wells spent the better part of the morning and early afternoon brooding at Derek's house, trying to prolong the last day of summer vacation. *Who was Monica to think she was so high and mighty? Where did she get off judging what I do with my time?* Wells thought. It was true he didn't invest nearly as much effort into school. And he'd much rather be taking pictures, playing soccer, or just about doing anything rather than sitting in a classroom like his sister.

Later that night, he ate supper with his family, speaking as little as possible. The thunder rumbled in the background and the lights in the house flickered as the storms lumbered through the river valley like giants taking a casual stroll, stopping to tap a few houses here and there with their large, electric clubs.

Wells' mind wandered to his new digital camera. Photography was one of the few things he truly enjoyed, and his parents had just given him a Canon PowerShot with a sixteen gigabyte SD memory card for his birthday. He was eager to try and capture a bolt of lightning if possible, and the storm was getting close.

"Wells, you haven't said much tonight. Are you alright?" Margaret asked as the kids dispersed from the kitchen like a football team breaking from a huddle.

"Yup. I'm good."

"Okay. Well, I just wanted to tell you, your father and I don't think you are floating through life, like Monica said. You are very special to us. All of you kids are." She wondered if this was the time to tell him about his gift. She'd tried to tell him so many times, but it never seemed right. She knew he hadn't been using it, at least not intentionally. She would have been able to tell. There was a look that the men in her family had once they'd begun to control it. It was an air of confidence, almost cocksure. You could see it in all the old photos. The eyes were wild with adventure. The smiles alluded to the secret they kept. Even the posture gave them away. She could see it in the photos of her brothers and her father who died when she was still a baby. In those pictures, the expressions on their faces looked as if they were gracing the camera with their presence. When she looked at Wells, Margaret saw none of these things. She saw a moody teenager who had few passions and very little childhood whimsy remaining on his plate. In that way, he was perfectly normal. Though her daughter may be correct, and, at times, he did seem like a cloud floating on the day's air currents. But what if she told him everything?

"Thanks, Mom." He barely made eye contact.

She watched him trudge up the stairs. So many times she'd watched her children walk away. Those were always the times she was most tempted to hold on. She'd have to talk to him soon. Maybe she and Charles could discuss it tonight. They could have Heather watch Leslie and take Wells out for pizza this week under the guise of celebrating the start of a new school year. They could try and explain it all to him.

Wells took the stairs one at a time and turned toward his room as the lightning flashing outside spilled into the hallway from his bedroom window. His mind was still stuck on Monica's criticisms from the morning. Her words poked at him like a rock in his shoe. What else did she expect him to be doing? He went to school. He got decent grades. He didn't get the best marks, but he did fine enough. And what was so bad about liking soccer, or video games for that matter?

He sat down on his bed and pulled the digital camera off his nightstand and looked out the window. The clouds weren't heavy enough to empty yet, so Wells figured this was his chance to grab a photo without ruining his new toy in a downpour. He closed the door to his room, slid open his window, and popped out the screen. The shingles met the house six inches below his windowsill. He swung a leg onto the roof and ducked through the frame. It was a narrow section of roof on the back side of the house. As long as no one walked into the backyard, he wouldn't be noticed or disturbed.

The clouds moved at the steady pace of honey pouring from a jar. The wind was cool, a noticeable change from August's heat. Another flash lit up the sky. Wells turned on the camera. One, one thousand. Two, one thousand. Three, one thousand. Rumble.

The clouds continued to roll toward Wells. He held up his camera and tried to frame the liquid crystal display screen on the sky above his backyard. After a few seconds, the tops of the towering clouds lit up with bolts of heat lighting, like snakes lashing out at an attacker. He clicked the shutter button and waited for the picture to light up the display. The pixelated image of the lightning-less clouds mocked him, and he scoffed.

"It's too slow."

Maybe another method would work. He pointed the camera at the towering cloud and held down the button. Each time a picture clicked, he released his finger and held it down again, hoping luck would be on his side and the timing would be just right.

Another flash laced through the sky. One, one thousand. Two, one thousand. Boom. He felt that one in his chest. The timing was better, and he thought he may have caught it just right.

He pressed the play button on the back surface of the camera and reviewed the shot.

"Nope."

The digital camera was just too slow. The charcoal clouds in the image were blushed with pink, maybe just before the large bolt, but it wasn't good enough. His reaction time would have to be perfect to capture what he saw in his mind's eye. He wanted to seize one of those photobook-worthy images of an

Olympian, jagged bolt of lightning crashing down from the heavens.

The storm was moving closer. A few large drops began tapping the roof. Wells sat with his knees up to his chest. The soles of his bare feet held him in place. Another bolt struck, this one closer and brighter. Wells thought his ears were buzzing.

One, one thousand.

Rumble, rumble, crash.

Wells tried to shimmy backward to inch closer to his window. His hand slipped and his left heel kicked out from beneath him. He fell onto his elbow and pain electrified his arm as the scrape of the shingle dug into his skin. Had the camera not been strapped to his right wrist, he might have tossed it into the yard. Thankfully, he caught himself and shifted back into position.

"That was close." He swallowed hard trying to calm himself and decided to give it one more shot.

A gust of wind picked up, and the air began to whir with electricity. It buzzed just like his mind when he and Monica were yelling at each other. Wells slipped again on the roof and his frustration rose thinking of Monica, his slow digital camera, and his inability to simply take a picture the way he wanted. Somewhere inside himself, he heard a soft rumble building momentum.

This time, the flash and crack happened in synchrony. The light was white, hot, and blinding, but the thunder was cut short like a power chord pulled from a loudspeaker. Wells held his eyes shut tight. His pulse tapped rhythmically in his ears. It was strange. He could no longer feel the wind. The leaves in the tall silver maple standing next to their house had stopped rustling. He swallowed the pooling saliva in his mouth and heard the noisy workings of his tongue and throat. Something was different. Misplaced. He opened his eyes expecting to be shrouded in the silence of the eye of a tornado, the funnel rushing around his neighborhood while simultaneously sheltering his home, but instead he found himself staring at a bolt of lightning connecting the sky to the small metal jungle gym in their backyard just twenty feet from where he was sitting.

The bolt reverberated with energy as if trying to escape from a straightjacket. The arctic blue color was filling the backyard, and Wells felt the fuzzy little hairs on his arms standing erect.

"What the?"

He retreated back to his window. The house, the street, the sky, everything stood still except for Wells and the simmering bolt of lightning. It was like living inside a painting. He fell backward with an awkward somersault onto the floor of his room. He stood up but kept his eyes fixed on the bolt.

"Mom," he shouted. No response. "Mom. Heather? Dad?" Still nothing. Wells turned around and walked into the hallway. The bathroom door was locked. He knocked on the door and put his ear against it. No sounds of the sink or shower. He tried the doorknob again. Nothing. *Maybe somebody locked it accidentally*, he thought.

He shot down the steps three at a time and walked into the kitchen. Charles was at the sink looking out the window. Wells was relieved to see his father and rushed over and started rambling.

"Dad, you should see this. I was out on the roof trying to take a picture of the lightning, which, yeah, I know I'm not supposed to do, but then this huge bolt just froze. It's still there. Did you see it? Dad?" Wells was right behind his father who's frame was statuesque. Charles held a coffee cup in his hand. A wisp of steam suspended itself like a rising flower above the mug.

"Dad? Are you okay?" Wells placed his hand on Charles' shoulder. It was warm. Solid. But his father didn't flinch. He stood still, eyes peering at the unleashing clouds.

"Mom!" Wells shouted, backing away and starting to lose his composure. Beginning to totally freak out was a bit more accurate. He raced into the living room where Margaret sat on the couch, absorbed in her book. She looked like a display in a storefront window.

Several years ago, his parents took all the kids to the Dayton's Christmas Holiday Show where they walked past scene after scene of mannequins acting out iconic images of the holiday season. Some were spectacular. Some were funny. Some were just plain creepy. Looking at his mom frozen like a wax figure brought the latter to mind.

He stumbled back to the stairs. Maybe the lightning bolt wasn't there anymore. Maybe he fell asleep, and this bizarre dream would end with the clap of the thunder. That had to be it. He just needed to wait for the sharp crack of that lightning bolt, and this would all fade back to normal.

"Wake up. Wake up," he repeated as he ran up the stairs.

Wells darted into his room and crawled through the window, and there it was. The shimmering bolt, almost too bright to look at, still suspended in his backyard.

The camera was still in his hand. With a dazed expression of disbelief he slowly lifted the camera up to this weird nightmare. He framed the shot and partially pressed the button down to focus on the lightning bolt. The camera lens made a soft whirring noise as the lens and aperture made their minute adjustments and pulled the image into focus. *At least the camera works in this alternate dream,* he thought.

He pushed the button down and looked at the viewfinder. It was black for a moment, but finally, the image popped up. It was the perfect shot of the bolt with its precise yet chaotic branching fractures like a river delta diving into the lawn. It was always hard to judge what the picture might look like on the tiny digital windows, but even on this two-inch by two-inch screen, he could tell this image was special.

Wells looked back up to the suspended electricity in front of him. The bolt was mesmerizing. He stared at it so long his eyes began to water, and he felt a tickle in his nose. The tickle turned into a rising pressure deep behind his nostrils, and he closed his eyes to sneeze. As he let out his big "ah-choo," the cracking thunder resumed, and rain pelted him in the face. The tidal wave of sounds rushed around him. He hadn't realized how silent it had become. The lightning bolt had disappeared leaving behind a steaming scorch mark in the grass. He could hear voices drifting out the window. His mom? Sisters?

Wells hid the camera under his shirt. *Did that really just happen?* He tried to think back to what he'd been doing when the bolt hit. He had been angry at his camera and was ruminating on his spat with Monica. He was focusing hard on the lightning.

He squeezed his eyes shut again to try and seize the storm. The rain continued to fall. He scrunched up his nose and felt water trickling down over his eyebrows like the overflowing gutters of the house. He could still hear the rain. He focused harder and tensed up, causing a rumble in his ears like wind rushing by your face while bombing a hill on a bicycle, and that was it. The rain suddenly stopped. The wind ceased. He opened his eyes. Drops of rain hung in the air in front of his face like bubbles of carbonation stuck to the side of a glass.

Wells opened his mouth and scooped up a drop with his tongue, smiling. He closed his eyes again and made the rumbling noise in his ears and the world started moving once more. It was like pressing a pause button on a video game over and over again.

After about five minutes of trying to capture another lightning bolt and getting completely drenched on the roof, he crawled back into his room.

His mind was racing, and he felt lightheaded. *Is this a dream?* His eyelids sagged with a heaviness almost too hard to fight. He wanted to go and see if his family had seen what just happened. *Do they know? Can they do it?*

His arms and legs were filled with lead, and his body began to shake. He wasn't cold, despite being soaked and now dripping all over the floor of his room. The dampening carpet resurrected the faint scent of their family dog that died two summers earlier.

Wells felt like he did after trying to beat the class record for the mile run in gym glass: utterly exhausted. Little sparks and lightning bolts were creeping into his peripheral vision as he moved to the bed. With a heavy thud, Wells fell face-first onto his mattress and sunk into a deep sleep. He dreamt he was floating through a glacial river, slowly bouncing off the bottom like a tumbling leaf and looking at the sky above while his family stood watching from the shoreline. There was no panic, only wonder and fascination as he twirled away from his parents and sisters.

CHAPTER 11: 1/5/20 EVERYWHERE ALL THE TIME

When I woke, the world was bright with noise and jittering activity. I had forgotten to close the window, so the community of finches, mourning doves, and woodpeckers that congregated at Mom's feeder were chattering with excitement at the breakfast buffet of millet and sunflower seeds. They were like the old men and women sharing gossip around the church coffee pot, thankful for any opportunity to be surrounded by peers.

Then came the muffled rush of the shower running down the hall. Leslie's high voice floated up from the kitchen. Dad was belting out one of his morning usuals hitting all the wrong notes. He repeated the only words to "I Dreamed a Dream" from Les Misérables that he knew. Through the wall, I could hear Monica's CD player and thumping footfalls as she paced back and forth in her bedroom, presumably shuffling through flashcards that had long ago been committed to memory.

This cacophony, though jarring, was a welcoming anchor, grounding me in my home. I pushed myself up from my bed and wiped the drool from the side of my face. Was it Saturday? Why was I still in my clothes from yesterday? I sat on the edge of the bed and looked around the room. I saw my digital camera on the floor next to me, and like fog clearing, my memory started to come into focus.

I picked up the camera and pressed the on/off button. The screen lit up. I tapped the PLAY button, and the last photo taken appeared. The jagged lightning bolt, blue and white with heat, stood still like a fire pole descending from the hand of Zeus, connecting the heavens to my small backyard in Southeast

Minnesota. With one look at the picture, everything from the night before flooded back, hitting me like a tidal wave.

Wells sat, mouth agape, staring in disbelief at the image on the screen. The small size of the picture betrayed the significance of what he had done. His feet rooted to the bedside carpet, he closed his eyes and tried to remember how he had made it happen. He squeezed his eyes shut and began grinding his teeth, whispering to himself as he did so.

"Do it. Do it. Do it."

He couldn't hear the birds in the backyard. The shower had stopped. Maybe that was it. He'd done it again. Wells hopped up and walked to his door. He peered into the empty hallway through the crack in the doorway. It sounded quiet. The house seemed still. Like a teenager sneaking past his sleeping parents, he made his way through the hallway, heartbeat accelerating. He began to smile. Whatever it was, he'd made it happen again.

"Lightning can strike twice," Wells said, feeling damn-well pleased with himself.

"What are you doing?"

"Jesus!" Wells yelled, jumping around to find his sister staring at him. Heather stood quizzically eying her brother.

"Why are you tiptoeing through the hall like that?" she asked.

"You scared the crap out of me." Disappointment began setting in and was followed by embarrassment.

"Well, you're being weird. And don't say 'Jesus.' You should probably change. You don't want to be late." Heather skirted around her brother and trotted downstairs to the kitchen where Leslie's voice could be heard ringing like a bell. Wells looked down at his wrinkled shirt and tried to retrace the night before. The rain, the camera, the lightning bolt. The details played over in his mind on repeat. He had flinched at the thunder and, later, accidentally resumed the storm.

Then it came to him, the feeling of pulling himself inward through the tip of his nose and the subtle vibration in his ears. He closed his eyes and began to focus as he heard the door handle to the bathroom begin to turn, but just as suddenly as it began, it ceased as the soft sound, like a gust of wind blowing across a seashore, filled his ears. The house fell truly silent. Monica's door was motionless, open barely a millimeter.

Wells walked through the hallway to the stairs. The creak of the steps and pops of his joints were eerily noisy and echoed through the house. He stepped into the kitchen to see Heather just about to sit next to Leslie at the table. She was squatting in midair. He saw his dad filling his mother's coffee cup, the black stream still as a marble statue and shining, reflecting the sunlight from the window and a small wisp of steam rising from her cup just like the night before.

"Hello?" A smile of wonder and disbelief spread on Wells' face as he waited for a reply, but none came. His family sat before him like a scene from a sitcom, paused in mid-act. A perfect picture of the domestic morning chaos on the first day of school.

"Mom? Dad?" He walked over to his parents and waved a hand in front of his mother's face. No response. He held his hand by his dad's ear and pinched his thumb and middle finger together. *Snap!*

Nothing. No blink. No flinch. No reprimand for scaring the living daylights out of his father or nearly giving his mother a heart attack, something they commonly claimed when the kids jumped out from behind a corner.

Wells laughed, amazed. He could stop the world, or at least the world around him. Glancing out the window, the clouds in the sky were no longer skating across the blue. He moved through the house. He went into the front yard; the neighborhood was at a standstill. Down the road, Mr. Jacobson was leaning over to pick up after his dog. A car was halfway down its driveway, stalled. He saw a squirrel on the side of the maple tree in their front yard. He walked right up to it and scratched its little head behind the ears.

"Hey there, little fella," he said. The fur was rough and wiry.

If it had moved, Wells would have crapped himself, but the squirrel didn't flinch.

Wells headed back into the house. Strolling straight through the kitchen and up the stairs, he walked into his bedroom. He threw yesterday's clothes into a pile in the corner. He put on a new shirt, a clean pair of pants, and pulled on his socks with an alternating one-legged hop. Something told him this was going to be an amazing day.

When he was back on the stairs, out of sight of the kitchen, he closed his eyes and pulled himself inward, jumpstarting the house around him. He paused to listen to his family in the kitchen below.

He heard the scrape of chair legs on the linoleum floor as Heather sat down at the table.

"Thanks, honey," his mom said. Wells heard her give his father a peck on the cheek in exchange for the fresh cup of coffee.

Behind him, Monica left the bathroom and darted into her room, already worrying about what study opportunities she may have lost while showering. Wells knew she had probably written down study facts in the fogged-up mirror to review while brushing her teeth. He's seen the remnants of her scribbles on a few occasions this summer.

"Mom, I think Wells will be late. He wasn't even dressed when he stumbled out of his room just now," Heather said.

"No, I won't," said Wells as he jumped down the stairs and into the kitchen, looking more bright-eyed than his family had seen him all summer.

Everyone turned to see Wells strut over to the counter and start pouring a bowl of cereal.

"Hey, Mom. Morning, Dad," he said, grinning.

"Morning, buddy." Charles' eyebrows were raised with a pleasant surprise that his son, who up until this point had proved every theory of teens not being morning people correct, was up and dressed for school and, more miraculously, in a good mood.

"Whoa, that was fast," said Heather as her brother sat down at the table. He shrugged and grinned as he took a heaping spoonful of cereal.

After Leslie caught the bus, Margaret watched through the screen door as Wells and Heather pulled out of the driveway in the old Toyota Corolla. She turned to Charles who was draining his cup of coffee, briefcase at his side.

"I think he knows," she said.

Charles tapped his pocket to confirm his keys were in their place.

"Who knows what?"

"Wells. I think he knows."

Charles paused, attention now drawn to his wife.

"You think?"

"He wasn't just excited for the first day of school. He was... different. He's been dreading the start of school since June. I don't know, but I wonder if last night, somehow, he figured it out."

Charles took a deep breath. He glanced at his watch. He would be late for his first meeting, but he knew this was important. The folks at work could wait. He thought of his little boy and that Christmas long ago. It seemed like it was light years away, in an entirely different lifetime. He honestly had hoped it was a fluke and maybe this all wouldn't happen. But now he considered, at some point, he had fallen into the trap of denial, the thought that the belief in a thing is the only part making it real. Disbelief, therefore, might keep it at bay.

"What should we do?" he asked, flatly. He was clearly stunned by being thrust into a new phase of their life as parents. "Should we take him out for pizza tonight and talk to him like you said?"

"Oh, Lord. Tonight? I don't know. Think how much could happen between now and then if we're right. I mean, really think about it. How many moments are in a day that he could get himself into trouble?"

"So what? Should we pull him from the first day of school? He's a good kid. I don't think he'll do anything too stupid. Maybe we should just wait."

"Really?" Margaret let out a tortured sigh. She ran her hands through her hair. "I'm going to drive myself crazy today. He might be using it right now."

"It'll be okay. I'm positive. I'm going to get to my meeting, and then I'll call and touch base. Okay? I really think we need to let him have his first day of school." He kissed her on the forehead and walked to the garage.

"Okay. Maybe you're right. I'll go grocery shopping and try not to eat everything in sight." She made a sound that was half laugh, half whimper, and smiled at him. Charles blew her a kiss and closed the door.

"Please, God. Please keep Wells out of trouble," Margaret prayed aloud.

Off and on, for the rest of the day, she recited this prayer just as she would for all of her children for years to come.

A few miles away, Wells was being as good as you could expect for a teenage boy with such a gift. The drive to school usually took a little less than ten minutes. Today, it seemed to last at least an hour for Wells who stopped the drive about once every block. He noticed, whenever he did this, the clock on the car's dash stayed still. It wasn't just the world around him he was stopping, but it seemed to be time itself. He looked out the window at the passing cars with the drivers checking their mirrors or picking their noses. He peered up at the birds suspended high above the car. He couldn't wipe the smile off his face as he relished in the simple wonders all around him.

"What is wrong with you?" Heather was staring at Wells as if he was stoned. He'd almost forgotten she was sitting next to him. He did it again and stared at her expression of worry and skepticism. He let her go, and the car moved again.

"I guess I'm just excited to go back to school," Wells said with a shrug and a half smile.

No matter how hard he tried, he couldn't stop smiling. Heather watched her brother suspiciously the rest of the drive,

85

settling on the thought that he might have a new girlfriend she didn't know about waiting in the parking lot.

Their small-town school was like a lot of other high schools in the United States on the first day back. It had the bustling energy of reuniting friends in fresh, trendy outfits, boys guffawing, girls pointing, outsiders skirting crowds, and teachers hushing. The distractions made it difficult to explore his new party trick, which still seemed fragile. Even though he'd been using it all morning, he worried there would come a point where he'd tire out and not be able to repeat this bizarre dream he'd been living for the last eighteen hours.

Among a crowd of friends clustering outside his morning homeroom class, Wells stopped the school just before the bell rang. He looked at the gang of teens around him and walked by each of his friends. They all had similar crips t-shirts and sharp-edged haircuts. He never really noticed how they all drifted toward the same clothing and hair styles before. It was almost comical in this frozen state; and a little unnerving.

Do I really look like this? Wells thought as he leaned in close to inspect the hair product lacquered on the head of his buddies. He wasn't sure he wanted to know the answer. If he asked his sisters, he knew they'd give an unequivocal "yes." They all looked like caricatures. They were frozen puppets, hanging by their silly expressions.

Wells encountered his first problem with stopping the world around him in this group of teens gathered outside homeroom. When he stopped the clock, he had been standing in the inner circle of his friends, right between Kyle and Stephen. He walked around the group, inspecting each of them for a few minutes, but when he pulled himself inward and stirred the sound in her ears, he was standing on the opposite side of the circle in the far back of the cluster of bodies.

The laughing and elbowing of rib cages resumed, and Wells watched Kyle and Stephen look to the space between them, surprised. Simultaneously, they looked around and spotted Wells across from them.

"Whoa, dude," Kyle chuckled. "What are you, a ninja?" He turned to Stephen as if to say, "Am I right, or what?"

Wells' stomach sank with the realization that something so simple as standing in a different place when he resumed time could lead to a flurry of difficult questions. Questions that he would have no idea how to answer. He knew he would have to be careful about restarting the world around him from now on if he wanted this to stay his little secret, which he was pretty sure he did. At least for now.

The morning bell gave a shrill ring, and the hallway bystanders began to funnel through the classroom doorways. As Stephen passed Wells, he pointed to a girl ahead of them in the classroom.

"Hey man, there she is. How'd you disappear like that, by the way?" Stephen didn't wait for Wells to reply. Instead, he walked into the classroom. He sat right behind the red-haired girl who he'd just pointed out to Wells. It was Katelyn Morrow, one of the coolest and most admired girls in their grade. Wells stood in the doorway as others moved around him. He couldn't tell if Kyle and Stephen really knew he had stopped time. They were acting too casual to have caught on to that. If they really had been paying attention, it probably would have looked like he teleported. Kyle and Stephen, now seated by one another just behind Katelyn, turned to smirk at Wells, and he felt a tinge of paranoia that they might just be onto him.

What are they smiling at, Wells thought? *They couldn't know. They would have freaked out. Right?*

Wells sat in the back of class and let the teacher move through the morning announcements. His mind was far away considering what his friends would think if they knew about the lightning bolt, his frozen family at the breakfast table, or him inspecting all of their imperfections in their morning huddle outside class. *Would they think it was cool? Would they think I was a freak? Would they try and get me to steal cigarettes from the gas station? DVDs from Best Buy?*

"Wells?" The teacher's voice pulled him out of his cloud and back to his seat.

"Ah, yes. Here."

Kyle and Stephen laughed. Wells flushed with embarrassment, clearly missing something.

"Thank you, Mr. Monasmith, but what I asked was, 'how was your summer break?'"

"Oh, sorry. Um, good. It was, um, good."

"And what was one thing new you tried this summer?" Wells looked around and thought of sitting on his roof in the storm and his mannequin parents with their coffee cups. He saw Katelyn turned around in her seat, waiting for his reply. Their eyes connected for one long second. She gave the smallest smile and turned back to face their teacher.

"Um," Wells said, "photography. I mean, I got a new digital camera, so I've been kinda, like, trying to take pictures and stuff."

Kyle and Stephen continued to quietly jeer Wells.

"Very nice, Mr. Monasmith. I look forward to seeing some of your work this year." The teacher continued interviewing students and then asked everyone to take out a sheet of paper and a pencil.

"I'd like you to write down how you will use what you learned this summer to make your life and the lives of those around you a little better. Don't show it to anyone. When you are done, I want you to fold it up and place it in the envelope I'll be handing out to each of you. Seal it and write your name on it. And don't worry; I won't open them," the teacher added as a few self-conscious looks were cast about the room. "I'll be handing these back to each of you at the end of the year, and we'll be able to see how you all did."

Wells got out a sheet of paper as instructed and looked over toward Katelyn. From his seat, her head was turned to the left just enough so he could see the corner of her eye behind her shining hair. She turned her face toward him ever so slightly, as if she could sense his gaze, but she didn't look. He stared into space, getting lost in her direction with his pencil hovered over his paper. His thoughts floated in that empty space of daydreaming where he bobbed up and down like a buoy at sea. The morning of stopping time had him a little more tired than usual. Though in reality it was only a little more than five minutes, Wells was surprised when the bell rang, indicating the end of the first period.

"Crap," said Wells, looking down at his blank sheet and the unlabeled envelope. The teacher began giving last-minute instructions. Where had the time gone? Suddenly, it occurred to Wells what he could do. He smiled and scrunched his nose. The room fell silent immediately. Some students were standing with bags flung over their shoulders. Others were dropping envelopes at the front of the room. Some were still seated.

He looked down at his paper and considered what to write. *Should I write the truth? What if the teacher read it?* That'd be a complete invasion of privacy, a betrayal of trust. He wouldn't do that. Wells couldn't be totally transparent, but maybe he could still pay homage to this new gift. Feeling a clever strike of inspiration and courage, he began to scribble on the sheet of paper.

This summer I learned how to use time. I hope I can use it better this year than I have in the past.

When he was finished, he folded the paper up and sealed it in his envelope as he walked up to the front of the class. He hopped and danced on his tiptoes around his classmates and dropped the envelope in the pile, feeling proud of himself for outsmarting his own unintentional procrastination. He looked over to Kyle and Stephen, half expecting them to congratulate him, but then remembered they, too, were frozen in their moment of packing up for the next class.

Sitting down in front of Stephen's chair was Katelyn. She was like a Greek statue, eyes fixed on her paper as if in deep thought. Her fingers were pressed firmly on the sheet, ready to slide sideways to define the fold. Wells walked over to her desk. She was achingly beautiful. The skin on her cheek was slightly blushed. Her eyelashes draped down with her gaze to the words yet uncovered. He could just make out some of what she had written:

...to listen and be a better friend before I ...

"Before you, what?" Wells asked himself.

His curiosity pulled him closer. As he stood at her desk, his eyes shifted from her paper upward and he could just about see down her blouse to the smooth skin where her neck met the top of her chest. He stepped back, feeling embarrassed but also a beat of excitement that stirred somewhere deep inside him. He looked at Stephen and Kyle. They hadn't moved. No one had. Heat and electricity burned through him, and he felt something close to sickness in his belly.

Hesitantly, he turned back and let his eyes fall toward the nape of her neck. In the shadows, he saw the soft white line of her bra. His stomach tightened.

Wells hadn't noticed how close he'd been leaning forward. As he was pulled toward the beauty before him, his thigh leaned into her desk just as he saw the shade of her tanned skin at the edge of her bra change color from summer tan to a hidden lighter shade.

A terrible screech shattered the silence in the room as the metal feet of Katelyn's desk stuttered across the tile floor.

"Holy shit!" Well shouted.

He jumped back and raced to his seat, trying to look normal. Trying to retreat from his trespassing glance. A tsunami of guilt flooded over him. Sweat beaded his forehead. He was sick with shame and wanted to vomit. He scanned the classmates around him. He looked to the front, and he locked eyes with the teacher. Everything was still frozen. His teacher had a sleepy, pleasant look on his face, but the eyes just happened to be barreling right into Wells, and at that moment, they looked like knowing eyes. Judging eyes.

"Oh my God. Oh my God. Oh my God," Wells sat back down on his desk and put his face in his hands for close to five minutes. He took out another sheet of paper and wrote a different note to himself.

Wells, don't ever do that again.

His pencil hovered over the page momentarily before writing two more words.

I'm sorry.

For the rest of the day, Wells had the persistent urge to wash his face and hands with scalding, soapy water, and his paranoia that he would be found out only grew. He didn't want to think about what might have happened had he not bumped into her desk. Deep down, he knew where it could have gone, but he wouldn't let himself travel too far down the train of thought. On the car ride home, Heather noticed the gloom that sat next to her in the passenger seat.

"What's going on with you? I thought you were all excited for the first day. Too much homework already?"

"No, I'm fine. Just tired is all," Wells said.

She didn't seem to buy it but decided not to press him. When they got home, Wells walked straight through the kitchen and up to his room, closing the door behind him. He dropped his backpack on the floor and crashed onto the bed trying to sleep away the knowledge that he would never be worthy of a girl like Katelyn Morrow. And he promised himself he wouldn't become an asshole who could take whatever he wanted. Wells began the day feeling excited, but he fell asleep feeling guilty and alone.

CHAPTER 12: 1/6/20 THE TALK

I realize it might be uncomfortable to read about that first morning in homeroom. Honestly, it's still hard for me to think about it, let alone write it down. But I can't change the past and that is how this all began. There were many things I did during those early years that were morally questionable or just plain wrong. But what do you expect when something like this is thrust upon a teenager?

And yes, the Katelyn I referred to is "that Katelyn." She moved away shortly after the school year started. Up until the day she left, her fire burned me with a twinge of guilt every day I walked into that classroom and saw her sitting in the front row. After she was gone, I felt just as much relief as I did loss for that crush. It was bittersweet to say goodbye to that flame.

And, of course, she did come back into my life in a significant way several years later, but I won't get into that yet.

For now, I want to tell you about two things. The first is something called the Baader-Meinhof phenomenon, and the second is something all teens fear. They fear it more than being the only one of their friends to fail the driver's license exam. More than peeing your pants at school in front of your biggest crush. More than getting caught masturbating by your sisters.

What they fear more than any of those things is the day their parent knocks on their bedroom door and tries to talk to them about sex. I'd wager nine out of ten teens would trade any of the above options over and over rather than have the uncomfortable conversation about sex with their mom and/or dad.

But before we get to my personal version of "the talk," we need to review the Baader-Meinhof phenomenon. Monica, maybe you've come across it in med school. Maybe not. I only stumbled across it by chance when sifting through some pages at that used bookstore in La Crosse. I'm sure you'll recognize the term once I describe it.

The Baader-Meinhof phenomenon is the illusion that things occur at an increased frequency once you have been made aware of them. For instance, I remember in high school when Karl Thompson—you remember Karl, right? Tall guy, played basketball, and painted his fingernails black like Dennis Rodman? Anyway, he told me he wanted to save up his money to buy a Honda CRX. A little sporty car that I'd pretty much never known existed, but in the months to follow, I felt like I was seeing them all over the place. I couldn't turn around without noticing one. On TV, biking to pick up sodas at the gas station, in the school parking lot. You and I know all too well, in our small community, there couldn't have been many of these cars. In reality, I was probably seeing the same two or three on repeat, but I could have sworn those zippy little autos had suddenly populated the entire town.

So, Monica, why am I wasting your time explaining the Baader-Meinhof phenomenon? Well, after I settled down from that first day and realized the opportunity to catch up on procrastinated work, the way I had done with the short, letter-writing assignment, I saw these chances everywhere. I felt like I'd been given a free pass. I didn't have to miss out on anything so long as I had a fraction of a second to stop time and finish my homework at my own pace. I used this all the way through college. It's honestly why I got such good grades and did so well on the ACT and SAT. I didn't cheat, per se. I just crammed every now and then, and if I needed more time on a standardized test, I just snuck a little in there to catch up. Did I have an unfair advantage that some might think was wrong? I guess. But was it evil? I don't believe so.

Now, back to the other topic: the talk.

Knock. Knock.

"Yeah," said Wells. He laid on his back with his eyes buried in the pit of his elbow. His legs dangled off the edge of the bed as if too heavy to lift. He was still feeling sick from looking down Katelyn's shirt. It wasn't that he didn't like it. The image in his mind's eye caused his pulse to quicken the moment he conjured it. But knowing that she couldn't stop it stirred up feelings of shame and self-loathing that pushed the color from his cheeks.

"Wells, can we come in?" His parents opened the door slowly.

"Yup." Wells' voice was monotone and unaffected, as if already half asleep. He was exhausted. It had been a long day, and his head felt dense with fog.

"Hey, sweetie." His parents walked in, and his mom sat on the side of the bed. His dad stayed standing. "Your dad and I were wondering if you wanted to go out for pizza tonight. To, you know, celebrate the first day of school and maybe talk about a few things." Margaret looked at Charles for support. They had rehearsed this, but it still felt awkward. Unveiling the invisible elephant in the room was going to be harder than they thought.

"I'm not really hungry, to be honest. I kinda just want to go to bed, if that's okay."

Margaret looked at her husband and tilted her head to signal it was now his turn.

"Wells, um, anything interesting happen at school today?" Charles shrugged and mouthed "I don't know" to Margaret with a lost expression that would have been comical had they been living in a sitcom.

Wells sighed and drove his palms into his eye sockets. The heavy silence filled the space of his small room as he waited for his parents to shift uncomfortably and finally ask if any of his friends were having sex. The air felt as pregnant as Marianne Baker, Heather's old childhood friend who served as the unfair and unwilling reminder of what can happen when teens "do it." No one ever seemed to remember the role Alex Hubert played in that story. *Whatever happened to that guy?* Wells wondered.

Exasperated, Wells gave up and spoke first.

"Nope." He slid his hands to the top of his shaggy head and stared at the ceiling, yawning. He thought of the lightning bolt and Katelyn. "Not really. Do *you guys* have something you'd like to talk about? Did something interesting happen to you today?"

There was another silence. This time, it was Margaret who took the lead when she couldn't take the silence any longer.

"You know, don't you, Wells?" she asked.

"Know what?" His response was as flat as the tires of his old bike in the back of their garage. Wells was still staring into the sky somewhere above his ceiling.

"You figured out how to stop time."

Wells blinked, and he pulled his attention down from the clouds like a kite on a string. He sat up and looked back and forth between his parents.

"What?"

"It's okay, honey. I know all about it," Margaret said.

Wells felt the shame rush in again. How could she know about the assignment? About Katelyn?

Margaret continued. "Was it last night or this morning that you discovered it?"

"How do you know about that? Were you spying on me or something?" he said defensively. He looked around the corners of his room, expecting to see a security camera. Wells quickly rounded back on his parents as fear and indignation were quickly driven out by anger. It's funny how, no matter how wrong their actions may have been, teens had a way of believing nothing was more evil and unjust than being spied on by their parents. Somehow that thought made his little time cheat and glance down an unknowing girl's shirt seem irrelevant.

"No, we didn't see you, but. . ." she stuttered, a little shocked at Wells' look of reproach. *Oh, my Lord. Has he done something awful already?* she thought. "I can just tell. My brothers could do it, too. This morning, you had the same look they did. Like you could see things we couldn't."

"And we didn't know when it would happen, but we thought it would be soon," Charles added hastily to bring the heat of the conversation back down. "Your uncles were about your age." Seeing Wells about to protest as he realized his parents knew all along, Charles quickly continued. "We had hoped, honestly, you wouldn't be able to do it. So, I guess that's why we didn't tell you. Just in case, you know?"

"Wait," said Wells trying to let his thoughts catch up with him. This wasn't the direction he thought this conversion would go. They weren't blaming him for anything. And they knew about it all. Should he be angry they didn't tell him? At least they weren't spying; that was a relief. But how could their family have this secret and nobody talk about it? "So, what is it? Can you guys do it, too? What about Monica or the others?"

"It comes from my side of the family, and it seems like only the boys can do it. Your father and your sisters can't. Your sisters don't even know about it yet. I can use it to a certain degree, but nothing like what my brothers could, or you. And honestly, I really try my best not to use it at all." Margaret watched as Wells took it in, wondering which of the many directions he might take the conversation.

"Why don't you want to use it, whatever it is?"

It was the question Margaret and Charles had hoped their son would save for last, but of course, it was his first.

"That's a little complicated, I suppose. Partly, I don't think I'm as good at it as you or my brothers were, so my experience is somewhat different. I can just slow things a bit, but they keep moving, and it doesn't last long. I guess that limits the use I have for it. Also, I've learned to live without it. I'm not... dependent on it, so I just don't need to do it. I think my brothers built their lives around it to an extent." She had wanted to say her brothers became addicted to it but was scared to use that word. Margaret worried if she said it out loud, it might come true for Wells, too.

"I guess the other reason is that I felt it wasn't fair. This is a personal decision—one you'll have to decide for yourself. I didn't feel comfortable trying to use it when others couldn't. It isn't wrong having this... ability, but I do feel how we use it is important. For instance, the times I've been most tempted to do it often have to do with things I love."

"Like what?" asked Wells with an expression as if he was about to be. "Like listening to Rod Stewart or something?" Wells knew his mom had an odd, almost frightening, fascination with the spiky-haired singer. He thought it was weird, as did all of the kids. Dad didn't seem to be threatened by the Brit. Margaret laughed.

"No. No. Other things, like my children. Like you. Watching your children grow up and away from you is one of the best and worst things about being a parent. So, sometimes, like when you were starting first grade, and I watched the bus roll up to the stop, I held on to you a little longer, just to cherish the sight of you smiling at me before you left." Wells saw his mother's eyes glisten. He looked to the ground.

"Okay, but that sounds like a special memory. So, like I said, why don't you want to use it, then?"

"Everything has a cost, Wells. I think you have an opportunity to see life a lot differently than other people. But, this power, or gift, or whatever you want to call it, just seems to be hard on our bodies. Both of my brothers died young. Long before you were born. And even now, when I use it, it seems to age me a little bit. Maybe it's like smoking cigarettes."

"Something you also should not do, by the way," interjected Charles.

"Yeah, Dad. I know."

"But it is true, Wells. That's the biggest thing we want you to hear. We can't tell you how to live your life. But we want you to be careful. We love you, and stopping time will take its toll. It has a cost."

After a final silence that signaled the end of his parent's speech, Wells received a "good-talk-son" pat on the shoulder and a tip-toed hug from his mother. After they left, Wells flopped face first onto his pillow. With his mind swimming, he was absolutely obliterated with exhaustion. Before his eyelids sank like a ship in a stormy sea, he thought of Katelyn. He thought of school. He thought he wouldn't tell his sisters, and maybe not even tell his friends. Swayed by the lingering voice of his parents, Wells also swore to himself he'd be careful and only stop time if he really needed it. Finally, he yawned with relief at least for now not to have to suffer through the mortifying discussion with his parents of how to avoid making a baby. Regardless of all that had happened, that talk would have made his day exponentially worse.

CHAPTER 13: 1/7/20 PHOTOGRAPHY, DREAMS, AND THE TOAD

We all have personal experiences that shape us, and they are often hidden from others. Each of you, Monica, Heather, and Leslie, I'm sure has something that you've done or has happened to you that has become so essential to your core that you see it as a sentinel event shaping the person you have become spiraling outward from that moment. Hopefully, it wasn't traumatizing and was a positive experience, but unfortunately that isn't always the case.

My intention with this story isn't to bore you, so if that's already happening, I'm sorry. Maybe take a quick walk around the block and come back to me. I am hoping that I might be able to give insight into those unseen parts of my life, the sentinel events I just spoke of. In doing so, I guess I also hope you might better understand who I was and why I wasn't always around, and even when I was, why I may have seemed distant. The other reason is something less selfish. If you have any sons or grandsons of your own one day, I'm hoping this rambling series of events might help guide the strange life they'll be living.

So, during high school and the few years I attempted college, there are three things I want to tell you about. The first has to do with photography. The second is dreams. Last is the story of one big, fat, warty toad.

———

Margaret and Charles always marveled at the unique interests of their children as most parents do, and no matter how much they tried to predict interests or direct them, the kids continued to surprise them. There was a time when Charles thought his children would be stars on the soccer field just as he had been. He bought Monica a little soccer jersey, took her to the high school games, and spent hours trying to get her to pass a ball back and forth in the backyard. However, no matter how much enthusiasm, bribery, and pressure he applied, Monica always ended up in tears. She simply had no desire to play soccer. Instead, she'd spend more time debating the absurdity of the rules. After all, who would make a game where you couldn't use your hands? It seemed ridiculous to her and discredited all soccer-related activities. She did go on to become a standout swimmer, however. Wells gave soccer a half-hearted attempt, but never really excelled. Heather gravitated toward gymnastics, and Leslie played ice hockey.

The childhood dreams of becoming a professional athlete were few and far between in the Monasmith household. Still, it was a shock to both parents when Wells decided to drop soccer the fall after he discovered his ability.

"Are you sure, Wells?" said Charles as the family sat around the dinner table eating steamed broccoli, chicken, and rice.

"Yeah. I'm sure." Wells drank from his tall glass of milk. "How'd you hear?"

"Coach called earlier when he didn't see your registration." Charles' eyes were soft with concern.

"Are you going to do anything instead?" Margaret was hoping there was another club that might take soccer's place. She had also noticed Wells withdrawing from his friends this year. High school was hard enough for kids. It was even worse if you walked that road alone.

"I guess. I was kind of thinking of seeing if the journalism teacher, Mrs. Anderson, would let me do some sports photography." Wells presented the suggestion hesitantly, as if it were a fragile offering that could break if not handled properly.

"What's a photographer do?" asked Leslie.

"It's someone who takes pictures of people," answered Heather.

"Oh. I thought you liked your soccer friends. Are they not, like, fun enough anymore?" Leslie's question was sincere, but the sliver of truth in it hurt.

"No. They're all fine," Wells said.

"Are you having problems with someone on the team?" Heather asked.

"No." The interrogation was starting to annoy him. He felt hot around the collar of his shirt.

Monica, who was back for the weekend, pushed away from the table and bussed her dishes. "Photography sure sounds nice and easy. Easier than sticking with something for once."

"What is that supposed to mean?"

"It means you're not dedicated."

"Shut up. No it doesn't."

"Hey, stop. Both of you," Charles said. "Wells, I think what we are all saying is that you've played soccer for so long. The team's going to miss you, and you'll probably miss it, too. You know, you could always try hockey. You're a good skater. It's not too late to pick it up." Charles, also an avid hockey fan, still had hopes one of his kids might be on a state high school tournament team. Even if Wells didn't pick it up, he'd still have a chance with Leslie. But it was worth a shot to see if Wells would start playing, too, and increase his chances.

"The team'll be fine, and I'm not that good at hockey. I just think taking pictures for the yearbook might be more fun. I bet I could probably get some good shots of the teams, like, since I've played sports and stuff, that might help me know when to shoot, you know? I... I think I'll have good timing." He looked at his parents who didn't catch his eye. He turned back to his food. The statement was delivered like a toe breaking the surface of a swimming pool. He thought maybe they would register the implication, an under-the-table request for permission, but it looked like the meaning behind the words was lost.

"I'm sure you will take wonderful photos, honey. We just know you've really liked playing, but of course we support you in whatever you decide to do. And who knows? Maybe you'll end up just taking the year off and play next year," said Margaret, playing the role of the ever-optimistic mother.

"That's true, you know. You could keep up your footwork, or even work on your stickhandling skills on the outdoor rink. I'm sure the boys would come out and skate with you. You could have Leslie come, too," Charles said.

When it came down to it, Wells had been looking for any opportunity to stop time. He knew his parents didn't approve of him being careless with it. It felt like they dropped passive-aggressive hints everywhere. But each night when he went to bed, he looked at the photo of the lightning bolt. He'd printed it off at Walmart so he could hold it in his hands. He didn't have any formal background in photography, but even he knew it was a remarkable shot. He would run his fingers along the edges of the crackling bolt. Wells could almost feel the shimmering, blue heat driving into their backyard.

If he could get signed up as a yearbook photographer, he could stop the players and get the pictures just right. The athletes in the photos would be crisp without the typical flaws of amateur photographers who published yearbook photos of poorly cropped, overexposed, and blurred subjects. The beauty of his idea was that he'd feel less guilty stopping time since he was doing it for school. Heck, he figured his parents would be proud of his altruistic motives.

By the end of the conversation, Wells had enough passive support to garner the courage to approach the journalism teacher the following day and within two weeks, he was sliding into the schedule of school sporting events with a photographer pass hanging around his neck. The first set of pictures Wells developed were from a Junior Varsity girls' soccer game. The more senior photography students had dibs on the two digital SLR cameras, so Wells was stuck picking one of the 35mm Nikon film cameras. He had a tutorial prior to the game with a few tips from the head school photographer.

"What's your name again?" asked a tall, black-haired girl named Jackie who had been taking photos for various school functions over the previous three years.

"It's Wells."

"Okay, so, Wells, I see how you are looking at the SLR. I know you want to use the digital cameras, but first, it's a seniority thing. All the first-timers get stuck on the film cameras initially. And second, if you do it right, the film camera will make you a better photographer in the long run. You'll have a better understanding of the entire process, especially when we go to the darkroom and you see all of your mistakes materialize before you."

"Mm-hmm"

After Jackie gave a short lecture on aperture settings and shutter speeds and handed Wells a *Photography for Dummies* book, she gave him a heavy shoulder bag and told him to be at the game at least a half hour early so he could practice by shooting warmups. Jackie gave him a look that was at best sympathetic but with too much of a grin as she was clearly enjoying playing a key role in this budding photographer's education. She watched him walk away as if she was throwing him to the lions in a gladiator's pit. Wells, however, walked away feeling like a well-equipped lion tamer ready to emerge victorious from the tunnels beneath the colosseum.

That night, beneath the washed-out floodlights of the soccer field, he used an entire roll of film. No more, no less. When he met back up with Jackie after the game, she shook her head in over-dramatic, unsurprised disappointment.

"I was watching you. You should've moved around more to get your shots, and don't be afraid to step onto the field. As long as play isn't close to you, they're pretty chill with us getting up close for a good shot. Plus, plan on, at best, maybe five of those shots being passable. Don't be too hard on yourself, though, if none of yours turn out this first time. This stuff is tricky, and most folks don't stick with it." To her, Wells was just one more kid jumping on the "journalism is an easy A" train, and, by the looks of how the night went, he wouldn't be there very long.

"That's good to know. Thanks," Wells said with a forced grin

From what Jackie saw, Wells barely moved all game. He walked around, slowly watching the plays unfold, and only raised the camera to his eye if a lot of action was happening. She'd needed to remind herself to tell him that, though the film cost money, one good shot was worth the price of a few rolls, so he should be liberal with his picture- taking attempts early on. A few times, she thought she saw him bring down the camera so suddenly she was worried he'd drop the ancient beast. It was as if he was avoiding taking the shots.

To Wells, the game didn't last ninety minutes. It took a hell of a lot longer and he loved every second of it. He'd stopped the game fifty or sixty times to get his camera to capture the perfect thirty-six photos before he ejected his film canister. Each time he stopped the game, he circled the players, the girls jumping up for a header goose necking for every millimeter, the goalie diving to stop a penalty shot grimacing as her fist punched the ball, the slide tackle spraying mud and grass into the air. It would be at least a day or two sitting in doubt before he'd know how it all developed.

When he finally looked at the film in the darkroom and the photographs were pulled by chemical reaction onto the smooth white paper, every shot was perfectly framed, focused, and gleamed with impeccable lighting. Mrs. Anderson looked at the photos with an astonished expression no teacher had ever directed toward him or his work.

"Wells, these are amazing. You didn't take a single bad photo. And you've never tried sports photography before?" She looked at him with an expression of part disbelief and part joy. Regardless of the subject, it was always a special moment as a teacher when you see a child with true, deep-rooted talent. Like finding a winning lottery ticket in the school parking lot.

"No, not really." Admitting he hadn't spent any formal time practicing photography felt good. Pride rose in him like the morning sun. His face lit up, but he tried to hide it as soon as he saw jealousy flash across Jackie's face. It was gone as quickly as it appeared, but Wells knew the look. The concern faded quickly. At that moment, he felt untouchable.

"Then you're a natural," said Mrs. Anderson matter of factly as she clapped her hands together. "You've got a gift. Keep it up, Mr. Monasmith."

"Mr. Monasmith?... Mr. Monasmith?"

"Yeah? Sorry." Wells came back from somewhere in outer space and looked into the kind eyes of a cardigan-wearing guidance counselor seated at a desk cluttered with pamphlets and magazines.

"You can come in now."

Wells walked into her office and sat down on the chair facing her. On the opposite wall, there was a picture of a kitten dangling from a tree branch with the caption "hang in there" written in pastel lettering. Wells wondered how many times someone had to dangle the kitten on the branch before they got that shot just right. Was there a pillow beneath the tree limb ready to catch the kitten if it fell? Or just a lot of kittens waiting to replace the fallen felines?

Over a year had passed since Wells started photography, and all of the juniors were required to have an appointment with Angela Thompson, the school guidance counselor. She was a warm-hearted woman with a couple kids who had also passed through the school halls in previous years. She wasn't afraid to give the hard-to-hear practical advice, but was also willing to nudge dreamers further into the clouds for the students willing to put in the work.

"Another Monasmith, is it? Are you the last one?" She smiled at Wells who gave a polite grin in return.

"No, there's one more." He didn't want to engage and prolong this any further than needed. Thinking about the future made Wells feel like he was standing in a canoe. Having no idea what he wanted to do after high school made him feel as if he could tip over at any moment. Everyone said "go to college," but Wells wasn't even sure what that meant. Monica was driven and knew from her fourth Halloween she'd wanted to be a doctor. Heather was interested in nursing, and it seemed like a good fit. She smiled whenever she came home for the weekend to do laundry and shared stories from her clinical rotations.

"You'll eventually meet my little sister, Leslie, but she's still in grade school, so you've got some time."

"That's good." Mrs. Thompson gave Wells a wink. She was good at banter but better at reading students. She could see he didn't want to talk, so she decided to cut to the chase. "So tell me, what is it that you want to do with your future, Mr. Monasmith? What do you want to do after high school?"

"Um, I'm not really sure, I guess."

"Your sisters are both going into healthcare, right? Heather is in nursing school, and Monica, is she in medical school?"

"She starts next year. She's going to the U."

"Is there any chance you'd like to follow in either of their footsteps? There are a lot of diverse opportunities in healthcare. You can find jobs almost anywhere if you like the idea of getting out and exploring."

"No. I don't think that interests me. Healthcare, I mean. Travel would be nice, I guess, but how do you get paid to travel?"

"Good question. Wouldn't that be a cool job? Getting paid to fly all over the country or even the world? Let's see." She opened a folder that was sitting on the desk. Wells hadn't noticed it until now. His name was written on the tab. She scanned a few papers and hummed to herself.

"Wow. It sounds like you've really done well in journalism."

"Photography," Wells corrected. "I don't really like writing, but I like taking pictures."

"Mrs. Anderson says here you're the best photography student she's had. Ever. That's really something. Have you ever thought about going to a school that would allow you to make photography your career? There are a lot of avenues to find that destination. You could enroll in an art or graphic design program. Journalism, just like you do know, is another good option. We have a lot of schools here in the area that might fit, depending on how far you'd like to be from home."

"Can you really take pictures for a living? I thought that was just, like, the people who take those awkward grade school photos everyone is embarrassed about."

"Well, that's one way you could go, but how do you think they get all of the photos for the newspaper? Or who do you think takes the photographs you see up on the billboards along the highway?" She let this settle in and looked back at Wells' file.

"Let's try another question. Do you want to go to college?"

"I mean, I guess. Isn't that what we're supposed to do?"

"Most people find you can earn a higher income over time if you have some type of college degree. So, in general, yes, we try to encourage all of our students to look into some type of college or training after high school, but that doesn't mean it's right for everyone."

Wells didn't answer. He picked his nails and looked up at her, not sure what to say. She gave him another nudge.

"If you could do anything after high school, what would it be? What do you dream about?"

Wells stared at his guidance counselor and closed his eyes as the rumbling reached a crescendo in his ears. Mrs. Thompson stared at him like a figure in a painting.

"Ugh. Just give me a second, okay?" Wells pushed his chair back from the desk. As far as dreams were considered, that's another question Wells hadn't explored yet. The idea of his dream job felt too big to clearly visualize, like a large cloud riding the horizon, always shifting and growing, but never showing its full, true shape.

"What are my dreams? Honestly?" He said, exasperated, to the counselor sitting in front of him like a storefront display for sensible teacher's attire. He pushed himself up and away from the desk and paced back and forth in the small office. "Well, I want to learn to surf and take a picture of a hurricane, or maybe learn how to play guitar like Jimi Hendrix, go sky diving, and visit another country. There's a million things." Even with her frozen in time, he felt too embarrassed to say "have sex" in front of a teacher, but that thought crossed his mind, too.

When the image of the red-haired girl manifested before him, he quickly pushed the thought far from his mind. Even though her family had moved away, he'd feared he had scarred himself from the incident during the previous year. Any time

111

the flirting with girls at school started to become something more, a small seed of guilt lying dormant began to sprout, and he retreated from whatever base he thought he might steal.

He stopped pacing and sat back down where he was when he froze her. She blinked again, still smiling, waiting for his answer.

"I think I do want to go... to college, that is. It'd be cool to learn more about photography and maybe somehow get a job doing that, I guess." Even though his voice wavered with hesitancy, Mrs. Thompson's face lit up with the committal.

"That's great! Now we're getting somewhere. So first, let's start brainstorming how close to home you'd like to be. There's pretty much three categories here. There's pop-in-for-dinner close, bring-laundry-home-on-the-weekends close, and I'll-see-you-at-Thanksgiving-and-Christmas close. Any ideas which type of close-to-home you'd like to be? And don't worry, we'll get to financial aid soon."

In the end, Wells walked out of Mrs. Thompson's office with a handful of pamphlets on a few midwestern schools, all within a three to five hours' drive. Each of the schools was capable of giving him an opportunity to study photography, study abroad, and one maybe even learn to surf. When it came to having sex, he had a feeling where you went to college made no difference so long as it wasn't online.

———

"Hey, Mom, I'm going out on a run."
"Okay, be careful. Wear light colors."

"Okay," Wells called back over his shoulder as he stepped out the front door of his parents' house and into the smothering twilight. The late summer sunset was showing the last of its colors. It was a battle cry of burning pastels, imploring the world to remember what might be summer's last stand. It was a fitting symbol for Wells' last summer at home before starting college. He had settled on a state school a few hours north that rested on the hill overlooking Lake Superior. The selling point of the school, besides the fact that neither Monica nor Heather had attended it, was that there was a student surfing club. If he wanted to check any of his dreams off his list and still be able to make it back home for an occasional laundry dump, this might be his best chance.

Wells looked down at his iPod and pulled up his latest playlist. The music began flowing through his headphones like a spring-fed creek. The guitar tumbled forward, followed shortly by the smooth voice of Gillian Welch. Wells stepped onto the road as Gillian sang like a tight copper wire, "time's the revelator." Jogging at dusk was now a routine for Wells. The summer air was warm as bathwater, and the bats skirted around in the dying light, scooping up bugs, fattening up for a long winter. He wondered if the music in his iPod would stop if he held onto the evening for the rest of his jog.

The sound of a passing car came to a halt as Wells stopped the little river town in its tracks. His music stopped, too. He looked at the screen and the paused play clock. He clicked the play button.

Nothing happened. Why was that? He focused on the numbers on the screen, careful not to let the world resume around him. He imagined the gray, pixelated numbers counting the seconds. Then, so suddenly that his ears hurt, the music

113

picked up right where it left off while the bats remained motionless like they were hung up with fishing line on his parents' porch at Halloween.

"Hm. Well look at that," he said. Shaking his head in amusement, he let the bats resume catching mosquitos and Apollo continue dragging the sun to someone else's horizon.

The wanderlust with his ability was still there from time to time, but the shine had worn off a bit. Over the last few years, he mostly stopped when he wanted to create more time to hang out with his friends playing video games or go fishing and, of course, if he was taking pictures. But even that wasn't as exhilarating as it had once been. It became so routine, even his parents, whom he was pretty sure could tell what he was doing, seemed to accept it. The most recent example in his memory was in spring before his final history assignment was due. Wells jumped down the last few stairs in the kitchen and moved quickly for the garage.

"Mom, I'm heading over to the river to meet Ryan! I'll be back after dinner."

"Wait, I thought you had that big history project still to do."

"No, I already got it done. Just finished it," he said with a grin. To his mother, he'd been home for just over twenty minutes. To Wells, who had put off the majority of his project until today, it had been hours of researching, writing, and rushing to pull together something decent enough to earn a solid B. The assignment was a third of his grade, after all, so he knew he needed to at least try a little harder than normal. He spent the better part of four hours during his mom's twenty minutes completing the project, and by the time he let go of the hold, he was ready for a well-deserved break.

"Wells, you just got home. How could you already be... Nevermind." She shook her head at him and looked over her glasses. "Just don't be late for supper."

Early on, when Charles and Margaret suspected his new homework routine, they held another intervention.

"Wells, you really need to be careful. What if someone thinks you're cheating? You could get in serious trouble," Margaret said, trying to focus on immediate consequences. They had found that pleading with him to stop because it was bad for his health had been fruitless. What teenager truly fears their mortality?

"First of all, even if I was, how could they prove that? And secondly, I'm not cheating. I'm doing the work."

"We know you are, Wells," said Charles. "But they don't. We just want you to be careful. Once you get accused of cheating, or anything for that matter, it's hard to shake that label."

Ironically, Wells' teachers didn't think he was cheating. Instead, they were wowed at his sudden dedication and natural intelligence that seemed to have blossomed as he matured. It also coincided with the exposure of his now-famous photography expertise. Some argued it was due to quitting soccer. Others happily took the credit that their teaching techniques finally got through to the stubborn student, and some just seemed to like the Cinderella story and didn't care about the explanation.

Now, jogging on the empty black top of the road heading in the opposite direction of the river and toward the bluffs, he took long strides away from his home. In a few short weeks, Wells would be moving into a dorm room in northern Minnesota to pursue an art degree with a focus on photography. He was starting to get excited to finally spend his time in school focusing on something he actually cared about. There was just something special about taking pictures of things when he froze them; it was like painting a still life. Seeing a deer in your backyard is one thing. Walking up to it as it stands as still as a bowl of apples on the table is another. School was finally going to mean something to him.

Out of the corner of his eye, Wells saw a fat American toad hop onto the road. The streetlights were on now, and the moths and a myriad of insects were beginning to fill the buffet for these amphibians and other bug-loving critters. Wells hopped over the toad, so as not to end its tiny life.

Suddenly, a horn honked, and Wells stopped in the middle of an intersection. A white minivan came to a screeching stop.

"Hey, watch out!" the driver yelled through the window.

"Take it easy, buddy," Wells shouted back and began running again, eyeing down the driver who sped away in the opposite direction. Wells was clearly in the wrong. While he wasn't paying attention, he had failed to scan the intersection, and the music in his headphones competed for the sounds of the oncoming car.

"Asshole," he said and sighed.

Wells kept running, shaking his head in frustration. He should have stopped time and messed up the car. He could have taken the keys out of the ignition and thrown them on a lawn or let the air out of the tires. He rubbed sweat from his brow and frowned. He wouldn't want the driver to get hurt. It was just aggravating that he didn't react quickly enough to stop time. What if the driver hadn't seen him? Would he have been able to stop the van before it hit him? He had the power to stop everything, so long as he was paying attention. This made Wells feel close to invincible.

Wells turned down another street and sped up. His legs pumped beneath him. He didn't see anyone around so he stopped and started time every fourth step. If someone had been watching, it likely looked like he was teleporting, or maybe running under a strobe light, skipping forward with a stuttering flash of movement. The thought made him run faster, propelling him forward, his quads starting to burn from the lactic acid. A plane roared up above as it made its way to the nearby airport.

He turned the corner back onto his parents' road and was just about to slow down when another toad hopped out from the shade and into the light of the streetlamp. It hopped right in his path.

"No!" Wells shouted.

He was in mid-stride. The toes of his right shoe were about to lift off the ground behind him, and his left heel was starting to descend on the pavement inches in front of where the toad had landed. Wells pulled the world inward to stop everything. The sound of the plane flying above ceased, the wind hushed instantly, the hum of the town died, and Wells' left foot landed.

Instead of landing on the hard pavement, his shoe slid and rolled over a soft lump that squished beneath his weight. Wells hopped to the side and skidded to a stop looking to see if, by some freak chance, the toad had survived. The skin was stripped from the back legs exposing the smooth, pink muscles. The belly was split, and a string of glossy purple and gray entrails lay behind the animal like a twisted umbilical cord. The toad lay on its back with the webbed front toes dangling in the air. The streetlight reflected off the pale lower jaw.

Wells groaned. His heart was thumping in his ears, and he tried to catch his breath. He kneeled down beside the toad, still as can be, with no knowledge of what had occurred. This had never happened to Wells before. He was always able to give himself the time he needed to control a situation. Whether he needed another hour to finish his homework, get home before curfew, or even run away from the police when they were called to Kyle's parents' house at the end-of-the-year senior party.

When Stephen ran down into the basement and yelled, "The cops are here!" Wells calmly got up and walked out the sliding door. Just as a flashlight started shining around the corner, he froze everything and nonchalantly walked away. He felt a little guilty once he was out of sight, so he sauntered back into the house and took all the beer out of Kyle's room and hid any empty cans or bottles out of plain sight. Kyle even had some weed that Wells took and returned later. That one saved Kyle from a lot of trouble.

Looking down at this dead toad, Wells felt a sickening realization that, even with his special power, the ability to stop the world in its tracks and walk through so many doors that would otherwise remain locked, he still might not be able to control everything. Unfortunately, Wells also possessed the power that courses through the arteries and veins of all eighteen-year-olds. The power to ignore the bigger picture. The power to forget that your actions affect others around you. The fallacy of invincibility and certainty of unlimited time.

CHAPTER 14: LESLIE

Text message:

Leslie: Have you read Wells' story yet?

Heather: Some of it. Started last night, but then Maya woke up and Adrienne climbed in bed with us. Didn't get too far. You?

Leslie: Yeah. I stayed up and finished it.

Heather: Wow! What do you think? I remember that Christmas. You probably don't.

Leslie: I think I'm still processing it, you know?

Heather: For sure. Do you believe it all? I mean, I love Wells, but I don't know. It's all so crazy.

Leslie: I do. I guess it just makes sense to me. You should finish it though, before we talk more about it.

Heather: K. Deal.

Leslie: You going to Wells' place on wed with mom?

Heather: Yeah. Christian is gonna stay with the kids. I'll try and finish by then. Do me a favor and pray the kids let this mama sleep for once.

Leslie: Got your back #whataresistersfor

Heather: lol. I'm so old. It takes me like 5 minutes to read hashtags. #Imsoold

Leslie: ha

Heather: see you wed

Leslie: k

Leslie set down her phone and looked at the polaroid sitting on her old bed. She read the message scratched on the back of the picture.

When you're ready, think of Wells, and imagine yourself doing backflips underwater.

"Wells, you're so weird." She tried to imagine herself underwater.

"Water. Heavy, cold water," she said, trying to follow his instructions. She slowed her breathing and listened to the beat of her heart. A snowblower started up somewhere outside. The heater at her bedside clicked on. The distractions were winning. She tried to focus again on the pool of cool water. She pictured the pond near her parents' house. Right now, it was frozen over. Snow shovels lay at the edge. Two hockey goals faced each other from opposite sides of the pond. Leslie imagined the ice beginning to melt and the nets tilting through the surface, sinking to the bottom. She imagined bare feet walking to the edge of the water. The snow had now melted, and the grass was fluorescent green. The surface of the water began to shimmer and lift and out walked Sara Hannon. Leslie stretched out a hand to her and then remembered what she was supposed to be doing. She opened her eyes. Her body was warm from dreaming of things she loved.

Leslie set the polaroid down and picked her phone back up. She scrolled through her favorite contacts and found Monica's number. Her thumb hovered over the name but shifted and tapped the name above. It rang twice before Margaret picked up.

"Hey there, sweetie."

"Hey, Mom. How's it going?"

"Oh, you know. Your dad is driving me crazy, as usual. We're trying to contact the lawyer to help deal with Wells' things. Are you planning on coming Wednesday?"

"Of course, Mom. Whatever I can do to help."

"Just being there is enough."

Leslie heard Margaret rinsing the dishes. She closed her eyes and could see her, dishrag sitting on the counter, taking the plates out of the sink one by one, wiping them clean, and placing them back in the cupboard over the old white Mr. Coffee drip machine. The coffee would be pale and weak, the way her parents preferred, as opposed to the dark full roasts that had become standard at most coffee shops over the years. You can't drink strong coffee all day long unless you're trucking eighteen wheels or working the third shift in the intensive care unit.

"Mom…"

"Yes, dear?"

"Why do you think Wells never told me?"

Across the line, the faucet turned off, and the shifting of clean dishes and silverware stopped.

"I don't know. I regret we didn't tell you sooner. But we really felt like we needed Wells' permission to do that. That's a dumb excuse, I know, but he's the one this has impacted the most. It's just such an odd thing to try and explain. And now that he's gone, it makes it harder. It makes me wish we had sat down with all of you many, many years ago." In the silence that followed, Margaret realized she hadn't answered her daughter's question.

"I know Wells wanted to tell each of you in person. In the end, I think he saw that he was running out of time, something Wells probably never expected would happen."

Leslie thought about this. She thought about all the times she wanted to say something, to Sara Hannon, or her sisters, or Wells, but didn't.

"Mom, I love you."

"I know." Her mom laughed.

"I know you know. I just wanted to say it."

"Well, thank you, dear. Oh my, your father's calling. I'd have all the time in the world if I didn't have to babysit him. I'll see you Wednesday then. Okay?"

"Okay, Mom. See you on Wednesday."

"Bye now."

Leslie heard Margaret shout at her father to put the hammer down before hanging up the phone. She smiled. She looked at the polaroid. She read the handwritten note from her brother. Leslie was exhausted from staying up all night, and she had to be at the bookstore at noon for her afternoon shift. She laid her head on the pillow and pulled the fleece blanket over herself.

I don't want to leave things unsaid, she thought. She peeked her head out from underneath the covers and spoke two words into the morning air of her bedroom before closing her eyes, smiling, and falling asleep in her naked, honest skin.

CHAPTER 15: 1/8/20 STARTING SMALL

It seems not even possessing the ability to stop time will keep regret at bay. There were so many different ways I could have spent my time. Honestly, I sometimes wonder if it would have been better for me to forget all about the stupid party trick and try to live a normal life spending more time at home with all of you. (Yes, I did mess with my college roommates many a night when they were pretty drunk. They couldn't figure out how I escaped the bathroom over and over.)

And still, how can I rationalize the ability to stop time as the reason I wasn't a good brother? Hell, I should have been able to spend more time with the people I love because I could take care of all the other mundane necessities of life when the clock had stopped. Of course, that wasn't my train of thought. Instead, I became obsessed with the act of stopping time and, in some ways, believed that stopping time would lead to solutions whenever I had a problem. I was hyper-focused on what I could control and ignored what I couldn't. I kept going back to my control over the music on that jog where I accidentally killed that toad. I started going on nightly runs with the world holding still while my music blared on. It only occurred to me halfway through college how significant that little act of pressing the play button truly was. When I realized it, I became hell-bent on finding how many things had their own "play button" to press while the rest of the world stood still.

You know, I've often thought about the difference between addiction and obsession. I do think, at times, my feet tiptoed in the territory of addiction. But, if the difference between the two is an illness versus a pleasure-driven compulsion, then I would say I barreled my way toward compulsion, and I loved every minute of it.

———

Wells sat in the darkroom beneath the blood-red lights just bright enough to see the details of the large prints coming into view as he bathed them in the developing fluid. This was a piece of the process he loved. The transition of what he had frozen for the perfect picture into something others could see as well. After two years in college, it was widely known that whenever Wells walked out of the darkroom, you were about to see something special. His photos had made their way into the enrollment paraphernalia and on the school website. Toward the end of freshman year, the university asked him to work as a school photographer which became a lucrative work-study gig. Shortly after sophomore year began, he was selling pictures to the city newspaper which quickly started covering his room and board costs. Both of these positions were held under the assumption he could keep his grades up, which, of course, he did.

"Dude, these are awesome." Ryan, Wells' sophomore roommate, was looking over his shoulder in the darkroom at the photos from last weekend's homecoming game. "I don't know how the hell you get these shots."

"Thanks, man," Wells said as he lifted the eight-by-eleven-inch shot out of the solution with the tongs and clipped it to the drying wire.

"Have you studied for the philosophy quiz yet? Professor Fitzburn sucks. The quizzes have been so hard."

"Yeah." Wells winced at the mention of the class. It mostly consisted of memorizing the several major philosophers and their theories that explained peoples' actions. Like many of the general credits he had to take, he felt little interest in the material thus far. It felt like most of the students and even the teacher knew it was simply a hoop to jump through.

"'Yeah,' you studied, or 'yeah,' you know he sucks?" Ryan smiled through the dim light.

"Yeah, it's hard, but no, I haven't started studying yet. I'll do it later. I wanted to go to the soccer game tonight and get a few shots, plus I want to get a jog in before the snow tomorrow."

"How do you have time to do all that, dude? Do you *ever* sleep?"

"I don't know. I don't need that much sleep, I guess. Plus lots of coffee."

"Coffee? Gross. Red Bull is where it's at, man. Or Rock Star. That stuff is wicked." Wells laughed. Ryan was Wells' freshman roommate, too. Just before they came back to college for their second year, Ryan watched the movie *Good Will Hunting* and had been describing everything as "wicked" since, typically adding a subpar Bostonian accent. Ryan was gawking at the photos hanging like prayer flags. He moved from shot to shot with reverence like walking through an art exhibit.

"I still can't believe you don't use a digital camera. It'd be so much faster. I mean, these are unbelievable, but still. This is a ton of work."

"Yeah, I don't know. This just feels more tangible. Closer to the moment it happened somehow."

"You can look at digital photos quicker, though, if that's what you're talking about."

"I know. They just feel diluted, I guess. Photoshop can do some crazy stuff, but it seems kinda like makeup. You're right, though. It would be nice to see things sooner. Having to come back and develop can be a pain."

"What if you could do those instant camera things for sports and stuff? What are those called? Where the picture sticks out like a tongue. There was a song about it, right?" Ryan started dancing around in the dark, shaking his hand back and forth.

"You mean a polaroid?"

"Yeah! That's it. But I bet those are pretty crappy, huh?"

Wells had never thought of using polaroids before. In truth, for all his love of photography, he'd never even held one. He decided he would pick one up if he could find a used one at the camera exchange shop in the Twin Cities. Otherwise, he could just look online.

"Alright, that's the last of em. Are you heading back to the dorm?"

"No," Ryan said. "I'm gonna go to the library. You should come, too; we can split up the practice questions. I already looked at them. This is gonna be a hard one."

"Nah. I'm going to stop at the stadium first. I'll try and catch up with you, though."

Wells only needed half the game to get the shots he wanted. The wind was picking up with the cold front moving in. He could smell the snow that was riding on the chilled breeze. The scent was more of a memory than an actual aroma. Like winter exhaling after a long sleep. If he wanted to get his jog in before the snow, he'd need to get moving.

After he got the photos he needed from the game, which, incidentally, only took him about five minutes of running time with his ability to stop play whenever he needed, he ran back to his dorm to get changed. Once dressed in his sweatshirt and jogging pants, he made his way back down to the quad. A few students skirted around him, burying their chins beneath their collars. Wells put in his headphones and began moving through the campus. He wanted to wait until he was in a spot with fewer people before stopping time. There had been a few occasions where he thought people noticed him shifting positions if they saw him stop and start time in a different location. It had never caused any problems or uncomfortable conversations, but there was no reason to tempt fate.

He ran around the back side of the field house and through an empty loading zone. He pulled out his iPod and stopped the cool gusting air and dimming night that was surrounding him. He pressed play and ran.

It was nice being back at school after the summer break, but there was a listless nature to his presence. He was making money selling his photography and could probably make a reasonable living as a freelance photographer or even working for the newspaper full-time. He was getting to know some of the staff there. They might hire him if he asked. Wells just had the feeling school wasn't the right place for him. The game of studying for tests on topics you had no affinity for seemed pointless. Especially when he could be doing things that were much more enjoyable, like checking out new bands downtown or searching for good waves to surf along the shore.

He was only able to try surfing once as a freshman. As a sophomore, Wells made a deal with himself to officially join the surfing club this year and go whenever he could. He hadn't been able to stand up yet, but the chase of that goal was addicting.

That first outing of the year, he couldn't even get himself to a crouch before he pearled down and bounced off the rocky bottom of the lake. After that first spill, he popped out of the water with an enormous smile on his face and knew he was hooked. The storm that was now moving in as he jogged was hopefully going to bring a few waves tomorrow. If he didn't have the philosophy quiz, he would've gone straight to the shore after breakfast.

Wells turned down a street lined with some fraternity houses. On the porch of one of the larger homes stood a cluster of broad-shouldered and big-chested boys still as statues. Wells recognized them as several of the starting football players. A few girls were scattered around them, watching one of the players taking a knee, gaze directed to the heavens while he clutched a clear plastic tube to his lips. The other end of the tube was attached to a red funnel into which his companion was emptying some shitty light beer. Once you've seen a few frat parties in diorama form, the absurdity makes it hard to want to participate.

As he ran on, a soft glow of orange tucked behind an untrimmed spruce caught Wells' attention. A red fox was huddled behind the tree, just out of sight from the cluster of partiers. The ears were perched high, and the back legs were locked and ready to spring if a retreat was needed. Wells stopped running and walked closer to the animal. He wiped the sweat from his forehead and crouched down next to the fox.

Wells reached out and petted the animal's fur. It was warm and glowed with an auburn luminance. It had a wiry quality to it as if cotton candy were made of fine steel wool. The music continued to play, but he didn't like the song that had queued up. He pressed pause and it stopped. That's when it occurred to him. If he could get the MP3 player to start and stop while everything else froze, maybe he could do that with other things, too.

Wells was in the snow on his knees now, looking at the fox intently. He stared so hard the fox might have burst into flames. The ears were tipped with black as if singed by its own fire, and the face was salt and peppered with short guard hairs. Wells ignored the frat parties and cold weather surrounding him and fixated on the animal standing before him.

Suddenly, the jet-black nose twitched, and a few long whiskers flickered. Like a large stone pushed down a hillside and slowly gaining momentum, Wells willed the fox to blink and begin to move again. The effort it took was surprising. This wasn't the same as gently pressing play on a device. Wells felt as if he was actually trying to move something heavy, like pushing a stalled car while in neutral. As the fox began to reanimate, the effort to propel him into movement abated. The black slit in the brass-colored eyes began to dilate and rolled toward the man hovering over him. In a sudden lurch of freight, the fox jumped back, hunching as if dodging a blow.

Wells shot upright as well, letting out a burst of surprised laughter. The drunken scene on the porch behind him was still just a poster on the wall. The fox looked around, unsure what was amiss in this new world he had just been transported to. Something was off.

He took another sniff in Wells' direction and bolted around the pine tree, disappearing between the row of houses.

"Awesome," whispered Wells as a wave of dizziness rushed over him like a heavy blanket. His head buzzed. It was like standing up too fast, and he liked it. The head rush began to fade. He clicked play on his iPod and let the partygoers resume their antics. As he ran, Wells wondered what else he could release while the world stayed still, and his mind drifted to the waves that would be crashing along the shores of Lake Superior tomorrow morning while the university recreation club gathered to find a little freedom from the doldrums of college life. The winds were picking up as the low-pressure system moved through the north lands, and the surfboards were calling out to those brave enough to ride.

That night, Wells dreamt of birds flying over his head. The birds were graceful as dancers with wings that stretched across the sky, silhouetted by a clementine sun in a dandelion atmosphere. The flock was soaring just out of his reach. The birds looked familiar, but his tongue couldn't unravel the name. Charcoal bodies and leathery legs draped over him. One of the birds circled him and dipped its head low, exposing a mask of crimson and lava feathers. He reached upward just as the bird turned and flew far into the horizon.

When he woke, the sky was dark. Ryan snored on the loft above the microwave. Wells threw on his swimsuit, then some sweats, grabbed his camera, towel, a few granola bars, and made a peanut butter and jelly sandwich before walking out the door. He jogged across campus through the spitting rain and wind of the early October morning. Wells strolled up to the 10-passenger van just as the recreation director was doing the final count.

"Hey, you just made it! Are you Wells?" He had a long shaggy goatee and smiling eyes.

"Yeah. This is the surf club, right?" Wells asked.

"You got it. Hop on in. We're about to get rolling."

Wells crawled into the back of the van and sat by a boy he didn't know.

"Sup, dude? I'm Dylan. First time?" This boy had shaggy blond hair and a permanent grin on his face. Wells had the feeling he had been curating his appearance the entire summer with this exact day in mind. He looked like the perfect picture of a surfer.

"Hey, I'm Wells. And, yeah, it's pretty much my first time."

"Aw, man. You're gonna love it. It's a bit tricky at first, but so awesome once you get it. I started surfing last year. My first time was rough, but if the waves are good, you should be okay. Have you ever skateboarded or used a longboard?"

Wells thought of the summer when he was home. He took Leslie's skateboard and rode it on the interstate all the way across the Mississippi River to Wisconsin, weaving between the cars and semis he had stopped. On his way back, he coasted down the exit ramp with his hands outstretched like he was about to take flight and join the bald eagles that surveyed the river.

"Yeah, I skate a little. This seems pretty different though. Or at least I thought so." Maybe it was the chilly morning air causing Wells to shiver, but he was pretty sure it was the nerves. Somehow he didn't think stopping time would really help him out while riding waves. It hadn't even occurred to him to try it last year when he failed at surfing so spectacularly.

The van pulled up behind a few cars parked along the lakeshore at a spot called Stony Point. A few kids were already suited up in black wetsuits made to withstand the frigid temperature of Lake Superior. They were pulling boards off the top of their cars.

"Alright everyone, before we get out into the chilly morning air, we're gonna go over a few basic things to remember. After that, we'll get suited up and make our way to the water for some drills and maybe catch a few waves. There's supposed to be a pretty decent swell today, so I think we are gonna get lucky. Now, did everyone read the homework assignment I emailed last week?" He looked expectantly around at the blank faces staring back at him and then laughed. "I'm just messing with you." Then, brandishing a clipboard, he continued, "The only homework you need to do today is to sign this waiver that says if you get hurt or die, you can't sue me or the school, capiche?"

The thick neoprene wetsuit he was putting on made Wells feel like a large seal ready to cut through the water. He imagined himself paddling out in the lake and watched as the water's surface erupted with one of those leaping great white sharks that cruise the coast of South Africa. It tossed his body like a rag doll in perfect National Geographic slow motion. Why he insisted on watching *Shark Week* every summer was now a complete mystery to him at this moment standing along the lake shore. The fact that this was a freshwater lake was pretty much irrelevant. The shaking climbing up his back was definitely his nerves threatening to get the best of him.

He suited up until the only pieces of his body not covered in rubber were his face and hands. All of the prep was happening extremely fast. The instructor was sizing up each of the students and handing them a freshly waxed board. He had them find a flat spot on the granite slabs to practice paddling on their bellies and jumping up to their feet.

Before Wells knew it, they were taking turns walking to the edge of the rocks, and one by one, jumping into the water onto their long white boards like a troop of penguins heading out in search of fresh fish. Wells put his feet on the edge of the granite. This was all moving so quickly. He couldn't remember half of the instructions. He didn't remember being so nervous last year.

Wells pulled himself inward and stole an extra moment for himself. The silence wrapped around him like an additional wetsuit.

"Come on, Wells," he said. "This is fine. You're gonna be fine. Why are you so nervous?" Feeling silly and childlike, he laughed at himself and the suspended waves before him. The glowing sun was leaping up from the horizon, scattering light across the surface. The lake was wearing the sun's rays like a movie star's dress at their big premiere. His anxiety was getting the best of him. Wells reminded himself he was still in the company of others before gritting his teeth and continuing his pep talk.

"Okay, you got this. We can do this. We can do this." He took a deep breath, restarted the world, and pounced onto his board. The boards the students were using were extra long and he glided across the water with surprising speed.

Even with his center of gravity as low as possible, he felt like he was riding a teeter totter, ready to tilt to either side at any moment. He tried to paddle forward, but couldn't quite find the balance point of the board. He felt his body lift as a wave passed under him. He stopped the water again.

"Come on." He moaned and shifted on his board trying to get his balance, but when he restarted time, his board had to compensate, and he tipped again. He swore under his breath.

"You alright, Wells?" said Dylan, who had noticed the floundering rookie lagging behind.

Wells laughed.

"This isn't as easy as those YouTube videos make it look," he said.

"You gotta work up to it. You'll get it, but until then it's kinda like trying to balance on a basketball while wearing a blindfold."

They both laughed this time, and Wells paddled after Dylan the best he could while the sharp teeth of the frigid water splashed up at his exposed cheeks.

To say Wells was exhausted after the morning of being tossed and tumbled by cold waves was an understatement. The fatigue, however, was the gracious kind, as pleasurable as a full belly after a holiday meal.

Wells sat up on his board. He was sitting outside of the break, watching the waves roll by toward the shore. Every ten waves, someone tried to catch one and ride. Sometimes they caught it. Sometimes they were a hair too late. Straddling his board in the slower water while the wind whipped around his body, Wells felt like he was riding a slowly loping horse. He took a deep breath and stopped the water and riders around him. His feet paddled in the lake, but he felt more stable now that the waves were holding their position. The water around him felt thicker than normal as his feet paddled back and forth.

"Man, I suck at this!" Wells shouted with a boisterous laugh. He slapped the water, sending a spray into the air that slowed to an unnatural stop before landing in the lake. The ability to stop time, while beneficial when it came to catching up on homework and getting the best photographs, had also brought him isolation and provided so much control to his world that Wells had lately been feeling like his life was somewhat mundane. So far, this experience surfing, even though he still was pretty much worthless, was exhilarating. A stark contrast to his recent routine. The frigid, steal-your-breath smack of water in the face every time he dove under a wave. The feeling of the ground being pulled out from underneath him while falling off the wave's crest only to be cradled again by the same water as if it was congratulating you just for trying. Surfing was something he had to earn. Something he first had to fail at miserably in order to improve. He loved it.

After a solid morning rolling around in the cold, the students returned to their vans and pulled off their neoprene hoods.

"You all did awesome," said the instructor. He'd been encouraging them non-stop even though they were as far from awesome as you'd expect a bunch of unpracticed surfers to be.

Dylan turned to Wells and slapped him on the back.

"Nice work, man. You seemed to be getting your balance on the board there at the end."

"It's hard." Wells couldn't wipe the smile off his face. "But I love it."

"The group meets again next month. You should totally come."

"Next month?" Wells asked. He didn't want to wait for an entire month. He wanted to surf more now, but since he didn't have his own gear and was still new to all of this, there was little he could do. He could stop time right now, but surfing in stationary waves was about as pointless as shooting pictures without a subject.

The image of the fox from the night before flashed in Wells' eyes. If he was able to release the fox while holding onto the rest of the world around him, could he do the same with the waves? A fox was an easily identifiable object with discrete boundaries. Wells could wrap his mind around each part of the animal, giving it the nudge it needed to reanimate.

The lake, however, was different. The shoreline was beyond his comprehension. He could imagine the shape of the lake from the Great Lakes sticker that was pasted to the board he'd been sitting on most of the morning, but its depths and the tributaries that fed the massive body of water were innumerable. However, if today's tough surfing lesson had taught him anything, the least he could do was to try.

Dylan was reaching into his backpack, rummaging for a granola bar. The other students were huddled around the back of the van reliving their brief seconds of surfing glory which surmounted to little more than standing up. The instructor was sliding a board back into its bag. A car was just pulling up with a board strapped to the top, the driver hidden in shadow.

Wells stopped them all. The pitter patter of the drizzle on his wetsuit and susurrant waves went quiet. The granite coast, alive with iron and the deep greens of the swaying pines and blues of the sky he saw before him. Wells weaved around Dylan and grabbed his satchel out of the car. He pulled out his camera and walked down to the shoreline. The pictures he took were nothing spectacular, but enough to capture the moment.

After eating one of his granola bars and taking a swig from his water bottle, Wells pulled his hood back over his head. His feet were heavy and numb, so he took the thermos of steaming water and poured, filling the neoprene booties. He slid his toes back in the stockings and felt the warmth spread over him as if he was dipping into a roadside hot spring. The board he'd been riding that morning was still unpacked and resting on the side of the van. He tucked it under his arm and walked down to the water's edge.

Wells looked at the waves, imagining the sound of them rushing over the slabs of granite, agates, and smooth pebbles covering the coast. It was as loud as holding his head out a car window while driving down a highway and as comforting as the whir of a fan cooling him down on a sweaty summer afternoon. He thought of the rivers he had crossed to get to the beach and imagined them feeding the lake like arteries feeding the heart of this great northern beast. He felt the rhythm of the waves rocking his body back and forth like a child cradled in a dim bedroom lying down for an afternoon nap.

The fox had fallen back into time starting with a twitch of the nose and whiskers. Wells was waiting for something similar in the great lake before him. Maybe it would be a little splash or a quick tumble of a wave. Nothing moved. He tried to press his mind into the stubborn water and clenched his teeth, grimacing. He held his breath. Lastly, he dreamed that he pulled the wind toward himself as if he was the center of the world's gravity. An iron core that all the water was drawn to.

Initially, it was hard to tell if the waves began to roll. The momentum grew so slowly. Like accumulating snow, the waves began to make progress toward the shore. The whisper of the water crept back into his ears. It reached its crescendo over the next thirty seconds. Wells smiled. He turned back to the van to make sure everyone was still in their place. Now he had the waves to himself. He dove onto his board and paddled out, watching the waves roll by as he waited for the perfect combination of confidence and timing. Every six or seven seconds, the waves pushed through, tumbling toward the shore.

The first wave sent Wells pearl diving over his board, rolling in the cold water like laundry in the washing machine. Once he chose his next wave, he began paddling as hard as he could but was too late and gave up as he felt the crest roll under him. Wells spun his board around and sat out the next few waves trying to regain his confidence and breath. The wind started to cut back, and he saw a clean wave moving toward him. He charged toward the shore with the wave behind, paddling as hard as he could. The water began lifting him up. He was thrust forward and jumped to his feet, landing in a low crouch as he and the board dropped into the palm of the wave and began skating across the surface of the lake.

Wells' mind was rushing as fast as he was sliding across the water. His knees shook as he settled into a more relaxed stance. Instincts took over as he rushed toward shore and carved to the left as the wave broke. He managed to keep his balance for a couple more seconds until he kicked the board out from beneath his feet and folded into the water. Wells stood up in waist high water. His feet may have been on the ground, but he felt like he was riding the clouds above him. A broad smile stretched across his face as he gathered his board and made his way back to the shore to catch his breath and let his joy seep into the rocks around him.

After about twenty minutes of watching the waves roll and the wind kissing his cheeks, he grabbed his board, satisfied with the small triumph, and walked back to the van. Wells returned to his position in front of Dylan and released the hold.

When all the boards were packed up and everyone was out of their wetsuits, the crew piled into the van. They slugged from water bottles and devoured snacks and sandwiches. Wells was certain this had been one of the best days he could remember since the evening on the roof with the lightning bolt. He was electric with joy and satisfaction. If he were a painting, he'd be a canvas covered in splashes glowing neon colors.

The van pulled away and Wells took one last look back at the waves that were still rolling in. He didn't need to freeze this moment, but he still wanted to remember it. The sun was starting to peek through the clouds and the waves might begin to ease up as the rain pushed out. The driver of the car that had parked behind them had just gotten out of the vehicle and was unfastening the board from the roof. Their hooded sweatshirt hung heavy over their head and their slender legs wore the necessary thick, dark wetsuit. The school van drove off, and the beach and parked car were almost out of sight when the hood fell back on the last surfer at the point. In the split second that the surfer was still in his view, Wells saw a long braid of fiery red hair uncovered by the falling hood. He tried to twist back to get a better look, but the surfer and lake were gone. He and the girl were not only too far away but also faced the opposite direction, so it was inconceivable that he could recognize them. But the combination of attraction and guilt made his heart race, and Wells had a feeling that someday, just maybe, he might see that red hair from his past once again.

CHAPTER 16: MONICA

"Ha," Monica scoffed. "Listen to this. '...life gets busy for all of us...' That's what he starts with. Wells. He starts with 'my life is *so* busy.' You know, I don't know if I'm going to be able to read this trash." Monica sat in bed, her back propped up against the headboard. Jack was curled under the covers with his back to her.

"I don't think it's that bad, actually," Jack said.

"You've read it already?" Monica sounded accusatory.

"Not all of it, but most. I think I just have a few pages left. I've read it off on and on for the last couple days."

"Well, aren't you just the overachiever?" Monica took a sip of her merlot and set the glass back on her bedside table. She reminded herself that one glass of wine per day when pregnant was most likely fine, and she needed at least one after the day she had.

Jack didn't answer.

"Are you asleep?"

"No," said Jack matter of factly.

"Jesus, this is long." She flipped through the pages. "I don't have time to read this fairytale. There's no way I'm going to get it done before Wednesday."

"I think it'd be good if you could. There's some decent stuff in there, even if this all seems a little far-fetched."

"Far-fetched? *Far-fetched?*" Monica's voice got higher pitched and louder as her irritation increased. "Stopping time?

Are you kidding me? What are we, in some Star Trek movie with Luke Skytalker?"

"I think you mean Star *Wars* and *Skywalker*," he said flatly.

"Oh, whatever. I haven't seen either of those movies. You know what I mean."

"Something that should be corrected as soon as you're done reading that."

"I'm just saying, this is insane, right? I mean, I can't be the only one to think that the idea of our family being a carrier for a genetic mutation that allows the boys, and 'some lucky girls' to freeze time is absurd, right?"

"Your mom seemed pretty lucid."

Monica puffed out an annoyed breath. She took another sip of wine, relishing in the little buzz she'd started which helped her float a few millimeters off the bed. She looked to the stack of papers and the polaroid of the girls. The sight of them tugged at her the same way they pulled her back to playgrounds and block towers when she would be standing nearby, lost in emails and responding to pages from the hospital. She picked up the stack of papers with her left hand and rubbed her belly instinctively with her right, cradling the memory of the bump that would begin to swell and show in the months to come.

"Whatever," she said and began to read again. She let out a sigh of skepticism with every turn of the page. Jack lay with his eyes closed and tried to ignore the cold distance growing in the inches between them.

Chapter 17: 1/9/20 Coffee

I think sometimes I have a habit of getting lost in my own world. There is some danger in that space created by stopping time. It's a bit like missing the forest for the trees. In that way, that tendency becomes a potentially treacherous thing... I guess I'm not sure how that relates to this part of the story. Let me start over.

This ability to stop time isn't just a gift. It is also an affliction. As you all know, I finished sophomore year and limped through junior year, but even completing that was mostly out of guilt. I had signed up for the classes and was paying for them, so I had to finish. My grades were fine, and I was even given some small art scholarships for my photography. But the truth was, I didn't see what the extra year would give me. Most of my assignments were completed last minute in the silent world I created, buying extra time at what I thought was a very favorable exchange rate. I was already making some money in photography, and I watched the weather for any sign of a swell in the lake that could be surfed.

Basically, the water and camera were all I lived for, and school felt like the wet sand keeping me walking when I wanted to sprint. So, I stopped going.

But, of course, because freelance photography can be a bit of a hit-and-miss gig, and there is always the bit about money and needing to pay rent and buy gas for my car and film for my cameras and eat food, well, I figured it made the most sense to finally get a regular job.

Coffee is also worth mentioning here because it became a very necessary thing. Every time I went surfing and stole the waves just for myself, I tended to get really exhausted, even if it was just for a few hours. I think stopping time and releasing the great lake was more work than I realized. In hindsight, it is all so obvious, but at the time, the thought of long-term consequences was a foreign concept.

So, in order to stay awake, I learned to love coffee. In that way, I have coffee to thank for the following things: one was a job working with some pretty wonderful people, the second was fewer hours spent dozing off, and the last was finding my way back to one of the most spectacular people I have ever met.

"What can I get for you?"

"Just a large dark roast, please. Oh, and a blueberry scone, too. Thanks."

"Sure thing. That'll be five-seventy-five." Wells ran the customer's credit card and handed him back a steaming mug of coffee and a fresh scone. He wiped away the scattered crystals of sugar that had fallen to the counter.

"Hey Lillian, I'm almost done. Do you want me to clean up some of the tables before I go?" Wells asked. Lillian had chocolate hair and eyes that smiled constantly. She was the owner of the quaint coffee shop and bakery located near the touristy waterfront area of Duluth.

"Oh, that'd be great. Thanks, Wells."

Wells walked through the cozy café which served as an escape for tourists and a hangout for artists. He cleared a few empty cups and crumb-covered plates, wiped down tables, and returned a book to the community bookshelf. Lillian was at the till helping a customer with a to-go order. Wells heard the clinking of change on the floor and heard the two women laugh. It was a pleasant sound. A song by Bright Eyes playing over the speakers caught his attention, and he reminded himself to send this band to Leslie. He thought she might like them.

He brought the bin of dirty dishes into the kitchen and returned with the empty tub.

"Shoot," said Lillian.

"What?" asked Wells.

"That gal who just came in, she left this. She must have set it down when she dropped her change."

Wells looked at that boxy, black polaroid camera. The thin black strap draped over the edge of the counter.

"Whoa, cool. I've always wanted one of these." Wells grinned at Lillian. "I'm kidding. Did you see which way she went? I'll run and try to catch up with her. I just need to grab my coat."

"I think to the left?"

The response was not convincing.

"Okay." Wells laughed, grabbed his jacket, and picked up the camera. He opened the door to the cool autumn air and turned back to Lillian. "I didn't really see her. What does she look like?"

"Um," said Lillian, trying to recreate the image of the patron. "Gosh. She had a dark-ish jacket and a nice laugh?"

"Oh my God. Okay, looks like I might be able to keep this after all. I'll just jog around the block, and if I can't find her, I'll bring it back."

Wells was pulling the door shut as Lillian shouted to him again.

"Red hair!"

Wells pushed the door back open and squinted as if it would help him hear Lillian's words better.

"I'm sorry. I didn't hear that."

"I said 'red hair.' I think she had redish hair peeking beneath her hat."

Wells shut the door and jogged out of the shop's entryway. He looked at the polaroid camera. It wasn't as heavy as he thought it would be. It was intriguing. It definitely felt retro. There was a small white sticker of a crashing wave stuck to the side near the shutter button. He walked to the sidewalk and glanced to his right. There was a couple pushing a stroller, but that was it.

"Excuse me," Wells heard the voice call from behind him. "I think that might be my camera."

Wells turned to see a tall woman standing before him. A few locks of auburn hair curled down the side of her face that shined with a faint red glow. There was something familiar about her. She stood with a self-assured confidence that was disarming.

"I think so. Did you leave it in the café just now?" It had been almost five years since that first day of school in tenth grade, but the features of this girl's face were starting to come together, and recognition was storming in. He didn't think he knew her from college, and the only red-haired girl he remembered from high school was...

"Wait," she said after taking the camera. "Did you grow up in La Crescent?"

"I did," Wells said hesitantly.

"Wells, right? It's Katelyn. Katelyn Anderson. I think we had homeroom together once."

"Ho. Ly. Shit," said Wells. "I mean, sorry. Holy crap."

Katelyn laughed. Wells blushed. He hoped the chilly air would be a good cover for the flush riding up his cheeks.

"How are you?" she asked.

"Good. I'm good." Wells was suddenly very aware of his wrinkled shirt and wished he had checked his hair. He had an urge to stop time to gather himself and his nerves, but held off as the memory of his first morning stopping the world flashed in his mind. His eyes were tempted to glance at the top button on her coat as if pursuing the memory, but he clenched his fist and kept looking into her eyes.

"Um, yeah. I just work over at the café, so I was making sure you got your camera." Wells swore at himself for sounding so stupid and not thinking of something more interesting to say.

"I love this thing," she said, holding up the camera. "I would have been destroyed if I'd lost it. Thank you."

"Yeah. No problem. So do you live here or something? Or are you just visiting?" Wells pleaded it was the former.

"Oh, I live here now. I just moved back."

"Moved back? Where were you?"

"My family lives in town. We moved here during sophomore year of high school. I was super dramatic about it. I told my parents I'd run away and all that, so when it came time for college I wanted to get as far away as possible. I moved out to Virginia and was there for a few years, but then there were some things back here going on, so it just made sense for me to come home. I just started working at the hospital doing communications work." Katelyn stopped abruptly, looking embarrassed, and then laughed. "Oh jeez. That was a lot. Sorry."

Wells liked that she rambled, and the sound of her laugh seemed to lift Wells into the air a few millimeters.

"I have to get back to work. I'm going to be late for a meeting. You said you work at the café?"

"Yeah, I'm off tomorrow, but I'm there most days. Unless I've got a shoot to do or the surf is good. Then I call in sick." If this was his only moment catching up, he wanted to get in as much information as possible so he wouldn't just be the guy who works at the café.

"You surf? Me, too! Okay, what's your number?" She pulled out her phone and handed it to Wells. He thumbed his number on her keypad and pressed the call button. The phone in his pocket buzzed. He pulled it out.

"This is you, I presume?" *I sound like an idiot*, Wells thought. But she laughed at the joke anyway.

"Okay, I really do have to go, but, if you get a chance, send me a text and maybe we can get a coffee, or, if the swell looks good, I can teach you a few things out on the water." Katelyn gave a taunting glance and began walking away.

If Wells hadn't known any better, she also had the ability to stop time and had just locked his feet to the cement. He stood speechless, watching her stride up the street. She had a brisk pace, but turned once and waved before getting into her car.

Transfixed, all he could do was raise his hand and smile. As she ducked into her car, he could have sworn he saw her smile, too.

CHAPTER 18: 1/10/20 THE GOOD STUFF

I imagine you have all heard about Katelyn at some point. She was the only girl I ever really mentioned to Mom and Dad. She was the only one that I was dating long enough to be worth mentioning, I suppose. Frankly, she was the only one worth mentioning at all. She was thoughtful, empathetic, introspective, and intelligent. She had one of those magnetic personalities that effortlessly made any room she walked into orbit around her. Though if you wonder why you can't picture her, it may be that she didn't have any siblings, so your paths wouldn't likely have crossed when she was living down by us.

As I reflect and write this all down, there are many things I regret. I regret that I didn't bring her to meet any of you. I regret that I didn't see her the way she wanted me to, and the way I should have. And I regret that, ultimately, I didn't take her advice. But this isn't the part of my story about regrets. Not yet, anyway. This is the part of the story where I tell you about the gifts she gave to me. Right now, it's about all the good stuff.

"So, you need to tell me, what is it you like so much about this camera?"

Wells was inspecting the polaroid Katelyn just set down on the table between them. They were sitting in a booth at Grandma's Saloon, their favorite kitschy burger joint where the walls were covered in neon signs and the stuffed head of a bull moose stared down at them from the wall. It had been about two months since the day at the café. Katelyn sipped beer from her pint glass and watched Wells peer through the viewfinder. This was their second date.

During their first outing, and on a few long phone calls after, they had been catching up on each other's families. Wells didn't have much to share.

"Monica's in medicine, blah blah blah. Heather, my other sister, is almost due with her first baby, a girl, I think? And Leslie is a pretty good soccer and hockey player in middle school. She's cool." said Wells.

Katelyn explained that her parents, who were older than his, were starting to have some health issues.

"I *loved* living in Norfolk. The coast, the food, the people. It was all so amazing, but, when my dad started getting sick, I just knew I had to come home so that I could be here to help and in case anything happened, you know?"

Wells agreed, but wondered if he would have been able to make the same decision. Katelyn had such a small family, and they were really close to each other. Wells' family was big by comparison, but he barely called any of them and only went home for holidays. Just long enough to catch up, but escaping before the criticism started. In Wells' opinion, now that the family talk was out of the way, the second date was going much better.

"You better not take a picture. That film is expensive." Katelyn's playful stare almost pushed Wells to try his luck. He put his forefinger on the shutter button.

"Oh yeah? How much?" Wells raised a flirting eyebrow.

"It's almost two bucks a photo."

"Jeez. Really? How much film does it hold?"

149

"Each package has eight shots."

"That's it?"

"Yeah. But honestly, I think that's one of the things I like about it."

"How so?" Wells understood the fascination with something less mainstream. After all, he still preferred film to digital, something many of his photography peers at school found perplexing. However, because he was now relying on freelance work to supplement his income, he found himself reluctantly leaning on his digital camera more and more. The practicality and benefits of Katelyn's bulky camera that only held eight expensive pictures was totally lost on him.

Katelyn looked at Wells hard before answering, as if trying to size him up. She squinted, and determined he might be worthy of her answer.

"With just eight pictures to take, and the cost being what it is, I feel like I have to be really aware of the shot." She saw this didn't register with Wells, so she tried again. "I mean, it's like when you're shooting a roll of film and are down to the last couple shots. If you are out on one of your photoshoots and the film is running low, you have a lot of pressure to be sure you capture the moment perfectly. You're more focused and intentional with those shots, right?"

"Yeah, I'd say that's true," Wells agreed. Truthfully, he could just stop time, making sure he *always* got his shot, but he understood the concept. And he liked the way she was willing to give an honest answer that had more depth than the typical small talk that lived in the shallows of his previous dating life.

"Right, so imagine that feeling or approach or whatever, the entire time. I feel like when I carry this around, I'm more present. I'm looking for the tiny moments worth appreciating and holding onto as opposed to drifting along and missing something special while I'm lost in a Facebook feed or something." She realized she had now entered the vulnerable side of truth and finished her statement with an embarrassed smile. "Does that make sense?"

"Yeah, that makes sense." He was trying to imagine her taking a polaroid photo the way he might stop time. He felt a wave of pity, realizing that she couldn't hold onto the moments as long as he could.

"Well, let me ask you this," she said. "Why do you like film? The developing process is such a pain. That must be kinda expensive." She pulled her camera back toward her. If he couldn't understand her, he wasn't worthy to hold it yet.

"It really doesn't cost *that* much, and I use my bathroom as the darkroom. I have the main floor of the duplex to myself, so I don't really bother anyone with the mess." Wells finished his pint. The beer tasted sweet, and his mind felt loose. "I guess it's sort of the same argument you're making. Like, digital is great for work and stuff. Because, the truth is, most of the photos the newspaper wants don't need to be spectacular. I can be a bit more carefree with digital than I would be with film, but not that much. Basically, everybody I work for wants me to email a jpeg or pdf or whatever. It is just much easier to download a photo to my computer and email it instead of bothering with scanning stuff." Wells was starting to get more animated as the alcohol seeped into his system. "But with film, I love seeing the photos develop when I drop the paper into the tray. The images come back to life in the darkroom, and you get to relive the moment, like, right there!"

"Shhh," Katelyn laughed. Wells didn't realize he was practically yelling. "I get it. I get it." She laughed again and grabbed his hand to calm him down. Her touch was as electrifying as the lightning bolt at his childhood home. "Yes, I think we are sort of saying the same thing. The only thing I'd fight for, where my little baby here has you beat," she tapped the black camera at her side like a lap dog, "is that I don't have to wait so long before I get to live in the moment. I just have to wait about fifteen minutes." She leaned back and turned on the camera, leaving Wells' hands on the table and him slightly drunk and grinning. In a single fluid motion, she raised the camera to her eye and a flash washed over Wells' face. The camera made a short whirring noise, and the photo shot out like a kid sticking out their tongue. She grabbed it and pocketed it before Wells knew what hit him. They both laughed.

Wells took a deep breath and fought the urge to freeze this moment. He wanted to take hold of it just as they both described. He hadn't stopped time again in her presence yet. He wasn't sure where the line of morality in that homeroom class back in high school lay, but the embarrassment and shame made him feel like he crossed it. He swore he wouldn't pause this or any moment around her without her knowing about it. And how could he tell her he could stop time? That definitely wasn't a second date type of conversation. Instead, he tried to stop thinking about his ability, and they held hands as they walked back to their cars.

"Is it ready? Can I see it?" Wells tried to reach for the photo, brushing her arm as he searched for her coat pocket. They were close enough to each other that he could have kissed her if the moment was right.

"No, get out of there!" Katelyn laughed and pushed him away playfully. You'll either have to hang out with me here for another five minutes, or just wait until date number three."

"So you want to see me again, then?"

"Well, I mean, it's a small town. I figure we'll have to run into one another at some point. Especially if I'm going to school you on the waves this winter."

"Oh ho! I see how it is. We haven't even talked about surfing yet." Wells took a step closer. Katelyn kept her feet locked to the ground.

"Four more minutes until the photo is ready. I don't know what we are going to do to keep busy." She pressed her lips together and raised an eyebrow. "Your move, Monasmith."

Wells wanted so badly to seize a moment to steel himself. He wanted to stop everything right now and gather the courage to kiss this beautiful girl who was challenging him like a hurricane, but he couldn't break that promise to himself. He closed his eyes and took in a deep breath. In spite of himself and thanks to the second pint of beer, he announced his obvious next move.

"Oh, God. I'm going to kiss you, if that's okay."

"You're such a dork." She laughed as he leaned in with all the nerves of a kindergartner on the first day of school and let him kiss her. It was soft and wet and uncoordinated, but it was wonderful.

"You surf smoother than your dating moves, right?" She added during a break from the parking lot kisses.

"Ha. Ah, yeah. Much smoother."

The photo was developed by the time they remembered to check it. Wells wasn't used to seeing himself as the subject of a photograph. The flash made him and the booth seem slightly overexposed. The vintage-soft colors touched Wells with

153

nostalgia for the date that had only just finished. His expression was happiness in its fullness. Whimsical and joyous.

Katelyn snagged the photo from his hands.

"Alright, alright. That's enough. This one is mine." She opened the door to her car and got into the driver's side. "Call me tomorrow?"

"Absolutely," Wells said.

Katelyn laughed and closed the door. Wells watched her until the car turned a corner and was out of sight. Only then did he stop time, pull out his iPod, and reenact Kevin Bacon's passionate dance scene from *Footloose* all throughout the parking lot.

———

"Holy shit, Katelyn. Wake up." Wells was tapping on the cracked screen on his phone. He turned and nudged the bare shoulder of Katelyn who lay in bed next to him, sleeping beneath the layers of blankets.

"Look at this," he said.

She rolled over, red hair burning bright against her porcelain skin. An archipelago of freckles danced across her shoulders. Wells imagined getting lost in those islands during the summertime when they would darken with the sun.

"Look at what?" she said. She held the phone closer, peering through the cobwebbed screen.

"You see that?" Wells asked with an are-you-ready smile.

Katelyn's eyes widened as she inspected the map of Lake Superior. The National Weather Service map showed a rainbow of colors across the lake. Wells pointed to the orange and yellow hues along their coast that indicated the areas of high wave activity.

"You wanna find some waves today?" He asked. They had been dating for almost six months. It took one month for them to talk about family. Two months to talk about her polaroid obsession, and four months for them to start sleeping at each other's places. But in all that time, in spite of all of their talk about surfing, Katelyn learning on "real waves" in Virginia, Wells stating it was his one true passion second only to photography and just maybe Katelyn (he'd say with a wink), they still hadn't hit the water together. The good waves never seemed to land on a day when they both were off of work.

Today was the day they would share something few people shared. The feeling of walking on a lake strong enough to humble the *Edmund Fitzgerald*. Katelyn jumped out of bed and danced her hips into the closest pair of pants within reach. True to his word, Wells still hadn't stopped time around Katelyn. There were times like this, however, times when he knew he was the luckiest man on Earth, the temptation would nearly barrel over him just like the waves they were about to tackle.

"Good Lord," Wells said as he watched Katelyn pull on her shirt over her bra. She looked at him, suspicious of what was turning over inside his head.

"What?"

"I just…" he shook his head and smiled at her. "You know, we could probably spare another half hour, if you wanted to… you know?" he nodded his head toward the space beside him that she had only just vacated.

"Priorities, priorities," she said. She picked up his shirt and threw it in his face. "Get dressed, lover boy. We're not gonna miss these waves today."

Katelyn scrambled the rooms packing her wetsuit, booties, and mittens, as well as some water, a towel, and a couple apples. Once outside, she strapped her board to the top of Wells' car, and they drove off together to grab Wells' gear before heading up the shore.

It was late April. The wind was picking up and snow was falling as the two pulled up to the beach. A few cars were already stacked up. A couple riders were paddling their way out from shore.

"We're not gonna be alone," Wells said, shaking his head.

"Are you ever alone out here? I feel like a forecast like this brings everybody out of the woodwork. I don't think I've ever had the water to myself. Not in Minnesota anyway."

Wells hadn't surfed with others for a while now. He didn't even surf with Dylan, who he had seen from time to time either in passing at surfing spots or at some of their old college haunts. Besides a few times while in college, Wells always found a way to keep the waves all to himself while the world around him remained at a standstill. He had grown to look forward to the times when he could have the entire world to himself. Whether it be a jog, photography, or riding waves, stopping time had become a habit that gave him an escape from responsibility and a sense of control when anything became stressful. But with Katelyn in his life, the desire to stop time was now satiated by something else. Whatever it was that stopping time seemed to feed inside him was now fed by her presence, and it felt wonderful. Still, as his feelings grew stronger for her, he was beginning to feel like this secret he was keeping was wedging itself between them. He wasn't sure how, but Wells knew he would have to tell her someday and possibly soon. He couldn't keep that part of his life from someone he cared for so much.

"Actually, most of the time I'm surfing without anyone around," Wells said.

"That's crazy. Cool, I mean. But I don't know, I like having a few other people there in case something goes wrong, I guess."

They jumped out of the car and started putting on their wetsuits beneath the overcast sky which had temporarily stopped dusting the shoreline. The air temps were just above freezing which was only slightly colder than the water. Wells stood with his bare feet on top of his shoes to protect himself from the chilly gravel. Katelyn leaned against the car door next to him, her bare feet touching the ground. He loved that about her. She was unafraid to touch the world around her, no matter the conditions.

A gust of wind blew in from offshore. It carried the smell of clean fresh water. Wells and Katelyn turned to face the breeze head on. They smiled at each other. Katelyn pulled her thick black hood over her head and stuffed a few stray strands of hair beneath the neoprene.

"Are you ready?" Katlyn asked.

"Let's do it."

They pulled on their boots and mittens and grabbed their boards.

"Ope, hey, I forgot one thing," Katelyn said. Wells stopped and looked back to see what she had forgotten. She saw a flicker of annoyance on his face, but decided it must have been the icy wind that had picked up again. He was already a few steps ahead of her, ready to charge the water. Katelyn caught up, leaned forward, and kissed him.

"Okay, now I'm ready," she said.

She laughed and ran past him through patches of brown grass and exposed light crimson mud and pebbles. Snow still littered the shoreline. Patches of slick ice were scattered here and there. Wells shouted after her and tried to catch up.

The two stopped on the smooth granite rock the size of a dinner table and looked across the massive body of water. After a nod of agreement, they walked to the edge of the water, jumped onto their boards, and paddled away from shore, bobbing up and down over the waves. The first time Wells dove under the water, his face was hit with a frigid blast. The cold reached into his lungs and yanked out every last breath of air. The rush of icy water spilt Wells and Katelyn wide open like peeling off a rigid chrysalis as they emerged above the water. They laughed and shouted, paddling with all of their strength to get out past the break where they could finally catch their breath as they sat on top of their boards with the line of other surfers.

"I don't know what it is about being out here, but I absolutely love it." Wells looked around and watched the scene play at full speed. He rarely took the time to watch the other surfers take their turns darting after waves. Most attempts were failed starts, but every once in a while, one of the riders would pop up and weave back and forth toward the tree-lined shore. If it weren't for Katelyn, he wouldn't be watching this scene. Instead, he would have waited until the perfect moment to keep it all to himself.

He pointed to a wave three crests away. "There, that one. You want it?"

Katelyn eyed the wave like a batter stepping up to a plate.

"Absolutely," she said with total confidence. She lowered her chest to the board and began to move into position.

Wells maneuvered himself to watch her work. Her arms propelled her forward. She angled the nose of her board to shore. She was turned just enough to see the wave as it began to lift her up.

Her poise was perfect. She paddled hard. Right arm. Left arm. Both arms. Both again. And again. The wave was lifting her up to its crest. At the last moment, the second when Wells thought she'd have to give up and miss her opportunity, she pushed herself up to a low crouch, left foot in front of the right. She cut through the water like a knife. She was a mythical creature. She was the daughter of Poseidon. Wells was overwhelmed with awe, and before he knew what he was doing, he pulled himself inward and heard the familiar rumble deep inside his head.

Everything stopped. The wind had been prying water off the tops of the waves. Wells saw Katelyn, frozen in the moment as she turned back into the wave to either rocket into the sky or cut back to shore. Wells wasn't sure which. It then occurred to him what he had done. He'd broken his promise and betrayed Katelyn.

"Shit," Wells slapped the water at his side. "Damnit." He looked down at his board, unsure what to do next. Should he tell Katelyn? Try and explain it all? She'd think he was completely crazy. He could try and prove it to her. He could let her enter his world. But what would she say? How would she react? Wells didn't know what to do, so he released the wheel of time and watched the scene around him come back to life, all the while keeping his eyes fixed on Katelyn to see what her next move would be.

CHAPTER 19: CHRISTIAN AND HEATHER

Christian put his ear to the door and listened. The paneled doors were thin. The winter was already getting away from him, and he hadn't gotten around to replacing them with solid wood yet, like he had planned. If he had replaced them, he wouldn't have been able to hear Heather on the other side, sitting on the edge of the bed. Crying.

"Honey?" He gently scratched the door with his fingernails. "Can I come in?"

"Yeah. It's okay. Come in." He heard her sniffle as he opened the door.

Christian walked into the bedroom. Heather wiped her nose with a tissue, looked up at him, and smiled.

"Hi," she said. "I'm sorry. I'm done. I finally finished it." She held up Wells' story and waved it in the air. The pages were ruffled and dotted with watermarks from her tears.

"Wow. Wells was that good of a writer?" he said. Heather didn't laugh, but the smile was a victory. "What are your thoughts?"

"It's just so sad," she said.

Christian had gotten good at reading his wife and knowing when to ask the questions and when to let her keep talking. Now was a time to let her forge forward on her own.

"I wish they would have told us earlier." She threw her hands up in the air, exasperated. "If he would have just talked to us, he wouldn't have had to go through this alone. I mean, he basically spent his entire adult life without us while he lived on an island in his own dimension."

She scrolled up Wells' story. She worked it in her hands like wringing out a rag, trying to see what other hidden pieces of her brother she might squeeze out.

"I just… I didn't really believe it at first, but now reading it, even if it isn't true, it makes me so sad to think we, his family, were here the entire time and could have helped him with whatever he was going through, but we didn't."

"Do you think he would make something like this up?" Christian asked.

"I don't know." Her tears had finally stopped. She sighed. "Mom and Dad believe it. And then there is this photo."

She picked up the polaroid. For such a small piece of paper, it seemed to weigh so much. It evoked so many emotions. She saw the joy in her own face and could almost hear her children laughing on the floor. Their legs and arms were tangled as they wrestled at her feet. She loved her family so much it hurt.

"I remember this." She held the picture so Christian could see it.

"Me, too."

"Wells was in there with us, right?"

"I thought so."

"So, did he stop time and take this picture? Is this his way of showing us?"

"I think? It sounds like that was how he was so good at photography. Think of all the pictures he sold to magazines over the years. Remember that spread on those birds in Nebraska last summer after he was in the hospital?"

"That's right. He talks about that in here," Heather said, unraveling the stack of papers.

"I think I just need to talk to Mom. And I want to be better about getting together with Monica's family and Leslie, too. This just reminds me how darn fast the kids are growing up."

She started to cry again. Christian sat beside her and put his arm around her back, pulling her into him. He kissed the top of her head.

"We might have to have an intervention with Monica if you want her to be around more." Christian thought this would serve to lighten the mood, but Heather didn't laugh. She held Wells' story in one hand and the polaroid in the other. She felt guilty she hadn't been closer to her brother. She felt sad for her parents who had been shouldering this burden for so long. And she felt thankful to be in the arms of her caring husband while the playful shrieks of their three wildly beautiful girls came barreling down the hall toward them.

CHAPTER 20: 1/11/20 THE HARD STUFF

Katelyn raced to the top of the wave and her board shot up and out from her feet. She flailed backward and tipped under the water. Her hooded head popped up looking for Wells. She waved and he could hear her laugh. Wells waved back and felt the familiar feeling of guilt resurface in perfect sync with Katelyn's reappearance. This time, however, it was worse. Before, she barely knew who he was, and he hadn't really comprehended what he was doing. Now, she trusted him. She might even love him. He thought he was better than this.

Wells paddled forward and caught the next wave. He popped up easily and rode toward her. It was a smooth, simple ride without finesse or panache. He dodged a paddling surfer and let himself fall off his board as he got close to the shallows.

"Hey, not too shabby, Monasmith. You ready to go again?"

"I'm ready if you are," he said. But Katelyn sensed a deflation that shouldn't be present in someone who just rode in on a wave like that.

"You okay?"

"Totally." He tried to smile like he believed himself. "I just... I'm just bummed I didn't ride that the way I wanted," he lied and chewed his lip while still debating what he should do. He didn't think he did anything wrong this time. It was innocent enough, but it still felt like something had fractured. You just don't keep secrets from the ones you love.

After an hour of fighting the wind and riding the waves, they sat on their boards and floated together, watching the last of the other riders head to shore. Katelyn's toes were starting to numb. The steaming water they poured into their booties only kept them feeling like they were surfing in the southern Pacific for so long. Wells wondered if this was the moment to tell her. He got light-headed just thinking about it.

"Um," Wells stammered.

Katelyn looked at him. She sensed it was a moment that was charged with the potential energy of whatever words were to follow. Was it an "I love you" pause or a "we should break up pause?" Or maybe "move away with me" or "I have cancer." Katelyn couldn't tell which way the words would fall, but she could tell whatever was on his mind was important. She also realized she didn't want him to say he loved her if he didn't mean it. She sensed he wasn't quite ready and didn't want to push him, especially since she wasn't sure where her feelings stood either.

"There's something I want to tell you. Something I've never really told anyone."

"Okay." Katelyn was still waiting to see what side of the hill this would roll down. Sometimes, he was just too hard to read.

"Um, so I have this, um, condition. It's going to sound really crazy, I know, but I just want you to know about it and, I don't know, we'll just go from there."

"Are you sick?" She felt slightly relieved he didn't say he was in love, but realizing the alternative might be a terminal illness was worse.

"No. No, not anything like that. You see," he hesitated and fiddled with the zipper on his wetsuit. "I have… I kind of have this thing where I can stop time?" He ended the statement like a question, not knowing exactly how to deliver this news. Katelyn squinted and her brow furrowed.

"What do you mean?" She asked cautiously. "Like metaphorically? Or literally?"

"Literally, I guess."

"I don't really understand."

"I didn't think you would." He sighed, feeling stupid and regretting this conversation. "So, I wanted to ask if it was okay for me to show you."

"Are you sure you're not high?" She knew Wells liked to smoke from time to time. She didn't like being high, but it didn't bother her that he did. It seemed to calm him down when he got anxious. To each their own, she figured.

Wells laughed. "No. No, I'm not stoned. I know it sounds totally weird, but I want to show you. Is that okay?"

Katelyn let out a skeptical laugh.

"I guess?"

The next moment unfolded very differently for each of them. For Wells, he closed his eyes and stilled the water, earth, and sky. All sound stopped. He stopped rocking back and forth on the waves. It was as if the horse beneath his saddle had turned to stone. He saw Katelyn before him, still and beautiful. He took a deep breath, not knowing if this would take the same effort as the fox or require the effort and concentration of awakening the Great Lake. He focused on Katelyn, sitting in front of him like one of her polaroids. He imagined her voice and looked at her eyelashes, dark and wet like the fine hairs of a flower petal. He thought of all the details hidden beneath her wetsuit he had come to adore. He could sense her heart, strong, healthy, loving. Wells felt his chest tighten, and she blinked.

Katelyn stared at Wells expectantly.

"Um, so are you going to show me, or…"

Wells watched as the changes around her began to sink in. They were no longer bobbing up and down like corks in a bathtub. The wind, jagged as a knife, had stopped cutting past them. She looked to shore and saw three seagulls hanging like a mobile from a child's ceiling. They were angled toward the surfers who had just climbed out of the water. Everything was dead still.

"What the hell is this?"

"It's okay," he said in a calming tone. "This is what I was saying. I can stop time."

"Wells, what the hell is happening?"

"Just relax. It's okay. I'm in control. I can start it all up again if you want me to." The panic in her voice was beginning to worry him. He didn't want her to fall off her board. The water wasn't behaving normally, and he didn't know how easy it would be to swim with it still like this.

"What do you mean you're *in control?*"

"I said it's okay. I'll restart it and try to explain everything. I know how insane this is, believe me."

She watched him clench his jaw, just like squeezing the hand of a person you have to let go one last time. Then he relaxed his shoulders and looked back up at Katelyn. The wind whipped and the water began to rock them side to side. Far away, the gulls screamed at the boys on the shoreline.

"Are you alright?" Wells asked slowly.

Katelyn stared at her board, head bobbing with the waves. Wells almost thought he hadn't fully released her, but then she looked up at him. Her eyes glistened with tears. She laid down and began the short paddle back to the rocky beach. She caught the next wave and rode on her belly as effortlessly as the birds flying above her.

"Shit." Wells laid down and raced after her. "Katelyn!" he shouted. "Wait up!"

Wells struggled to catch a wave. He had to awkwardly bodysurf back to the shallows and stumbled to shore. He found Katelyn sitting on the rocks, her hood pulled back, and her arms around her knees. He sat down beside her, but didn't speak.

"It feels weird, Wells." She looked shaken and unsteady. She wiped her eyes.

"I know. It's odd at first, but you'll get used to it."

"No, I mean, I feel sick. Like, my body can't handle that. Do you do that a lot? Do you use that around me, like, without me knowing?" There was fear in her voice. She had the urge to move herself further from Wells, but resisted after seeing the concerned look he wore.

"No. I mean, I used to do it a lot. Not around you, of course," he clarified. "But since we've met, I stop time much less. I've been able to do it for years, okay? I use it for taking pictures and catching up on homework and surfing and stuff, but nothing, like, bad, okay? I'm serious."

"So you've *never* done it around me?" She stared deep into Wells' eyes, looking for any sign of hesitation. She found it. He opened his mouth, but the words were still buried deep in his throat. That was all she needed to know right now. She stood up. She felt exposed and embarrassed.

"No, look. I can explain. Please." He reached for her hand, but she yanked it away. "Katelyn, it's happened twice around you, I swear."

"Okay, so when? Tell me. I want to know. Was I, like, in the shower, or changing clothes?"

"No, of course not, jeez." This was exactly the reaction Wells was afraid of, but what else could he expect?

"It just happened today, okay? When we were surfing. It was right after you caught your first wave. You were so graceful and gorgeous, I was just watching you and so amazed, I didn't realize what I had done until it happened. I knew I had to tell you, so I immediately let time speed up again."

She looked at him doubtfully. "And the other time?"

Wells began to sweat. Pins and needles were radiating down his back, the way he felt after puking when he drank too much in college.

"The first time was years and years ago, back in high school when we were in homeroom together. It was the first day of class. I had a huge crush on you but was too afraid to tell you about it before you moved away."

"And?" Her mouth barely opened and her voice clipped. The drizzle now falling on her red hair dampened it just enough to make it look dark as blood.

"The night before that day was the first time I'd figured out how to use it. That morning in class, I stopped time to get that letter project done. You know, the one where we wrote letters to ourselves?"

"Okay, and that's it?" She knew there was more. If that was all there was, he wouldn't look so like an ashamed dog standing in front of her.

"I was so amazed by the ability. I finished my letter and just walked around the class looking at the scene. I was in total shock at what I could do. You know, like today, how that felt to you?

It was crazy, right?" She didn't respond. Her silence was forcing the confession to move forward. "I just... You looked so amazing, and then I saw you folding up your letter, and I wondered what it said, so I..."

"You looked at my letter?!" Her mouth hung open in shock.

"I only saw part of it, about being a better friend or something, and then I stopped. Listen," he pleaded as she started to walk away again. "There's more, and I want to tell you everything. I also... like, I did kind of see a little bit down your shirt. I didn't, like, touch you or anything. Honestly, I didn't see anything, and I felt so awful and guilty, like I had betrayed you even though I didn't even really know you then. So that's why I never talked to you after that. I just... I couldn't. I'm sorry. It was so stupid, and I was an idiot. I let it get out of control." He reached for her hand.

"Let me go." She pulled away. "I... I can't talk to you right now."

She turned and hurried up to the road where the other boarders were packing up.

"Wait." Wells tucked his board under his arm and jogged after her. "Please."

"No, Wells. Please don't follow me. And don't do that again." Her stomach still felt queasy. Her body shuddered. "I just need to go home and process this. I'll call you later, but I can't talk to you right now."

"But what are you gonna do for a ride?"

"I'll be fine. Just stay there. Please," she pleaded. She trudged up to the parking area. Wells watched her wave at the other boarders packing up their van. She talked with the group for a moment, gesturing to Wells. The group nodded to her and

169

began shifting some bags around in their van so she could fit her things inside after strapping her board to the rack.

"Damnit," Wells said as he watched the van pull away and drive out of sight.

CHAPTER 21: 1/12/20 PRIORITIES

It really is an exercise in frustration to consider the "what ifs" and "if onlys," but I have no problem admitting one small thing—well, two small things I wish we would have done more often as a family. Cribbage and coffee.

I mean, coffee might be more of a stretch as we didn't drink that as kids for obvious reasons. But, I mean, cribbage? Come on! Didn't we play that every summer when we rented those cabins up north? If not Cribbage, it was War or Hearts or Spoons or King's Corner. I have vivid memories of the adults sitting at the kitchen table late into the night, counting out points on the rectangular board while we sat on the floor stealing spoons and praying for a war where we might steal an ace.

Anyway, the point is, I wonder if we got together more often for coffee and cards, would our conversations have been better and our differences been softened by our shared enjoyment of the little things being handed between us?

And maybe not. Maybe I would have still tried to escape, but turning those small things into priorities can be the difference between something special and something ordinary. At least that's what I believe Katelyn wanted me to understand.

———

Wells tapped his hand nervously on the table. He picked up his phone and looked at the time. He was early. Five minutes early. He sipped his coffee. He wondered if he should get

Katelyn a scone. White chocolate raspberry was her favorite. She'd probably like that. He thought about getting up, but then decided he didn't want to look too pathetic. He remained seated and checked his phone again.

It had only been three weeks since the day they went surfing, but it might as well have been an eternity. Wells had texted and called Katelyn every day. Most attempts to reach her went unanswered. Finally, after a week, she replied to his messages.

Katelyn: I'm sorry I haven't responded, but this has been a lot to process.

Wells: I know. I'm sorry.

Wells: Can I see you?

Katelyn: I don't think I'm quite ready yet. I want to see you, too, but I just need more time.

Wells: Okay. Take all the time you need.

Wells waited for a reply. Nothing came, so he typed a few words and hovered over the "send" key.

Wells: I love you.

Wells felt light-headed and sick waiting for a reply. He was pretty sure he loved her. At least, it seemed like something close to love. Even if it was motivated by the fear of what might be lost, maybe that was enough. He waited while his text sat fermenting in his stomach like sour milk. Finally, Katelyn responded.

Katelyn: Thank you. Maybe we can meet for coffee or something soon. I'll text you. Like I said, I just need more time. This is really, really crazy. I think you know that. I really care about you. My parents need some help this week and work is nuts. Maybe we can meet up next week. I'll text you.

Reading her words felt like swallowing a large pill with a throat that was far too dry. Trying to respond to them with restraint was even harder. Wells set his phone down so his reply wouldn't be too quick and his desperation wouldn't be any more obvious than it already was. He loved surfing and he had a decent job here in Duluth, but, basically, Katelyn was the only thing worth staying for when it came down to it. If she broke up with him, well, he didn't know what he would do with himself.

He picked his phone back up and typed out several different responses before finally settling on the one that appeared the most casual.

Wells: Sounds great! Have a good week, okay?

No response.

Now, sitting in the same café where their paths first reconnected, Wells waited to finally see her again. The door to the café opened, and Wells sat up straight only to be disappointed to see an older couple walk in, laughing and holding hands. His fingers shook as he lifted the cup of coffee to his lips for another sip.

"Shit. Come on," he said, scolding himself after a wave of coffee spilled over the rim of his mug and splashed onto the table. He stopped time. The café transformed from a cozy, bustling space with music playing over the speakers to a haunted asylum housing only Wells' anxiety. He cleaned off the table, pushed his chair back, stood up, and began pacing around his chair.

"Alright, alright. Just relax. This is going to be fine. We are going to talk through this. It will all be *just fine.*" He clenched and unclenched his fists as if this was enough to shake off his nerves. He took in a deep breath and went back to his seat.

"Okay. I'm good. I'm good." He sat back down, folded his hands in his lap, and the sounds of the espresso machine came whooshing back to life, followed by the banging of the barista emptying the coffee grounds. The door to the café opened, and Katelyn walked in. She saw Wells and walked over to his table. He jumped up and skipped toward her.

"Hey," he said, smiling and leaning in for a hug.

"Hi. You haven't been waiting long, I hope." She hugged him back, but her body was stiff and didn't fall into his the way it usually did.

"No, no. Just got here a few minutes ago. I got you a coffee."

"Oh, you didn't have to do that. Thank you." She took off her coat and hung her bag over the back of her chair. They both sat down. She sipped her drink.

"Mmm. That's good. Thank you. You didn't have to do that," Katelyn said again.

"Oh no, it's not a problem. So, how are you? How are your parents?" Wells rocked forward, tapping his toes nervously.

"Oh, they're good, you know. They're fighting over the same stuff, whether or not to trade in their old Buick. The car is older than I am. That's just how they are, I guess. But you've gotta love them with their old and crazy ways." She took another drink. She had paused for a fraction of a second after saying the word love as if she wished she had chosen another word. "How about you?"

"Oh, work is fine. I sold a few more pictures to the newspaper, so that was good. You know, I've missed you a lot." Wells watched Katelyn for any sign that she would reciprocate his feelings. She stared into her coffee long enough that he almost thought he accidentally stopped time again. Finally, she looked up.

"Listen, Wells. I don't really know if I'll ever be comfortable with what happened. I'm not mad at you for showing me," she added quickly, seeing Wells about to interject. "I realize the significance of what you were doing and am honored you took me into that world with you. And I forgive you for back in high school." Wells let out a big breath of air and smiled back at her, looking relieved.

"Look, I can't even imagine what it is like to carry this around with you," Katelyn continued. Her eyes darted around the café as if looking for the courage to proceed with the point she'd been practicing for the last week. "But I still think you have to be careful with it. You get to see things no one else sees. I'm sure there are things so amazing others could only experience by watching a movie or something, but you don't even know what it does to your body, Wells. I still feel off. Something deep inside of me just doesn't feel aligned. Like my heart isn't beating in time with the song my body sings, if that makes sense. I don't know. I just think this is a really big deal, and it's worth being thoughtful about it."

"Listen, Katelyn, I'm fine. It doesn't affect me. I am thoughtful, and I can stop if you want me to. I just won't do it anymore. It's easy. I'm done." Wells reached across the table and grabbed her hands. She slid them away and set them in her lap. Katelyn could see the sincerity in his eyes. She realized he probably believed he could stop.

"But that's the thing, I can't really ever know, and I think this is a part of you. I think it will be really hard to stop, and I can't ask you to. That's not fair, and I won't do that. But when you're in that space, just think of what you're missing out here," she waved her hands around her.

"I don't understand what you're saying."

"I don't want you to regret spending your time that way." She fidgeted with a bracelet on her wrist. "Or rather, I think being able to do something as mind-bogglingly significant as what you can do deserves some forethought. The implications of it all are huge, Wells. I know there is an entire world you get to see when you stop things, but every moment you're in there is a moment alone and away from everything else. Everyone else."

"But that's the thing, Katelyn, I have *all the time*. I have as much time as I want, and I can give that to you, too. You're the only person I've ever shown this to. We can do that together. Explore the world together on our own time. You've always said you wanted to hike the Superior Trail, or what was that other one in Virginia?

"The Appalachian Trail," Katelyn said, like batting away a fly.

"Yeah! The Appalachian Trail. We could do that. We could find the best weather and hike an entire day in less than a moment. Isn't that amazing?" Wells' voice was dangling somewhere between offering and pleading.

"No, Wells. Look, I do love you, but I don't want to spend my time in that other space. I want to be out here taking care of my parents and working, which I actually like right now for once. Of course the trail sounds amazing, but I don't want to do it that way. I want to suffer through the rain and watch the sun move across the sky. I want to feel the pressure of the deadlines. I want to surf and watch everyone around me taking turns on the waves. And I have the feeling you don't want to do things the hard way or, maybe, can't. Listen, I think we should take a break so you can try and find a way to balance this. I'm worried it isn't healthy, and I want you to be safe. Maybe you should go spend time with your family. Your niece is almost due. You should try and be there for that. But I mean it. I need a break. A break from this. A break from us."

Wells sat motionless, taking in Katelyn's breakup speech. To be fair, he realized he'd never been on the receiving end of one of these. At least she was there in person and it wasn't simply a ghosted text. At first, he thought he might break down in the middle of the café and melt into a puddle of whimpering tears. Instead, sour anger was churning in his gut.

He closed his eyes and stopped the breakup.

"This is bullshit," he said.

If he had been on his toes, he could have stopped the conversation five minutes earlier. He looked at Katelyn. She stared back at him. Her unblinking eyes looked concerned for the man sitting before her. Wells thought he even saw some pity in the small ridges of her forehead lifting her eyebrows. Something caught his eye from the inside of Katelyn's bag. It was her polaroid camera.

Before he could stop himself, Wells reached over and pulled it out. He flicked the on button and a set of small lights told him there were three shots left. He lifted the viewfinder to his eye and looked at the woman sitting before him. The edges of her hair burned in the light shining through the windows. He pressed the shutter, and the flash went off. The camera spit out the picture.

Wells grabbed it and shoved it into his back pocket. He felt the sting of tears filling his eyes. He sat up, leaned forward, and pressed his lips to her forehead. It was warm. It felt like home, and he started to cry.

"I love you," he said. Wells shoved the camera back into her bag, turned around and walked out of the café. He didn't restart time until he was back in his room. He fell onto his bed and pulled the photo out of his pocket. It was the face of someone who was worried about him. It was the face of someone who loved him. It was the face of someone who had just broken his heart. It was the face of someone who didn't understand him.

"Bullshit," he said as he tossed the picture onto the floor before rolling onto his side and crying himself to sleep.

CHAPTER 22: 1/13/20 DYLAN, LITERATURE, AND THE APPALACHIAN TRAIL

Was it childish to take Katelyn's picture? Of course. It went against everything I'd been trying to avoid. What can I say? I was mad. Not mad as in angry but mad as in momentarily insane.

That week, I quit my job at the coffee shop. I had a few outstanding projects with the newspaper and the tourism bureau for their summer magazine. Besides those tasks, I had no desire to accomplish anything. I was depressed. I took pictures when I needed to pay the bills and surfed the waves while others waited to blink. I ran at night in between the moments through the deserted back alleys of industrial Duluth, and drank often, which was most nights for the better part of three years. If you want to make time move fast, spend it intoxicated and depressed. The lines between the days, weeks, and months will blur like Monet's Waterlilies. If you are depressed and intoxicated, it is like flying at light speed on the Millennium Falcon. You can pass a lot of time doing very little.

A lot happened to your families during this time. Heather and Monica, I think I wasn't that pleasant when I came home to meet Mary and Michelle when they were born. I'm sorry about that. It was, of course, amazing to see them. And now, looking back, it is astounding how much all the kids have changed in those few short years. I have to imagine that being a parent is one of those truly terrifying and joyful experiences where the desire to watch time pass and simultaneously hold it still is an immense battle. I'm sorry I wasn't more present during what must have been a very special time for you both.

But I digress. If you've stayed with me this long, I want to be mindful of your time, and I've still got a few more stories to share that I hope will be insightful.

———

"Hey, Wells?'

Wells was sliding his surfboard back into the long, insulated bag resting on top of his car. He looked over to see the cluster of kids piling out of the university's ten-passenger van. A blond-haired man with a goatee was walking his way. He looked vaguely familiar, but Wells couldn't think of anyone he knew with a goatee.

"Yeah?" Wells said. His face was numb, and his eyelids were covered in tiny icicles. He'd just finished a long solo surf in near-zero temperatures. He had hoped the cold waves would have buffered his hangover, but the headache was returning in full force. All he wanted to do now was to go home, sleep, and not talk to anyone.

"Hey, dude! I thought that was you." The man walked right up to Wells and slapped him on the shoulder.

"Dude! It's Dylan from the U! Shit, it's been like, what? Five, six years? I didn't know you were still around."

It took Wells a moment to sift through the facial hair, puffier face, and muddled memories, but finally the image of a younger, skinnier Dylan surfaced.

"Oh, hey. How's it going, man?" The complete lack of enthusiasm from Wells went unnoticed by Dylan who turned to instruct a younger kid to unload the boards from the van.

"Oh, it's great. So great." Dylan lifted up his hands as if motioning to everything around them.

"Are you helping out with the students, then? Or teaching or something?"

"Yeah, man! I'm the surf instructor and coordinator for a bunch of the water sports for the U. It's a wicked gig." Several of the boards tumbled down to the ground, stealing Dylan's attention. "Oh, man, I gotta help them out. But, hey, let's go get a beer later or something. Catch up?"

Wells didn't have any reason to say no. His social life had been non-existent for the past few years since breaking up with Katelyn. He had some photos to edit before tomorrow, but could put that off.

"Sure, why not?"

Dylan shared his number. Wells texted his information, and the two agreed to connect later in the afternoon.

When Wells walked into the bar where they planned to meet, he didn't even have to open his eyes to find Dylan. He could easily hear the boisterous laughter and jeering at the hockey game broadcasting from the television above the bartender. Dylan looked over and spotted Wells. He waved him over, slapping his hand on the bar stool next to him.

"Yes! You made it!"

Wells had a feeling Dylan was one to speak in mostly exclamatory statements regardless of his surroundings. He'd be just as likely to shout hello in a library as in a noisy bar.

"Sure did," Wells said and gave a little laugh.

"What are you drinking? No, no, no. Let me get this one," Dylan said as Wells began pulling out his wallet.

"Um, just whatever you're having is fine."

"Hey, Andy. Another double gin and tonic for this fine gentleman right here."

Wells wasn't sure if it was a good or bad sign to be on a first name basis with the bartender, but at the very least it meant his drink came quickly as the tall pour was set on top of a napkin before Wells could take off his coat. Wells took a sip and felt the sweet flavor of juniper berries trickle down his throat.

The two drank, talked, and caught up on each other's lives, marveling at the fact they hadn't run into each other sooner in all that time. It was especially odd, considering the surfing scene was such a small group. Since Katelyn, however, Wells had made a point to keep the waves to himself.

After surfing, they discussed everything from the college hockey team who was making a national championship seem like more and more of a reality, to family history, and namesakes.

"So, Dylan?" Wells asked. "Did your parents have a thing for Bob Dylan? He's from around here, right? Come gather round, people, wherever you roam," Wells sang.

"Oh, no. That'd make sense though," said Dylan. "Yeah, he's from around here. But no. I'm named after the other famous Dylan."

"Like Jakob Dylan? The 'One Headlight,' guy? That's Bob's son, right?"

"Ha. Yeah, but still no. Dylan Thomas, the Welsh poet." Dylan looked for an indication in Wells' face that he recognized the name. Wells shook his head, expressionless.

"RAGE!" shouted Dylan, raising his glass. Several patrons bellied up to the bar and looked over to Dylan who was now declaring himself to be potentially the most obnoxious person in the establishment. He looked around at his audience and continued while donning a sing-songy British accent. "RAGE! RAGE! Rage against the dying light! Do not go quietly into that dark night!"

Dylan finished the oration by slamming his drink down on the counter and looked at Wells who stared blankly back.

"Really? Honestly? Alright, okay." Dylan put on a concerned look and grabbed Wells by the shoulders. They both swayed a little, the drinks having done their best to make them dizzy.

"Wells, tomorrow, or this week, or whenever, you need to go pick up a copy of Dylan Thomas' poetry. Seriously." Dylan looked intense enough to make Wells slightly uncomfortable and slightly more sober.

"Yeah, sure. I will." Wells had lost track of how many drinks they'd had. He felt a warm layer of whirring fuzz wrap around his head, and his stomach churned. He didn't eat much for supper. The trip to the restroom made his state of inebriation apparent as he felt the urge to spit in the urinal. He needed to leave and find some food on his way home. The awareness of his intoxication led to a flush of anxiety. He hadn't been this social in years. He walked out of the restroom and tried to stop time, but his concentration was hard to gather up. It was like trying to scoop up an egg that had cracked on the counter. His ability was slipping away from him as the alcohol worked its way through his body. The walls of the bar seemed to be closing in, Wells was sure there were twice as many people packed in tightly as there had been when he first arrived.

"Whoa, there, buddy." Dylan came up to Wells and put his arm around his shoulder. "You alright?" Wells' attention snapped back into focus.

"Yea-up, I'm-alright." His words were smashing together and slurred. Not a good sign. "I think I just need some food. I'll be good."

"They've got poutine here. It'll cancel out three drinks, for sure. I'll put in an order," Dylan didn't seem drunk at all. Instead, he seemed extremely thoughtful and concerned about Wells. Wells realized he really was a nice guy. It probably would be worth spending more time together in the future. He might be a good influence on Wells who had essentially given up on making friends.

"No. No. I'm just gonna walk down to the gas station and find something."

Dylan surveyed Wells, trying to determine if he'd really be walking.

"How 'bout I call you a cab, dude? It's slick out there," said Dylan.

"That's alright, buddy. I'll text you when I get home. Thanks again for getting me out, honestly." Wells was going to wave, but Dylan pulled him in for a hug and slapped Wells hard on the back. He then grabbed Wells by both shoulders and looked sternly into his eyes.

"RAGE!" Dylan roared one more time.

Wells laughed and walked out of the bar. He felt the cold blade of the winter wind slice through him. It was sobering. Sobering enough that he started to think driving would probably be fine. After all, it really wasn't that far. He could just eat when he got home and save the cash.

Wells fumbled with his car keys, trying to unlock the door and dropped them twice. When he finally started the engine, he turned up the radio, tapped his hand on the steering wheel twice to psych himself up, and pulled out of the parking lot. A horn blared at him from his left, and Wells slammed his foot on the brake. A blue pickup sped past him, fishtailing around his front bumper. The front seat passenger, a woman who must have been in her forties, gave him the bird and a look of disgust as they passed.

"Shit," said Wells.

He looked to his right, watching the car drive down the road toward the intersection. A police officer pulled up to the opposite stoplight. "I'm not gonna chance this." Wells gritted his teeth and tried his best to stop the clock on his dash and the cars driving by. The alcohol was working against him. He took a deep breath and gripped the steering wheel, knuckles turning white.

It worked. The truck with the angry passenger was stalled in a right turn. The police officer was stuck, staring at her dashboard with a radio in her hand. A few sparkling snowflakes glittered in the air above him. He turned his focus to his own car and thought about the mechanisms under the hood, the pistons, breaks, and fuel lines. The engine revved back to life, and Wells gently put his foot on the gas, pulling out of the parking lot.

As Wells approached the intersection and weaved between the stopped cars, he prayed his adrenaline was enough to keep time still. As soon as he could, he turned off the main road leaving the law behind and thumping over the curb as he did so. His home was just a few blocks ahead. The road looked darker than usual. Wells leaned forward and looked up to see if the moon was out but failed to find it. The mailboxes kept catching him off guard as they approached. In the black of the night, their silhouettes jumped out at him like teenagers darting into the road. His eyelids hung low, and his vision was starting to double. A fireball shot across the road and suddenly a vision of a person was in front of his car. He swerved and slammed on the breaks, skidding out in a three-hundred-sixty-degree spin.

The effect of the alcohol was accumulating like the snow. His hands shook as he shifted the car into park. He swung open the door and stepped onto the middle of the road, ready to beg for forgiveness from whoever he had possibly just killed. Maybe it was just someone's dog or, better yet, a deer. He walked behind the car and looked down the road. There was nothing but a few parked cars. The snowstorm was still suspended above him. The neighborhood was quiet. There were no streaks of blood-stained snow scattered through his tracks. He bent over and spit on the ground. He wanted to throw up but fought it with the last sober part of his brain.

Wells inspected the front of the car just to be sure. Anger and embarrassment met him when he saw his headlights were off. He felt stupid. He felt sick. He felt like every asshole he'd seen in the newspaper who killed someone while driving drunk. Wells walked over to the snowbank on the edge of the road and grabbed a handful of snow and rubbed it into his face until his eyelids and cheeks burned. It cleared the heavy fog of gin and self-loathing just enough to get back into the car, put it in drive, and slowly swerve the few blocks home. He parked the car, staggered into the house, and climbed in bed before releasing time and passing out.

———

The sun shone onto Wells' face, waking up a throbbing pain that thumped with every beat of his heart. Wells kept his eyes closed and reached for his water bottle that he kept by the bed. He drank. His mouth felt like it was filled with dryer lint. The water was cold and eased his nausea. *Did I really drive home?* His old friends, shame and guilt, took away any good the water had done. *I should have just let Dylan call me a cab. So stupid.*

Still, in spite of the regret, it did feel good to go out last night and see a friend. Wells lay in bed, trying to rehash the conversations, searching for anything meaningful behind the echoes of Dylan's laughter and shouts at the hockey game. Then came the words forming like condensation on a window pane. Rage. Rage. Wells smiled at the image of Dylan raising his fist, orating to his subjects at the bar.

Who was that author? Dylan Thompson?

Maybe he would walk to the local bookstore today to figure it out. He didn't have anything to do anyway.

"Crap." Wells sat up. He had forgotten his deadline. He still had pictures to edit. He picked up his phone and checked the time and saw he had one missed call and two unread text messages. It was eight-thirty. The photos needed to be in by nine. The call and one of the messages were from Dylan telling him last night was a blast and wanting to make sure he got home. The other message was from his mom. Wells wrote back an apology to Dylan and sat up. He looked at the text from his mom who was "just checking in." He didn't have the energy to reply.

He wasn't sure he could stand without getting sick, but he had to meet the deadline. His clothes were crumpled in a pile at the end of his bed. He kicked them into the corner, threw on some sweatpants and a shirt and stopped the clock at eight thirty-two. Wells could taste bile inching its way up his throat. He needed food before he could focus on the photographs.

Wells walked into the kitchen and opened the fridge. Looking at some leftover pizza on the middle shelf, he felt his stomach pulsate as if daring him to try it. In the door, he saw one last can of beer. That would help ease the hangover. He hated himself a little bit for following through with this little trick, but he figured if it was socially acceptable for people to go and buy a mimosa or bloody mary, what was the difference between him having a can of Busch Light with his eggs and coffee? *The difference*, he thought, *is that I'm alone in my house and not out with a bunch of friends, and this also happens weekly.* The Saturday and Sunday hangover was pretty much the only reason he kept beer in the fridge.

Either way, by the time Wells forced down half of the can, his hangover began to wash away like an outgoing tide. The relief felt so good, it seemed iodic not to drink the rest with his breakfast.

He finished eating and finally got to the edits he'd promised to return by this morning. The journalism team would be annoyed that it was last minute, but his shots were always so exceptional that they couldn't complain too much. He was their award-winning photographer. They needed him.

The clock on his phone still read eight thirty-two as he finalized his edits. He released time and sent off the email. All in all, he was feeling much better. The worst of the hangover had abated, and, even though he was a little tired and still smelled like alcohol and night sweats, the idea of finding Dylan's book was appealing enough to make that his plan for the day. He texted Dylan and asked the name of the author again before heading for the shower.

Two hours later, Wells walked out of a cozy indie bookshop with a collection of poems by Dylan Thomas. He thought about buying a few other books of poetry but decided against it, given he'd never read any before outside of a couple random college assignments. On his way out of the store, another book from the window display caught his eye. On the cover, a furry muzzle and a pair of dark eyes peered out at him from a lush forest. It was a stark contrast to the gray, cold winter day on the shores of Lake Superior. He read the title: "A Walk in the Woods: Rediscovering America on the Appalachian Trail."

The brown bear on the cover stared at him. He thought of Katelyn. He'd seen her twice, but always stopped time and tried to avoid her. Both times he felt small and pathetic because of his avoidance. Just like when he cheated on tests. Just like when he drove home drunk. Just like that day in homeroom. Time, whether conventional or his version of it, wasn't a salve to the pain of those scars. When he looked at the book, something from a conversation with Katelyn long ago tugged at him.

What if I hiked the trail? He thought. *Why not? I've got enough saved up. I could sell some photographs from the trip.*

Wells walked back to the checkout clerk and purchased the book. It had been a long time since he read any books. It was just barely noon, and he had already had a full day. He would probably need a nap after the first paragraph.

Sure enough, just after he finished reading Dylan's favorite poem which pleaded to all sorts of men not to go quietly into that dark night, he set the book down and closed his eyes to let the poem marinate. He wondered what Dylan Thomas would think of his life. Was he going about it quietly? Was he making enough noise? He drained the last of his water bottle and cozied into the couch. The heaviness of sleep moved quickly upon him. The last thing Wells' conscious mind saw was a red-haired woman walking into the lush woods on a long winding trail, beckoning him to follow.

CHAPTER 24: 1/14/20 NORFOLK

Three hundred and seventy-five days. That's how many days since my last drink. Some days it is terribly difficult. There are days I want my mind to shut off and the hours to pass while my back is turned, minutes disappearing while I'm not watching. Time slipping away like the entire picnic as the ants go marching one-by-one, carrying away one side dish at a time.

But for all the difficult days, there is good in the clarity given to me each morning that follows a night capped off with a cup of tea rather than three fingers of whisky. I didn't quit drinking right after I left Minnesota, but the hiking sure gave me a head start. It gave me a break from the revolving door I had been trapped in since college.

Oh, did I actually hike the entire Appalachian Trail, you ask? Hell yes, I did! Armed with the encouragement of Dylan Thomas and Bill Bryson, I made for the Georgia starting line that spring. It took a lot of poor planning followed by a lot of lessons often partially learned and a silly amount of camping gear, but I most certainly finished.

I thought about writing more about the hike, but honestly, you'd be better served by reading Bill Bryson's book yourself. It would be, by far, more entertaining. However, there are a few details that are pertinent. First, I hiked the trail in world-record time. The current reported record is something like forty-one days. I did it in twenty-seven if you're following the calendar. But, as you've gathered by now, I didn't operate under the same set of rules. I stretched my good days into weeks. In reality, it probably took me five months. So, technically, I guess I hiked it just like everyone else.

If I had the time, and my body could take it, I would have loved to try it one more time. I began moving through the hike like a boxer hungry for a chance at the title. I was focused on the finish line. What I learned, even in my solitary ways, was that the trail is an extremely social experience. Especially for thru-hikers. On the nights when I would camp with these fellow hikers, I listened to their stories, explanations of nicknames given, commiserating on the challenges, and rejoicing at the triumphs that came every day in the form of burnt meals, torn rain flies, better than expected weather, and surprising connections between complete strangers.

Unfortunately, I didn't share in any of these conversations. I was a mere fly on the wall. As I said, I was traveling with a different perspective and under a sun that barely moved on many of the days. Even with my tunnel vision, I had long gotten used to concealing my past and ability. The key to making the entire trip work came down to three things: one new skill, one lie told repeatedly, and one hard-to-follow rule.

First, I had to figure out how to keep time still while I slept. You see, every time I fell asleep while time was stopped, it seemed to restart at some point when I woke. I had built up a tolerance for holding time and releasing certain objects, Lake Superior, Katelyn, or the fox, for instance, but I had never tried holding while I was asleep, assuming it would be too difficult for my subconscious to handle.

However, I found if I fell asleep with all my imagination and focus holding the hands of a clock frozen in time, usually the time shown by the digital numbers on my twelve-dollar Casio watch, I could drift away for six or seven hours and wake to shadows that hadn't shifted. My biggest fear with this was that I would wake up as a modern-day Rip Van Winkle in the hills of Appalachia, weathered, gray, and covered in snow. I didn't know if it was possible to freeze myself unintentionally. If I did, would I ever wake up? The fear of what might happen when I fell asleep in a world held still like an unplugged turntable drove me to hike faster and faster, avoiding stopping more than necessary.

This is where the lie came in. As I said, hiking the trail is a social affair. You really aren't isolated the way one might find themselves in the wilderness of, say, Alaska. There are day hikers, thru-hikers, lost hikers, fishermen, birders, and summer interns all working their way back and forth over the trail from Georgia to Maine. In this community, people talk not just to each other, but also about each other. If I wanted to be noticed as little as possible, I had to come up with a believable story.

I decided if I was pushed for my hiking plans, it was best to tell folks I was just hiking a few days. I usually added there might be a chance I would drive or fly further up the trail and section hike it. This was usually accepted without much interest. People were always wanting to share their own misadventures, and uncomfortable questioning could often be derailed with a single question.

"If you could eat anything for supper tonight, what would it be?"

When you are away from the amenities of home for more than a few days, the simplest of things become the topics of the most passionate conversations, most notably food, a warm bed, and a clean bathroom.

The last trick of the trail was something that wouldn't have been a problem had I hiked ten years earlier. The only thing that would have forced me to explain my perplexing travel speed would be if I were caught on camera by different groups who might compare photos and stories later. For instance, if I had breakfast with one group and posed for a group shot only to stop time, hike twenty miles, and sit down for a cup of coffee with another group, I might find myself in a situation where that group wants another group photo. If they pass the camp with the first group in the afternoon and start sharing pictures… You can see how this gets confusing.

Again, because of the generally friendly nature of hikers and the cameras and cellphones in almost everyone's pocket, I had to insist on more than one occasion that I didn't want to be in a photo. I'm sure there were plenty of hikers who classified me as one of the "odd ones" because of it. But, as far as I know, there were no tales of a guy who time-warped across the Appalachian Trail that summer, so it worked.

When I got to Maine and reached the top of Mt. Katahdin, I was exhausted and relieved. I stood alone next to the brown and white sign on top of Baxter Peak. I started the ascent at ten thirty on a bluebird morning with no wind. I had already hiked two eight-hour sections since sunrise and gone to bed twice. I passed several hikers heading up and down, looking either fresh or weather-worn. I skirted around them and had the summit to myself. I took one obligatory photo with my travel camera so as to completely document the trail, and I released the world to spin once again.

The wind picked up, and I watched a few clouds roll toward me. What surprised me most was how anticlimactic it all felt. Sure, the view is expansive, but, in my opinion, there were prettier spots on the trail compared to this craggy summit covered in lichen. But I suppose everyone has a different favorite experience during their time on the trail. I think a significant part of my disappointment was from being alone. Not having anyone to celebrate with left me with nothing to do but watch others ascend to their happiness and stand on the sign, hands in the air, tears streaming for the camera.

The other problem with the trip was that I only figured out after another cross-country journey that I did this entire thing for someone who didn't care about it. I hiked the trail for Katelyn. Not for me. On top of that mountain, I even felt the urge to contact her on Facebook and send a picture. I had looked her up prior to the trip. She was engaged. Part of me thought the universe might somehow use my energy spent hiking to realign our stars. I concocted a million scenarios on the hike about how she might break up with her fiancé and we might reunite upon my return to Duluth as I strolled into town weathered and wizened. Let's just say I was a bit self-aggrandizing.

On top of Katahdin, I powered on my phone and looked through my contacts for Katelyn's name. I wondered what the hell I was doing with my life. I had spent the last several years depressed about a girl I dated for less than twelve months. I drank, surfed, and sobered up enough to sell some pictures and then repeated the process all over again. I started a friendship again with Dylan, but then I left to walk alone in the woods, trying to outrun the sun and pretty much anyone else willing to say hello.

It was like I took to the trail using that rage Dylan Thomas wrote about trying to chase some idea of escapism en route to happiness. But, ultimately, the figure I was pursuing ended up being faceless.

I sat on that rock and decided I needed more change than the hike. I needed to empty my side of the duplex, pack up my car, and leave Duluth. I needed to get out of the Midwest. With my mind walking the threads attached to Katelyn, I settled on Norfolk, Virginia. I had enough saved up to get by for a while, and I had hoped to sell a selection of Appalachian Trail photos as large prints online or possibly even put together a book for gift shops and the like.

I looked back at my phone, scrolled away from Katelyn's name, and sent a message to Mom letting her know I was planning on *moving and would be driving through next week, so I would try to stop by if I could.*

Heather, I know you were there when I came by. It was great to see the kids and how they had grown. Thank you so much for bringing them. Leslie, I think you couldn't get away from school. Monica, you were in the thick of it with work and the little ones. I guess now is as good of a time as any to tell each of you I am fully aware I did not prioritize you. For that, I'm sorry. I wish I would have...

You know what? I'm getting ahead of myself again. I have a little more writing to do before I can share all of my apologies and regrets. They aren't difficult to write down, but there is a bit more to my story I still have to tell that will close the circle. The end starts close to where it started.

CHAPTER 26: 1/15/20 LITERATURE AND THE LAST DIVE BAR

It wasn't hard to pack up my belongings and leave Duluth. I rented a U-Haul for the little furniture I had, bed, dresser, etc., and put my car on a trailer so I could drive it out to Norfolk.

I searched online and found a place to rent on the beach. Not the ocean, but the north-facing shore of the Chesapeake Bay. The photos online were phenomenal. The apartment was a little weathered and filled with lots of kids either in or recently out of college. It made for a noisy place to live, but all was forgotten when I saw my first sunset.

I stepped off the uneven boards of the boardwalk and moved past the eroding grassy dunes as I walked toward the blazing sky on that first night. It was like walking around in an impressionistic painting. The clouds and the sky were on fire and the water reflected it back just to further press the point. It was one of those moments where I froze time thinking, "This is it. This... This is the most beautiful moment," only to freeze the sunset again a minute later. And again. And again. And again until the darkening gray from the east chased the violet into the western horizon.

I was twenty-eight. I found a part-time job as a medical photographer at a hospital in the heart of Norfolk right near the old shipyards. I could get to the oceanfront from my apartment in a little over thirty minutes to find some surf. If I drove fifteen minutes the other direction, there was a trendy coffee shop with a cat and a well-kept bookshelf. I finally felt ready to turn a corner and walk away from the rut I'd been living in the last few years that had now been broken by my time on the trail.

———

"Jeez. This place is awesome," Leslie said as she walked around Wells' bayside apartment.

"I know, right? I mean, it's small, but, you know," he pointed out the screen door, "that's the beach. It's right there."

"I think your mom and I will just move in, if you don't mind. You can have the couch," Charles joked as he peered out over the bay at a large shipping container moving across the horizon.

"Sounds good to me," said Margaret.

Wells had been living in Virginia for a few months when Charles and Margaret decided he had settled in enough that they could visit. Leslie was enjoying her first summer as a college graduate, so she joined, too. To her, this trip sounded like the perfect reward before she took her GRE and started applying to graduate school.

"I know you just got in, but are you hungry? There is a cool divey place just down the road that always has live music on Fridays," Wells asked.

"I'm always up for a good dive bar," Leslie said, clapping her hands together.

"Always, sweetie?" asked Margaret with a grin.

"Well, I mean, just for, like, the last year, of course," Leslie corrected.

"Of course," Charles said and winked at his youngest daughter.

An hour later, the four Monasmiths were seated under a thatched roof on a pier in the back of a nearby marina. The sun was just about to touch the tops of the sail and fishing boats docked all around them. The air was warm, salty, and carried the faint smell of the tide, a mixture of shellfish and seaweed. It was a smell that was completely new to Wells before Virginia, and he had grown to love it over the course of the summer.

The waitress, a tan woman with a fading tattoo of a Chinese character behind her ear, walked over with a pad of paper and a pencil in her hand.

"Hey, ya'll. What can I get ya to drink?"

"Can we get a pitcher of Yuengling and a bucket of shrimp? Actually, let's get two orders of shrimp. And lots of paper towels." Wells rubbed his hands together, grinning. It had been years since he hosted his parents in Duluth. They came up to visit, but usually stayed at a hotel. To save them money on this trip, he offered his bed to his parents, and he and Leslie took the couch and futon in the living room.

"This place is fun," said Margaret, smiling. She nodded her head back and forth and rocked her shoulders to the husband-and-wife duo strumming a James Taylor song. The beer arrived and Leslie filled four plastic cups to the top.

"Thanks for coming out, guys," Wells said as they raised their glasses and tapped them together. The beer was cold, watery, and refreshing.

The shrimp came a short while later, and Wells showed them the messy process of picking the crustaceans. The shrimp were covered in melted butter and Old Bay Seasoning. The paper towels piled up, stained with orange fingerprints, and the family was into their third pitcher of beer. The sun had set, but the humidity hung around the marina like a blanket. Charles and

Margaret were red in the cheeks and laughed with each other telling old stories of the children. Stories Leslie and Wells had heard one hundred times over, but in the heat and with the buzz of the beer, the old tales were funnier and more nostalgic. To Charles and Margaret, the stories were the chord that still tied them to the long-gone days when the adoration between parent and child was equal before it had grown so lopsided.

The band took a break and now recorded music poured through the speakers. The voice of the singer had the edge of rock-n-roll but was still thick and sweet.

"What is this?" asked Leslie. She was closing her eyes, taking in the words "*Come on girl, you've got to give it up! You've got to hoooooooold on...*" Leslie rocked back and forth, ignoring her parents who were tipsy and leaning into each other, sharing a moment.

"Oh," said Wells, enjoying the memories of time spent with an old album. "This is Brittany Howard and the Alabama Shakes. So, so good."

Leslie kept her eyes closed and took another sip of her beer. Wells had to piss. He'd been holding it for a few minutes already, but this moment was just too good to miss. He couldn't remember many moments with his family where he felt so content. He pulled inward and took hold of time. He looked at his frozen parents and sister and smiled.

Wells walked around the edge of the seating area. There was an uncovered section of walkway about two feet wide that skirted the small pier that housed the tiny bar. He made his way back to the dark parking lot and peed on the side of a dumpster. The moon was cresting over the upscale apartment buildings that stood across from the bar. He grinned, thinking of his parents and sister. It was nice having them visit. He thought, under the right circumstances, even Heather and Monica could enjoy it, assuming Heather could bear to leave her kids' side for more than a few hours and Monica could let someone else take control at the hospital for once.

Wells kicked some gravel over the puddle he created and walked back to the bar. Strings of lights hung from the roof, illuminating the walkway and reflecting off the water which looked black as the night sky. He sat back in his seat and filled his glass, emptying the pitcher. He took a sip, enjoying the cool alcohol and warm buzz. He hadn't drank since before his time on the trail. Most of last year, alcohol ended up making him feel sad and depressed, but now, he felt glorious.

He took another drink and released time. Leslie was listening to Brittany Howard's voice slow down as the song ended. His parents were laughing at a joke. Charles reached for the pitcher, surprised to see it was empty.

"Wow. Was that our third?" he said.

"That was quick," said Margaret. She looked over to her son who looked glassy-eyed. "Wells, are you alright?"

Wells blinked; his vision dimmed for a moment, but he was pulled back by the sound of his mom's voice.

"Yeah. Yeah, I'm fine." He stood up and finished his beer in three gulps and smiled at his family. "Just a head rush. Should we get the check? I've got a pizza in the freezer if we want more to munch on. We can pop that in the oven when we get back."

They walked the two miles back to Wells' place. Leslie and Charles played cards while Wells put the pizza in the oven and did a few dishes. He went to open the screen door on the small back porch that overlooked the bay. He stepped outside to look at the stars and took a sip of his fresh beer. He stared out into the dark sky and at the trail of blinking lights in the distance where the Chesapeake Bay Bridge Tunnel led to the Eastern Shore of Virginia.

"How often do you use it?" Margaret leaned onto the railing next to her son and looked into the night. A plane flashed its lights high above them, leaving the airport. She hadn't talked to Wells about his gift since high school. Maybe it was the alcohol or maybe it was the little spell Wells had at the bar, but she felt like she needed to ask about it.

"It varies, I guess." He glanced over his shoulder. Leslie and Charles were accusing one another of cheating. Wells smiled. "If I added it all up, it'd probably be a lot of time, years worth maybe. Why do you ask?"

"I was just wondering. Tonight, I thought maybe you used it." She waited to see if he was willing to share more. Wells looked at her with a guilty grin and shrugged his shoulders.

"You caught that?"

"I was wondering how that pitcher emptied so quickly"

Wells laughed.

"I'm usually pretty careful about that sort of thing. I was just having such a good time and I had to pee. I didn't want to miss the moment. So I bought a little time, excused myself, returned, and refilled my glass. Well worth it."

"Do you get lightheaded like that a lot?"

"Oh, that? That was nothing. No, I'm fine." He sipped his beer again.

Margaret looked at him. Her eyes softened with concern.

"Really, Mom. I'm fine. You don't have to worry."

"You say that, but you remember what I told you about my brothers."

"I don't think it's the same. Really, I'm healthy. I jog all the time. I really don't drink like this anymore. I don't smoke, and besides a bit of a weakness for late night Taco Bell, I eat alright." He looked directly at his mother who still didn't look convinced. "Listen, I'm *fine*. Don't worry, Mom." He gave her a hug and walked inside to his sister and Charles to help settle the ongoing dispute.

Margaret watched him walk away, joining Leslie and her husband. She understood the temptation. She imagined, given his cavalier attitude toward using his gift, it must be easier for him to use it than it was for her. It took her immense concentration, and even then, she only had the strength to hold a moment like this, her two youngest children sitting at a table laughing with the love of her life, for a short period. It was an image she was tempted to seize just as someone lost in the desert reaches for a mirage. Instead, with even greater effort, she walked back into the apartment and joined her family as they continued to laugh.

———

"Leslie, should we pick up some coffee before Mom and Dad get up?"

"Sure. Sounds great." She hopped off the couch and started putting on her shoes. Their parents were a little slow to wake up after the night of libations and playing cards that lasted well past their usual bedtime.

Wells grabbed a bottle of ibuprofen out of the medicine cabinet and set it by the bathroom sink before he and Leslie headed out to the parking lot for whenever his parents decided to emerge from their bedroom.

"What's this?" Leslie held up a book sitting on the dashboard of Wells' car and read the cover. "An Introduction to Genetics. And I thought I was the one studying for the GRE."

"Oh, I picked it up from the coffee shop. I'm just trying to read a bit more, I guess."

"Yeah, but *genetics*? Really?" She leafed through the book and opened to a dog-eared page titled "Lyonization."

"Ah, it wasn't that bad." Wells glanced over and saw Leslie scanning the page that he supposed might hold the secrets that coursed through his veins. He suddenly felt self-conscious, like Leslie might realize what was wrong with her brother. Somewhere further in the back of his brain, he wondered what combination of activated genes lived inside his sister. A bookmark fell to her feet as she sifted through the pages. Wells leaned over and snatched the polaroid that had fallen face down on the floor.

"What's that?" asked Leslie.

"Oh, nothing. Just an old photo," he said, sliding the picture into his shirt pocket.

It was just a shade over fifteen minutes' drive to Fair Grounds Coffee Shop in Ghent, the old Norfolk neighborhood district.

"What do you want for coffee?" Wells said as they walked into the coffeehouse. The chairs were plush and cushioned and there were several turkish rugs on the creaking, wooden floor giving the entire room a soft, cozy feel.

"Um, I guess just a dark roast. No cream. Thanks."

Wells stopped by the bookshelf and slid the genetics book back in place. Leslie started running her finger over the spines of the books. She pulled out one with a satisfied expression.

"Oh, this is a great one. Have you read Dylan Thomas?" Wells laughed.

"Yeah, that's my copy. I donated it when I first came here. A friend of mine back in Duluth turned me on to Thomas." The book was extremely weathered. Some of the pages were warped from water damage. The book was the only luxury besides his camera Wells carried with him as he hiked the Trail. Even protected in a Ziplock bag, the book took its hits. Worn pages were the true sign of a loved book.

"Really? Do you read a lot of poetry?" Leslie asked. She pulled another book from the shelf. Wells didn't recognize the cover. "Now this one. Have you read it? I love Bukowski."

Wells looked at the unfamiliar name "No. Not that one. Not yet, anyway." He picked up a memoir of Bob Dylan. "I had my eye on this next. Have you listened to The Freewheelin' yet?'

"Ugh, no. I've been meaning to, though, since you told me about it. I move through music pretty slowly, you know. It takes me a while to let it all soak in."

"Well, you better get on that. It'll change your life," Wells nodded and tucked the memoir under his arm. Leslie slid the Bukowski book back onto the shelf.

"When do you think you'll come back to visit? Christmas?" Leslie bent down and petted a cat that came to inspect the new customers. She rolled her fingers over the soft fur as the cat rubbed her leg. She felt the vibration of his purring against her calf. It was a comfortable and familiar feeling. A sting of loneliness stabbed at her chest as she found herself wishing she had someone who wrapped around her like that.

"I don't know. Maybe," Wells said. "I'm looking forward to this fall. Hurricane season means good waves. That was one of my goals for moving out here. See a hurricane. Surf it. Photograph it."

"Ha. Don't most people *not* want to experience a natural disaster?"

"I guess," said Wells, shrugging. They grabbed the coffees and pastries and walked out of the shop. "I'm not sure when I'll make it back to Minnesota. I mean, I don't plan on living here forever. I'll come back, I'm sure, but I just wanted a change. Something different. I guess I'm just realizing there are so many cool things to do, and if I don't start doing them... I... There is just a lot I want to do and see. And not just here. A cross-country trip would be cool, too. Hike in Utah and Colorado. Maybe visit Seattle. I've always wanted to do that."

"You're still young. You've got time."

Wells nodded as the two got into the car so they could return to feed and caffeinate their hungover parents.

"Large cappuccino and a white chocolate raspberry scone for Wells." The barista set the items on the counter and leaned forward to look over to the corner where Wells usually sat on Saturday mornings. Wells walked over and picked up his order, giving her a smile before walking back to his seat.

Last weekend, he finished Bob Dylan's autobiography. Today, he opened Leslie's recommendation, Charles Bukowski.

"The Last Night of the Earth," Wells said, reading the title. He took a bite of his scone, swept the crumbs onto his napkin, and started to read. Wells had some research ahead of him because he wasn't very familiar with this author. When he first read Dylan Thomas, he learned the poems were more satisfying when he had some context and knew a little about the poet's life. Bukowski was completely unknown to him.

The reading was going slowly, but after an hour, he started to get the sense Bukowski's life was a hard one. Women. Booze. An insightful pessimist, maybe. Wells' attention turned to a conversation at a nearby table where Zeeba, the café cat, was now visiting.

"Are you going to stay in town?" asked a young woman in her early thirties. She wore a bright purple fleece and sipped a frothy drink.

"No. I just feel kinda nervous. It's a little scary." The woman replying was dressed similarly. Trendy outdoor clothes durable enough to withstand the elements but unlikely to ever be put in the harsh weather situation they were intended for. "Lots of folks are talking about buying generators and boarding up windows. I think I'd rather just evacuate before the governor gives the actual order."

"It'll probably be fine. It always ends up just being a lot of rain and a few flooded intersections."

Hurricane Shannon was expected to make landfall in just a few days. The November waters had turned cold. It likely would be the last major storm of the season before the nor'easters started. The swell was starting to pick up. All the storms so far that had flirted with the coasts north of the Carolinas had either died down before getting close enough to make an impact in the Norfolk area or made last-minute turns out to sea. Wells was wondering if he'd have to stay in Virginia through next year's hurricane season to get his chance at taking on a storm. After the hurricanes Patricia, Quinn, and Roberta had each failed to manifest any exceptional surf, he wasn't holding his breath for Shannon.

Still, there was always a chance. He blocked out the continuing conversation at the nearby table and pulled out his phone. He sifted through his unread texts. There was one from his father asking if it had started raining yet. Another from Heather, sent yesterday, asking if he was coming back for Christmas this year. She knew it was early but was hoping to start planning a family get-together. A message from a co-worker reminding him about an upcoming deadline. Wells replied to that one first and then his dad's message. He ignored Heather's. He wasn't sure what his plans were yet. He'd respond later.

He closed his messages and pulled up Facebook to scroll through a few posts. He rarely ever shared pictures or updates, but he still found himself drawn to the strange gratification from hypnotic scrolling through pictures of people's food, travels, and relationship updates of old acquaintances. Getting stuck exploring the site was like eating ice cream straight from the carton. It was never quite obvious how much you consumed until you finally looked up and realized you'd just eaten most of the container and twenty minutes had flown by. Katelyn was no longer engaged, and Wells hated himself for spending thirty minutes in a spiral of stalking the profiles of her friends in hopes he might figure out which ones had feelings for her by the way they commented on her photos. Annoyed with himself, he scoffed and opened up his weather app to check the latest landfall predictions.

Wells spent the next two days preparing for Shannon's landfall. He went to the beach several times and surfed as the swells grew. Fewer and fewer surfers were braving the water as the calm, pre-storm swell turned harsh and erratic. The rain was ceaseless and ran constantly over his eyes. He needed to stop time frequently to catch his breath from the exhaustion that came after paddling against the waves that were becoming angrier and more dangerous. His falls, too, were more intense as his body was thrown through the tumbling surf. If it was already this difficult, how much harder would it be when Shannon made landfall? She was teetering between a category three and four storm and swinging straight toward Virginia Beach, the coastal city that neighbored Norfolk. If the winds really picked up and the waves grew much larger, there was a chance Wells couldn't handle the surf. After all, he wasn't anything special when it came to surfing. He just had the luxury of taking the time he needed to get set up properly to drop into the right waves.

A queasiness fell over him as he finished a few assignments for the newspaper, and he realized there was a chance even he might not be able to take on Shannon's tallest waves. The consolation prize would be photography. It gave him some relief to know he would be sharing some of the most striking shots of the storm. He might even get an award if they thought he had put himself in harm's way for the paper. At the very least he'd get a bonus if the photos gained national recognition. This was the opportunity Wells had been waiting for: a chance to face the violence of the storm from a front-row seat, camera in one hand and a surfboard tucked under the other.

In just less than twenty-four hours, Wells would walk along the 86th street boardwalk, well north of the city strip, and stride face-first into swirling winds that would do their best to rip his board out of his hands and tear the skin from his cheeks. What Shannon didn't know was that no matter how hard she tried to cast Wells off, time was always on his side.

I wish I could tell you I walked onto that beach and conquered those waves like a surfing god. In actuality, the entire thing was rather anticlimactic, comedic even. I couldn't even hang onto my board. It took the better part of five minutes for me to freeze time. The chaos of the pelting rain and blasting sand, blades of sharp dune grass whipping around me, and the roar of the wind was disorienting. And the minute I did finally bring it all to an eerie pause, sure, I trudged through the hundred yards of high surf until I reached a spot where I could paddle, but once I let time go, I was clobbered by gusts of wind over seventy miles per hour. My board ripped out of my hands, flipped through the air, and the black leash tethered to my ankle went taught, pulling my leg out from under me. With each attempt, I was outgunned and put back in my place like a toddler playing in the National Football League. I finally had to accept there was no way I was going to ride this storm's waves and live to tell the tale.

Ultimately, I crouched down and tried with all my might to calm Shannon again so I could walk back to my car, grab my camera, and hope to photograph her fury before she tore herself from my grasp and continued her assault on coastal Virginia.

All in all, it was an exercise in frustration. I took some impressive photographs that my boss loved. But it turns out even hurricanes are forgotten over time, no matter how strongly they make landfall. They move on and die out, and people quickly resume their lives once the flood damage has been dealt with and only vaguely remember the storm when it comes time to name the next one.

I drove back to my apartment, defeated and unsure if all my efforts to hold onto Shannon's calamity had been worth it. I mean, I moved across the country for this, and what did it give me?

I walked straight to the fridge and finished a half-eaten pizza. My mind buzzed with fatigue, and the vision in my right eye went black for a moment. I tried to shake off the head rush, but I ended up laying down and passing out on my futon, unable to muster the energy to walk the twenty feet to the bedroom.

When I woke, the window was dark, but the sound of rain told me Shannon was still dancing outside in the darkness. The wind wasn't as intense, so her restlessness must have been calming as she moved inland.

I stumbled through the apartment, shaking off disorientation. I brewed a cup of tea in the kitchen and leaned over the countertop, breathing in the grassy smell of the steaming tannins. I felt heavy with sadness. The hurricane wasn't anything close to the triumph I had hoped for. What I thought might have been the perfect match for my powers was overwhelming and left me feeling hollow. I took a sip from my cup and realized my vision was back to normal. It's funny how you can be unaware of something as obvious and important as vision. Because I have two eyes, the painless loss and return of sight from one of them was barely worth noting.

Bukowski's book was sitting on the counter next to me. I looked at the charcoal and red cover of his book of poems and picked it up. I opened it to my last saved spot, where the photograph served as my bookmark. Katelyn's piercing eyes and burning hair stared back at me. Her lips were barely parted. Her expression of concern was sincere. The picture pulled me right back to that table in Duluth. I had to look away.

I turned the picture upside down and flipped the page to the next poem and began to read.

———————

"Nirvana," Wells said. The word sounded full, comforting, and dream-like. It curled around him like the warm waves of the Chesapeake Bay in August. It was the opposite of how he felt now, chilled from Shannon's thrashing and empty from the failure of his adventure.

The words on the page resonated through Wells like an echo in a culvert. He imagined himself as the young man in the poem sitting on the bus, entering a café in the snowy hills of North

Carolina, not far from where he sat now, not far relative to where he came from, anyway. He'd never ridden a bus across the country, but he could see himself, listening to the conversations, the yawning, and coughing. He could see himself leaning his head to the side and staring out the window watching the scenery slowly change, flickering by like an old film reel.

In the poem, the young man catches a glimpse of the perfect moment in a roadside diner. Snow falls on the street outside the window. The waitress is down-to-earth and uninfluenced by the chaos of the world around her. She smiles. The cook and dishwasher trade laughs from somewhere in the back. All too soon, the driver calls the rider back to the bus to continue their journey. The young man is pulled from the perfect moment.

Wells read the words over and over. He laid in bed and closed his eyes, imagining the waitress behind the counter filling his coffee while he finished his slice of blueberry pie. He could almost taste the thick, dark syrup and soft berries rolling over his tongue. In Bukowski's poem, the young man, sensing the beauty of the place, hesitated when asked to get back on the bus. Wells read the man's words out loud: "I'll just stay here. I'll just stay here."

Wells felt the young man knew he couldn't stay. He knew the moment was fleeting. He had stepped into something magical, and no one else saw it. He was the silent observer of a piece of heaven living on earth, but he couldn't hold on.

Taking another sip of tea, Wells set the book down. He slid Katelyn's photo into the valley between the two pages and closed the book. If he had been that young man, Wells could have stopped time. He could have bottled that moment of idyllic peace and lived inside it. He was sure of it. He was the only person in the world who could seize something like that and really appreciate it. The only things keeping him from setting off across the country were a job he didn't care for and a bus ticket he hadn't bought yet. If he wanted to, he could take care of both of those things tomorrow.

CHAPTER 28: MARGARET AND CHARLES MONASMITH

"Do you think this will be enough?" Charles stacked the last of the empty boxes in the back of the Subaru.

"I think so. If not, we can make another run," Margaret said. "We just have to empty the apartment by next week."

"And I suppose we can make a couple trips if need be," Charles added.

They backed out of the garage and started driving toward the river. Wells' apartment in Wisconsin was only ten minutes away from their home on the Minnesota side of the river, but Margaret wanted to be sure they got to his place before any of the kids.

"Do we know when Monica is arriving?" Charles asked. The question carried the subtext that there was still a fair chance she might cancel at the last minute.

"Not yet. I asked her yesterday if she could still make it, and she said she would. When I asked what time, she just wrote back 'not sure yet.' I talked to Jack though, and he said she was reading Wells' story, so that is good."

The car drove over the big blue bridge that crossed the Mississippi and Margaret looked at the big river below them. Large sheets of ice shifted and steam rose from the exposed pockets of flowing water. The sun was bright today. Margaret thought that was a good sign. A sunny day in late January was a blessing. No matter how cold it was, the sharp sunlight always looked warm through the window, and that was something.

"Did you talk to Heather this morning?" Charles asked.

Margaret smiled. Her husband was always good at keeping the conversation going.

"I did."

"How's she doing?"

"She's okay. You know. She feels guilty and responsible for not reaching out to Wells more. And for not noticing the burden she thinks he was carrying all this time."

"Oh, Heather," Charles said. "I love her desire to take care of everyone, but there is no sense in her punishing herself. I realize it may be a natural reaction, to feel guilty, that is, but I just hope she can move on from it."

"She will. Today will be good, I think."

"Do you think we should have told them sooner?" Charles asked.

"Of course I do," Margaret said. "Or rather, I wish we didn't have to go through this now, but how would that have gone? No one would have believed us. Wells would've had to do something to prove it. I could have, too, I suppose, but I think it would have just freaked everyone out. Anyway, Wells wasn't ready to talk about it until recently."

Charles let out a sigh.

"You're right. I don't know how we could've told them earlier."

"I'm always right," Margaret said, patting her husband's leg and giving him a wink as they pulled into the parking lot of Wells' apartment. "I thought you'd learned that by now."

CHAPTER 29: 1/17/20 CHASING NIRVANA

Bukowski's poem became a mantra for me and the idea of crossing the country by bus, an obsession. (If you haven't read it, by the way, now would be a good time.) The one thing that annoyed me, however, was the pain of having to actually sit on a slow-moving bus. It was a situation that took control out of my hands. Additionally, there was the hassle of deciding what to do with my job, apartment, car, and belongings. I stayed on with the newspaper through the winter, but when February came, I gave my notice and hired a shipping company to store, ship, and deliver my car and everything I owned to wherever I would end up. I was thinking of heading to the Pacific Northwest. The idea of exploring the Pacific Crest Trail crossed my mind. I had recently watched that movie with Reese Witherspoon where she hiked alone along the trail, and it sparked my interest, but I wasn't quite sure at that point if venturing on another long hike was how I wanted to spend my time.

On the bus, I brought cash, camping gear, and my camera. Basically, I made sure I had enough to last until I figured out what my next move would be. What would I do when I found the diner? What if I found it before I got to Denver? Would I stay when I found the paradise from Bukowski's poem? Maybe I would. Maybe I would just stay.

Wells walked up to the Tinee Giant gas station off Brambleton Avenue in Norfolk, Virginia. It was a Saturday in March. The morning air carried the sweet, optimistic smell of early spring. Of course, where he was heading, the weather could still be very wintery, so he savored this last taste of warm weather before driving into the Midwest where spring weather was a complete gamble.

Wells had a hiking duffel full of clothes and camping gear, as well as a backpack with his camera, laptop, and a few granola bars. He pulled the printed receipt of his bus ticket out of his pocket and handed it to the driver. Wells wove through the center aisle and found his window seat near the back. He specifically chose the passenger side so he could watch the scenery scroll by his window unimpeded by the center median of the highways they would be traveling.

In the end, and mostly out of indecision, he picked Denver as his initial landing pad. From there, depending on which way the wind was blowing, he'd decide on either California or Washington. If he did decide to hike the Pacific Crest Trail, it made the most sense to move south. Given the bus ride was a sixty-hour trip, he would have more than enough time to determine where to go after he found the diner, and for now, food was his primary focus.

"Ladies and gentlemen, please take your seats, as we will be departing from Norfolk in five minutes. Thank you again for choosing Greyhound bus lines. My name is Miles, and I will be your driver." Miles continued with the rules and his expectations of the riders, and as the bus pulled onto the interstate, the hum of the tires lulled Wells to sleep.

The ride was boring and the seat uncomfortable. Each stop throughout the day was sterile and offered generic eateries far from what Wells imagined from Bukowski's poem. The perpetual drone of the bus seemed to hypnotize the riders. Wells studied the blank stares, nodding heads, and gaping mouths of those around him. His hope in finding Bukowski's slice of 1950s heaven was dwindling. It went on like this for hours as they drove westward through the night.

"Ladies and gentlemen," interrupted the driver. Miles had been replaced by a stout, gray-haired woman with a soft southern accent who was now leading them through the Midwest and ever closer to the great plains. "We are just pulling into Danville, Illinois. Unfortunately, the check engine light has turned on. I've talked to dispatch and they will be working with us to either find a replacement bus or see if this one will be able to get you to your destination. We will be extending our five-minute stop to forty-five while we come up with a solution. We apologize for the delay and appreciate your patience."

Wells stepped off the bus and onto the cold, slushy pavement. It amazed him that just a day ago, he was in the balmy spring weather of the Virginia Tidewater. It was the time of year when spring was trying to gather up the courage to kick winter out like an old friend that had overstayed their welcome. The erratic temperatures and revolving doors of storms meant unpredictable travel and wet shoes for anyone walking. This chilled, damp weather was closer to what he had grown up with in Minnesota.

He opened the door to the Greyhound depot and approached the desk where the lone staff member sat, looking more like a prisoner than an employee.

"Excuse me, do you know if there is anywhere nearby to grab a bite to eat?"

"Vending machines around the corner and McDonald's across the street." The attendant went back to the luminescent glow of his phone while his thumb repeatedly flicked at the screen.

"I was thinking more of a diner or sit-down place. I've got some time to kill." Wells stared at the top of the attendant's head. It was littered with dandruff, and he didn't acknowledge the comment. Just as Wells was about to try a second time, the man spoke.

"You could try Leon's. A little place over in town. You'll need to take a cab, though." The man tapped away at his phone and gestured his head toward the station window. Wells could see two gray and white sedans idling in the lot, white clouds of exhaust rolling out from the back tailpipes.

"How far is it?" Wells asked.

"Um, five miles or so. Straight down Main Street and north a couple blocks by the river."

Wells thanked the attendant who murmured a response.

"What was that?" asked Wells.

"You on the Denver bus?" the attendant said again, still not looking up.

"I am."

"Best to grab something close by then. You'll miss your bus if you go all the way to town. Won't make it back in time." The attendant finally looked up at Wells. His eyes had sickly, dark violet bags beneath them. They were the eyes of someone who stayed up all night executing online gaming campaigns fueled by caffeinated soda, chips, and gas station pizza.

"Thanks," said Wells. Then, shaking his head and shrugging, he said, "There's never enough time, huh?"

The attendant nodded and returned to the screen in his hands.

The moment Wells was outside, he scanned the parking lot for anyone looking in his direction and then stopped time and started walking in the direction of town, swinging his backpack over his shoulder. It was only a few minutes after seven in the morning and his stomach ached for breakfast. As he walked, he imagined greasy potatoes, shredded and flattened into a large pancake shape. He could practically smell the salty, smoky bacon that was so savory it infused your clothes with its heavy scent. When Wells finished mopping up his eggs with his buttered toast, he would order a slice of pie no matter how early it was.

Leon's wasn't that difficult to find. In fact, it was just as the inattentive attendant described. Wells walked straight down the highway, passing the stalled cars silenced in his own postcard version of Danville, Illinois. The highway eventually turned into a sidewalked Main Street which meant fewer puddles of slush to walk through, but the damage had been done; his feet were soaked and numb. Still, after sitting in a bus for over thirty hours, it just felt good to move around a bit, and five miles was nothing compared to where his feet had taken him. Wells kept to the sidewalk, passing an auto dealership followed by a gas station. Just before the bridge went over the river, he turned north on Logan Street. A couple blocks up, his feet sore and the novelty of the walk long gone, he saw the red and white lettering of Leon's Diner. It was a small building still dressed in its 1950s decor. Its white facade stood out against the brick building it was nestling up against. Wells had the impression it was a relic that had likely gone in and out of fashion several times during its lifespan but still managed to survive in this middle-America town.

He looked at his phone.

"Seven-o-four," he read.

Wells set his backpack down and took out his camera. He stepped back onto the street to get the framing right and took his shot. He looked around to be sure no cars were coming up or down the neighborhood street, and he released his hold on the town of Danville. He walked up to the glass door that led into the small diner. This was it. He could feel it. Before pulling on the door handle, a cold gust blew against his back and a few small snowflakes swirled around him.

"Nirvana," he said to himself, grinning.

He welcomed the chill that ran across his shoulders and opened the door, stepping into the entryway and being met by the cozy warmth of the heater blasting from the upper corner of the diner. Besides the scuffed tile floor, Leon's was as red and white as a candy cane. Several of the booths along the back wall were filled with families. A portly gray-haired man with a Korean War Veteran jacket sat at the far end of the licorice-red linoleum countertop. The waitress walked out of the kitchen and looked at the newcomer.

"Just take a seat anywhere, and I'll be right with you." She carried a pot of coffee in her left hand and a pencil was tucked behind her right ear. It was perfect. Wells couldn't help but smile. The Veteran furrowed his brow at this intruding stranger who showed unnecessary signs of happiness.

"More coffee, Frank?"

"Sure, Darlene. Thanks," said the Vet who had a striking resemblance to Santa Claus. This only added to the perfection of the scene for Wells who sat down one stool away from the man.

"We're out of bacon, in case you are wondering," Darlene said as she dropped a menu in front of Wells. "Would you like some coffee, sweetie?"

"I'd love some." Wells flashed a wide grin. He couldn't have picked a better name for his waitress nor a more picture-perfect diner. It was a snapshot in time from the sock-hop era with a grizzled war veteran at his side. The romance of it all was almost overwhelming.

"You know," Wells said to Darlene as she flooded his white ceramic mug with steaming coffee. "I'll just take the Saturday special with sausage. Patties if you've got them." Wells pointed to the checkered sign on the wall. The day's special was two eggs, two bacon, hash browns, and toast.

"How would you like your eggs?"

"Over easy, Ma'am."

"White or wheat toast?"

"Wheat, please." Wells slid the menu back into the rack with the other menus next to the napkins, salt, pepper, and ketchup.

"Coming right up." She turned around and set the coffeepot back on the heat. She leaned into the open doorway that led back to the kitchen. "Miguel, one easy, wheat special, with patties, please."

"You got it," said a male voice from somewhere back.

Wells took a sip of his coffee.

"Ah, this is great," he said.

"It's the little things, ain't it?" The veteran who had been watching Wells lifted his cup in a cheers motion to Wells.

"It sure is. You've been here before, I take it?" asked Wells.

"Every Saturday since I got back from the war."

"We just can't seem to get rid of you, can we, Frank?" Darlene chimed in. She leaned against the counter like she had done a thousand times and gave Frank a playful smile. He laughed.

"Sweetheart, you never will as long as you keep making that delicious pie." He laughed again.

Wells stopped this moment. It was absolute perfection. He couldn't believe it had worked. His gamble had panned out. This little neighborhood diner five miles from the bus stop was a hidden jewel. He pulled out his camera and switched to his 35mm lens. He stood and tried to find an angle that could frame this moment appropriately. He didn't know when he'd have the opportunity to develop this shot, but Wells knew this scene would be there waiting for him whenever he found his next home.

He sat back down on the stool, put his camera away, and drank his coffee. Darlene and Frank had the look of old friends. Frank looked like he could be twenty years older than Darlene, but age was always hard to tell for Wells. He imagined they had a flirtatious relationship, but Darlene never let it go any further. Wells let time begin to turn again.

"Any chance you have pie on the menu today?" asked Wells.

"Oh, Sweetie," Darlene said, giving Wells a look of amused pity as if she was looking at a child who didn't know any better, "pie is *always* on the menu."

Wells laughed, and a bell rang somewhere in the back. Darlene disappeared into the kitchen and returned with Wells' order. The toast glistened with butter, and the yolks shifted like a waterbed beneath their white, over easy covering. He salted and peppered his eggs. Darlene delivered an order to a family in a booth on the back wall. Frank scoffed at a story in the local newspaper. Wells ate a piece of sausage, egg, and toast all in one bite. He closed his eyes and stopped time again. He held onto the moment with all his might and swallowed his mouthful. The yolk was smooth and fatty, layering his tongue. It evened out the salty sausage and gave contrast to the toast with its crispy texture.

He took another photo, this time with both his camera and his phone. He despised panoramic photographs that warped the truth in the image, but today he wanted to show the view from his seat. It was a view he couldn't grasp with his 30mm.

Wells returned to his meal and let Darlene and Frank continue their Saturday morning dance. They were like two old high school sweethearts who never quite got their timing right, but every Saturday morning, they had the opportunity to reimagine what life would have been like had Frank asked Darlene to the winter dance instead of Judy Casperson, and if Darlene would have let Frank drive her home from that humid summer party out by the barn after their senior year just before he went off to basic training. Wells imagined how things might have been different for them. Maybe Frank wouldn't still wake up in a cold sweat from reliving the gunfire that tore his platoon in half, and maybe Darlene wouldn't have lost her daughter in that car accident fifteen years earlier.

"Can I still get you that slice of pie?" Darlene lifted the empty plate sitting in front of Wells and refilled his coffee.

"Yes, please." He looked up at the clock ticking away on the wall. It was seven thirty-two. "Shit," Wells said.

"You gotta be somewhere?" Frank asked.

"I've got a bus to catch pretty soon."

"The pie is worth it." Frank winked as Darlene set down the wedge of pumpkin pie topped with a generous swirl of whipped cream.

Wells looked up at Darlene. By the expression on her face, Wells could see she was waiting for him to take his first bite and tell her how wonderful it was. Wells bought one more moment to himself. He really didn't want to miss the bus, but he had to have this moment. No one could take this from him. No one could have gotten here and found this blissful moment of nirvana. Not like he had done. The young man from Bukowski's poem was torn away from the window that peered into heaven, but Wells had the power to buy this time from the gods.

He closed his eyes and ate the pie, bite after bite. He finished the last of his coffee and set the cup down on the countertop. It was perfect. Utterly perfect. Wells was living out the poem right there with the sun dancing through the window like a kaleidoscope of happiness. He closed his eyes and let it settle.

As the glow sank in, the bitter aftertaste of the cheap coffee hung in the back of his mouth. Wells wished he had ordered a glass of water, but he had nothing to wash that last taste away. Before he knew what was happening, the magic of the moment began to fade, just as a snow globe settles. Wells looked at the stains on Darlene's apron and saw a liver spot on the side of Frank's face that likely needed a dermatologist before its borders invaded any more of his cheek. The longer he looked at the world around him, the more he saw the wrinkles and imperfections in it.

One more time, Wells could restart the moment and thank Frank for his service. He could let Darlene know that the slice of pumpkin pie she gave him was the best he had ever tasted. He could even tell the two they looked good together and should find time for a long overdue date. Or, Wells could set a twenty on the counter, give one last look at this kind, unaffected waitress and the worn, overfed veteran and capture this fraction of time to take with him and develop his photographs wherever he decided home would be next.

Just as Wells was about to restart time and give his thanks and say his goodbyes, he noticed a pin on the lapel of Darlene's apron. It was a pair of dancing sandhill cranes, necks intertwined. The crimson caps burned bright against her muted clothing. There was something intimate about the way the two birds rested on one another like two lovers who had seen the worst of each other and still managed to stay tied together. His thoughts flew to Katelyn, and he suddenly had the urge to cry. Somewhere, Wells had heard sandhill cranes journey together with their mate year after year every spring and fall. They were never alone, no matter what storms came their way. A wave of sadness rushed over him like a cold blast from Lake Superior.

His skin began to prickle. He needed to leave. Somehow, this moment of perfection was spinning out of control and twisted itself into a mocking jest, throwing Wells' Garden of Eden back into his face. Wells pushed himself back from the counter and tossed down his twenty. He could care less what Darlene and Frank would say when he restarted the clock and the man before them had evaporated into thin air leaving behind an empty plate, a modest tip, and a story everyone wouldn't believe.

It was now seven thirty-eight in the morning and a new bus was stuck in time while pulling into the station as Wells entered the parking area slightly out of breath. Cold sweat made his shirt cling to his body, and his heart fluttered erratically like a dancer out of step with the music. The gray sky lacked any definition, reflecting his now sullen mood. He let his clutch on the clock relax, and the roar of the bus's engine erupted. It was startling compared to the silence he'd been walking in, but if the engine

227

was running, that meant the bus was warm, and Wells was ready to find a comforting, lonely seat, close his eyes, and let the anxious feeling in his chest settle down. What the hell was he thinking riding a bus across the country in search of a lost image written by a dead poet? He threw insults at himself and let them echo and ricochet in his head as the bus pulled back onto the interstate. Maybe he would just go back to Minnesota after he got to Denver.

The last year had been a search for something great. Something beautiful. He had thru-hiked the Appalachian Trail. He stared a hurricane in the face. He found a scene of pure Americana only poets can capture, yet he still had no clue what he was doing with his life.

The day had slipped past while Wells tried to sleep away the bus ride that now felt more like a trap than an adventure. The sunlight was beginning to burn across the sky as it eased into the horizon when the driver came over the intercom and pulled Wells from his ruminations.

"Well, we have a little bit of a treat for you as we approach Kearney, Nebraska. If you look out to our left, you can see we are hitting the peak of the sandhill crane migration. We'll have a short stop in about fifteen minutes in Kearney where you'll be able to step out and get a glimpse of these gorgeous birds just before it gets dark."

The riders all turned in their seats, some standing to see the distant flocks of birds swirling around the grassy field. The orange sky was reflecting off puddles in the marshy landscape. Some riders pulled out their cell phones and tried to capture the birds and the sunset, but Wells knew there was nothing those phones could do to give the image justice.

He thought of the pin on the waitress' apron. The two birds tangled up in their embrace. Why couldn't he find someone to hold him like that? Someone to migrate with him from north to south between winters and summers.

The interstate was busy and the intensity of the peach, orange, and blues was increasing with each passing car. Wells wondered if this could be the consolation prize to what had begun to feel like a wasted pilgrimage. He snatched his camera and grabbed a couple extra rolls of film as he stopped the traffic on Interstate-80.

"How quickly an opportunity presents itself." Wells thought optimistically.

He hopped down the aisle of the bus and forced the doors open, jumping onto the hard, cold cement dusted with salt crystals and sand. Wells walked across the median between the west and eastbound traffic, his shoes noisily squelching through the wet grass. A sound that could only be heard now that the interstate traffic sat motionless.

Wells was running across the road again in the oncoming lane and slid his hand over the hood of a white Prius. The vast sky of Nebraska's Great Plains was wearing a blazing cloak of fire. It reminded Wells of the salty sunsets that ignited the Chesapeake Bay outside his apartment in Virginia. But here, he was rushing toward thousands of dancing, feeding, preening, and flying cranes instead of a few seagulls and shorebirds. He shivered with excitement as he walked down into the ditch and approached the field.

Wells slipped and caught himself, driving a hand into the mud, but kept moving. He was out of breath and his left arm began to tingle. He was surprised the cold was getting to him this easily, but he ignored the heavy feeling of his dangling hand as he ducked between the wires of a long fence line running parallel to the interstate for what seemed to be eternity.

He entered the field where the birds had congregated and moved into the crowd of light charcoal bodies covered in feathers like thousands of slate shingles. The vibrant crimson covering their heads gave them the appearance of regal dancers at a masquerade ball. Wells raised his camera and finished the rest of his roll of film, shooting the birds from several angles backlit by the setting sun with the Platte River winding away in the distance.

Next, he came to a pair of cranes suspended in midair, wings spread wide as if about to dive deep into each other's arms. He clumsily wiped the muddy hand on his pants and painted his fingers across the bird's strong wings and stiff feathers. The ground here was drier, so Wells laid down on his back to see what the earth saw when the birds celebrated over her head.

The cranes were almost screaming with happiness as they danced. Wells put the viewfinder to his eye and framed the silhouettes of the birds. The tips of their feathers transilluminated the rays of the setting sun. Far, far up in the sky, something shimmered, disrupting Well's shot. He manually adjusted the focus on the lens and saw the metallic wings of a large airliner flying to the east come into focus. He shifted on the ground slightly to place one of the cranes in front of the intruding airplane.

Surrounded by these winged creatures who traveled far and wide with the ones they loved, Wells thought of Katelyn, and he wished he hadn't messed things up with her so completely all those years ago. He thought of Frank and Darlene and their imagined missed chances. He thought of all the unanswered texts and calls from his parents and sisters and of his lonely belongings waiting to be shipped to a yet-to-be-known final destination. He was suddenly homesick. He struggled to swallow, and tears filled his eyes. Wells wanted someone to hold and wanted someone to hold him back. He wanted to have more to show for himself than a stack of photographs and newspaper clippings.

"What the hell am I doing? What am I doing with my life?" Wells lobbed the question up to the sky, but the stillness of the scene mocked him.

He sat up and gently ran the fingers of his right hand down the neck of the crane closest to him. His left hand was still heavy and numb. He tried to shake the feeling off and looked into the bird's piercing eye that held more depth than such a small thing should be able to carry.

"I just want to go home."

When Wells got off the bus hours later in Denver, Colorado, he grabbed his bags from the lower storage container and got into the first taxi he could find.

"Where to?" asked the driver while resetting the meter.

"Denver International, please," said Wells.

"From the bus to the airplane, huh? You must like spending your time traveling."

"I'm just trying to find my way back home," Wells said as he absentmindedly massaged the feeling back into his hand.

CHAPTER 30: 1/18/20 AIR ABOVE THE CLOUDS

Do you know, I'd never flown in a plane up until that point? We always drove to vacations as kids, and, like the bus, I didn't like the idea of giving up control to another driver. So to say the experience of buying a ticket, checking luggage, and navigating security was foreign would be an understatement.

I slept at the airport that night and boarded a six A.M. flight bound for Minneapolis the following morning. When the vacuumed-sealed doors closed on the big rocket set to launch into the sky, I nearly had a panic attack. I had isolated myself for the better part of that year, and being trapped in an airplane with all of those strangers crammed in tightly scared the crap out of me. With the bus, at least I could get off at the next stop.

Hands shaking and forehead sweating, I felt my stomach lurch as our wheels left the ground and began pulling away from the streets of the Mile High City. My mouth flooded with saliva. I nervously folded and unfolded the paper doggy bag that was tucked in the seat pocket. I was certain I would throw up before the flight was over as we shook our way upward through the air.

All of that changed, however, when we broke through the clouds and I saw the rising sun.

———

Wells stared at the cotton candy landscape before him. Wisps of clouds swirled past the tips of the wings. The plane was more like a ship at sea than an airliner as the wings cut through the thick bed of clouds like waves in the ocean. Without hesitation, Wells stopped time again. The picture before him was just as gorgeous, but he quickly realized it was the act of moving through the clouds that was so mesmerizing. He let it go again and watched the plane's engines skate across the tops of the clouds. The sun was radiating from somewhere ahead of them now, sending streaks of gold and orange glimmering across their surroundings. The glare ricocheted off his window, sporadically causing him to squint. If only he could view more than what the little oval viewfinder at his side let him see. He pushed up on the shade. It jammed a third of the way up. *Of course.* He pushed harder, but it didn't relent. He tried again by pulling down and lifting swiftly, but even with the running start, the shade got stuck in the same place, hanging like a stroke victim's eyelid.

Wells knew how fast magical moments like this passed you by and left you forever with your regret. He stopped time and frantically pulled his backpack out from beneath the seat in front of him. He yanked out his camera and tried framing shots with several different lenses but each time, he cursed the damn close quarters of the cramped seating arrangements. Annoyingly, his phone almost did a better job than his SLR. The little cameras had gotten so good they made everyone an amateur photographer, and that bugged the crap out of him. He drove his feet into the seat in front of him to push his body as far back as possible and try to slice the angle through the window, but the double pane and glare found its way into every shot.

"Damnit." Wells set his camera in his lap and let time resume. The engines droned on and his ears rang. If only he could get his camera mounted outside the plane. An image of the old barnstormers flew into his mind, the open cockpit biplanes with stunt women braced to the wings. A thought occurred to him.

What if I could get out there? What if I could stand on the wings?

Wells watched the ocean of clouds move by his window. He knew the plane was flying hundreds of miles per hour, but the clouds seemed to float by at a lolling pace. Wells felt a little tired from starting and stopping time repeatedly, so it took significant effort and focus to drown out the engines and ringing in his ears and bring it all to a standstill once again.

The passengers halted. The engine stopped. The bells chiming in his head continued for a moment but soon faded away. He grabbed his camera, unsure what the hell he was about to do, and hopped over the sleeping man who occupied the aisle seat.

Wells walked up through the rear cabin and to the exit row. He looked up to first class where a flight attendant was filling a cart with breakfast for the first class passengers. The cockpit door was closed. A large emergency exit sign hung above the door to his left. A large red lever sat in the locked position, looking like an arm ready to wrestle whoever dared try to get past the threshold. Wells stuck his arm and head through the camera's shoulder strap and shifted it so the body of the camera rested on his back.

"This is so stupid," Wells said aloud as he found the door's safety lock and put his hands on the latch. He immediately thought of every movie he had seen where passengers were sucked out of the plane when a hole tore open from some type of explosion. And then he remembered something from high school physics class. It was a vague memory exploring daily applications of pressure. Something told him he might not even be able to open the door, given how high they were flying and the pressure gradient between the thin atmosphere outside and the warm pressurized air of the cabin.

But things worked differently when Wells held the world in his hands, and if he could stop Lake Superior and a hurricane, he might just be able to get the door open.

"Only one way to find out," he said as he forced the latch upward and felt the door give. He pushed and it swung forward with surprising ease. He nearly fell through the doorway and onto the wing and only just caught himself in time. He grabbed the edge of the door frame and took a hesitant, shaky step forwards onto the wing. Wells could now fully see the vast expanse of pillowy clouds all around the plane. They looked deceptively solid. If he slipped and fell, it looked as if he would be landing on a thick, velvety, down comforter. He was half tempted to try, but he shook the idea before the temptation grabbed too much of a hold. If he tumbled and died, so would everyone else in this airplane.

Stepping onto the wing sent a shiver through his body as if sliding into a cold bath. He half pulled himself back into the warmth of the fuselage. He blinked twice, took a deep breath and stepped back onto the wing and looked toward the rising sun. The air was thin, and the ringing started in his ears again. He held his camera up and strained to look through the viewfinder with the lens held steady by his palm.

His vision began to blur and the golden sun started to turn into hundreds of sparks like fireworks. He pressed the shutter button just as he dropped his camera. It bumped off his chest and swung under his armpit and onto his back only saved by the thin black strap of nylon around his neck. His head began to fog, and he groped with his right hand in the warm cabin for something to guide him back to safety. Wells found a long handle adjacent to the doorframe and heaved himself back inside.

The plane began to shutter. He could hear the very beginnings of an air current being pulled toward the open door like the whisper of air being sucked through a straw. He was out of breath, weak, and his world was spinning, but Wells managed to stand and reach for the red handle. He leaned back and felt the door swing into place. He used all of his weight to pull down the door latch before everything went black, and Wells Monasmith crashed onto the floor of the cabin.

Out of the darkness and heavy, numbing cold, Wells watched the angel, cloaked in white, lean over his body and speak in a strange language while she laid her silver coin onto his chest. *It must be the payment for the gates of Heaven*, Wells thought. The coin was heavy and frigid. He let out a gasp at the freezing pressure on his chest and the white-robed angel faded into the clean lab coat of the resident physician who gave a sympathetic smile.

"It's okay, sir. Mr. Monasmith, I'm Doctor Murray, one of the residents taking care of you. You're in the hospital. Just try and relax, okay?" She laid her hands on Wells' shoulders. He was trying to sit up and clearly panicking as he took in the foreign surroundings. He was so weak, her gentle push laid him flat into the waxy bed. He became acutely aware of the uncomfortable plastic tubing around his ears and jammed into his nostrils. The doctor moved to his right and she disappeared. *What the hell?* Wells thought. *Where'd she go?* He turned his head toward her, and there she stood, her straight dark hair was pulled into a ponytail and she had three pagers clipped to the bulging pocket of her white coat. Wells turned his head to the left again, and she disappeared again. He tried closing his right eye and then his left. No matter what, he could only see her if he turned his head straight toward her. He tried to lift his left hand and wave it in front of his face, but it was too difficult. His arm was resisting his command. When he finally did so, his arm raised clumsily, but it confirmed that his vision on the left seemed fine.

"Wa...," Wells tried to say, but his throat was dry and his voice sounded jagged, like ice breaking in Duluth harbor. He looked around for water, but there was none on the plastic table at his side. "Water," he said.

"I'm sorry, sir. You have to pass your swallow study before we can let you drink. You had a pretty significant stroke, sir. Especially for your age. For anybody's age, really."

"Stroke?" Wells repeated. He was trying to piece together what happened. He remembered the flight and the sunrise. He remembered the cold air and could see his feet standing on the wing of the plane, but then it was all empty. He thought maybe there was an ambulance, but that could have been his imagination filling in the gaps.

"Where am I?" he asked.

"You're at Creighton University Medical Center in Omaha, Nebraska. Your plane had to make an emergency landing when they found you unconscious. No one is quite sure how you got out of your seat or why you have frostbite on your fingers. We wondered if you had tried to open the exit to the plane, but that would have been physically impossible. Were you hiking in Colorado before the flight? Camping in the mountains, maybe?"

"No. Just got off the bus and decided to fly home."

"Where's home, sir?"

Wells didn't like that she kept calling him sir. He was probably the same age as her, but the title made him feel ancient.

"Virginia, or, no, Minnesota," Wells said.

"Okay, well, try and rest. We have a few more tests to run today. My attending physician and the team will be rounding a little later. I'll let them know you've woken up. If you have any questions, please let your nurse know, and she can get in touch with me."

Wells nodded and she moved toward the door. She turned around and opened her mouth to speak but the words stuck in her throat. Wells had the feeling she was about to ask a question she'd been wanting to ask for the entirety of their encounter.

"Sir, I do have another question, and it would really help if you were honest. Have you or do you use any IV drugs or illicit substances?" Quickly, as if she wanted to be sure he knew the security of the doctor-patient relationship, she added, "You won't be in any trouble if you say yes. We want to give you the best care possible, and the more we know about your. . .," she paused here choosing her words carefully, "your... history, the better."

"No," Wells said. "No drugs. I used to drink and smoke a little, but I stopped almost a year ago."

Dr. Murray's smile dropped ever so slightly. He could have sworn she looked disappointed at his response, as if she didn't believe him. She thanked him and walked out. His nurse came in and emptied something at the foot of his bed. It was then he realized that the bag she emptied was attached to a tube that entered his penis. His cheeks flushed. This was humiliating. He felt helpless. He had the urge to stop time and try to escape. He made an attempt, but he was too tired. Instead, he shut his eyes and tried to ignore the tubes and monitors he now realized covered his body. Slowly, Wells fell back asleep.

When he next woke, Dr. Murray was at his bedside again, this time with a cluster of more white coats, some short and some long. He thought his vision had improved and he could see more of the objects on his right, but he couldn't be sure. A stocky man with dark skin, a five-o'clock shadow, and a stethoscope around his neck stepped forward. From the way the rest of the team stood around him, he appeared to be the attending physician.

"Hello, Mr. Monasmith. We heard you were awake. This is good to see."

Wells tried to sit up. It took a tremendous effort to push himself up with his left arm, but he managed to do so. The limb felt clumsy and club-like.

"You gave everyone on the plane quite the scare." The attending moved to the side of the bed and began tapping Wells' extremities to check reflexes. "I believe Dr. Murray explained to you that you have had a stroke, correct?"

"Yes," Wells said.

"Okay. Any time we have someone your age have a stroke, we need to look carefully for a cause because it is not typical." The physician moved to the other side of the bed and slipped out of Wells' field of vision. Wells had to turn his head extra far to watch the doctor continue his examination. "Now, do you ever use cocaine or any other illicit drugs?"

"No."

"Have you ever been diagnosed with any heart disease or irregular heart rhythm?"

"No."

"Do you have any family history of stroke or blood vessel disease at an early age?"

"Maybe. My mom had some brothers who died young, but one of those was from alcohol."

"Hmm," the physician stepped back from the bed and put his hands in the pocket of his lab coat. "Well, the imaging of your head showed pretty extensive signs of previous blood vessel disease. It is something we would expect to see in some of our eighty and ninety-year-old patients with high blood pressure and elevated cholesterol, or maybe diabetes, but not in someone like yourself who is young and looks rather fit.

"Have you ever had any numbness or tingling in your arms or legs? Any slurred speech or episodes of vision loss?"

"Maybe some vision loss for a few minutes in one eye. No slurred speech," Wells said. His thoughts were still foggy. He remembered the tingling in his hand while watching the sandhill cranes, but was too tired to bring it up.

"Well, there is no doubt you've had a stroke, but, hopefully, as you are young, you'll rebound quick enough with a little rehabilitation. We're still not quite sure what happened on that plane. Besides what your blood vessels look like, everything else appears pretty normal. No heart disease. Normal cholesterol. The vessels in your neck are acceptable, a little blocked which is, at the least, worth noting, but they are okay. No clotting disorders that we could find, though you'll need to stay on a blood thinner for now, obviously. Where is home for you, Mr. Monasmith? Dr. Murray says Minnesota?"

"Yeah, I guess." Everything the doctor was saying was soaring over his head. Piece by piece, images of the last few days started flashing back. He remembered the diner, the cranes, and the sunrise above the clouds, all failed attempts at finding Bukowski's nirvana. "I was trying to fly back. I'm sort of in the middle of figuring out where home is."

"Okay. Okay. We can have social work assist with that if needed. For now, we will let you continue to rest and regain your strength. We have a few more evaluations for you today. Physical therapy and your swallow study, which by the sound of your speech, should be fine, and we will try and get that thing out of you." He pointed at the foley and Wells shifted uncomfortably, trying not to think about the catheter.

The crowd began shuffling out, and Wells laid back down. Just as he was about to leave, the attending turned back.

"Oh yes, is there anyone you'd like us to call for you? I expect you'll need some assistance getting back home."

Wells considered his options. His most recent acquaintances in Virginia were out of the question for sure. He hadn't kept in touch with anyone from Duluth. It had been a year since he last heard from Dylan. There was Leslie, but he didn't want to put this on her.

"My parents, probably. I've got their number in my cell phone." He looked around and realized he had no idea where his belongings were.

"Don't worry; we've got your things here. We were able to get the backpack from the airline as well as your duffle. I'll have your nurse find your phone." He tapped his knuckles on the frame of the door. "We're going to get you better, Mr. Monasmith. You're too young to be having strokes. You've got a lot of life to live yet."

Wells considered the parting words. "A lot of life to live." Somewhere inside, he heard himself cast skepticism. His nurse brought him his phone. He powered it on and fumbled through his contacts realizing his life might be almost over and he barely had anyone to call for help. He had come dangerously close to dying alone in a hospital in Nebraska. How long would it have been before his family learned about what had happened?

He'd always been able to make more time and manage everything on his own. In the process of doing so, it seemed he'd built his life on an island. Over the years, he must have burned the boat that he sailed to get there. For now, he was stuck without a safe way back to mainland.

Wells looked back to his phone and held it slightly to his left so he could read the entire screen. He found his parents' home number, then he took a deep breath and dialed.

CHAPTER 31: HEATHER

"I'm sorry, Mom. I know it's late, but I'm still trying to figure this all out." Heather paced around the dining room table in her home, her cell phone pressed tightly to her ear. The children were sound asleep, and the lights of their Christmas tree cast a soft glow that emanated from the living room. Heather loved keeping the tree up all the way until Easter. It was a comforting reminder of the connection between Jesus' birth, death, and resurrection.

"No, that's alright, dear. What's your question?" Margaret asked.

"So last summer, on the Fourth of July, when Wells had been back for a while, and we had finally gotten everyone together, you were planning on telling us then?"

"Wells had wanted to, but I think he believed things were getting better. His physical therapy had gone really well. His vision was even improving, and he was driving again. Just look at the Fourth. No one could even tell he'd had that stroke."

"Yeah, I couldn't tell. Do you think Monica could?"

"Um, if she did, she didn't mention it to me. But you know, Monica and Wells have never really seen eye to eye. They are so different from one another. Wells was pretty sure she judged him for coming back to live with us when he did. He thought she had a very low opinion of him, and to be honest, I think he was right." Margaret said this very matter of factly. Heather was impressed by how objective her mother could be at times. "But unfortunately, when you are in your late twenties and have to move back in with your parents, it's easy to start believing the way others see you. Wells was probably depressed about it and didn't start feeling better until he had his own apartment later in the summer."

"I wish I would have known. I would have gone to see him more. I would have taken the kids. Heck, I would have dragged Monica over there so they could hammer out their issues."

"I know you would have, dear. I think Monica will work through this in her own way, just as we all are. Now that you all finally know, we sort of have to face this." Margaret considered how this revelation could be something that either brings the family closer together or highlights their differences and drives them further apart. Heather pulled her back from these ruminations.

"You could have told us, Mom. You know?" Heather said. "It would have been okay."

"I could have. Maybe I should have, but would any of you have believed me? I know it's easy to think, 'what if we had talked about this earlier?' I don't know. There are days I think it couldn't have gone any other way, and there are days I think Wells could still be here, and we would all carry this condition with honor like our family crest. But it still doesn't change anything. I could apologize for days, but I'm glad you know now. I think we are in as good of a position as any to address and accept it. I'm just hoping your father and I will be able to give you girls enough guidance on what to tell your kids when the time comes."

"Oh gosh. The last thing I'd want is them running around trying to tell their friends they have special powers." Heather shivered, just imagining the parent-teacher conferences that could ensue. Daily, she found ways to fear the world as a potential beast seeking to sink its teeth into her children. This was just one more battle she would have to fight for them.

"It would probably be fine. But, yes, telling them is not as simple as it sounds. I know you'll do what's best for your family though, when the time comes."

"I hope so," Heather said.

"Well, I'm going to get to bed. Your father beat me to it again, I'm afraid. I'll see you tomorrow at Wells' place, okay?"

"Sounds good, Mom. Love you."

"Love you, too, dear. Night."

"Night, Mom."

CHAPTER 32: 1/19/20 HOME

Exploring regret in search of resolution at the end of your life is like swimming through a dark tunnel. Your arms are getting weak. You want to give up. You're running out of air, and it would be easier to stop fighting than to chase the speck of light calling out in the darkness. It takes an immense amount of hard work to surface on the other side where contentment awaits to greet you like that first breath of fresh air flowing into your wasted lungs. You feel the weight lift, but your body is still heavy with exhaustion. The journey is so difficult that you often question whether it was worth it.

It isn't that I didn't expect to someday reach the end of my timeline. And to be fair, I had been warned that this might happen, that I could die young. And I don't think I could've stopped using it even if I wanted to.

It's a fact, my sisters, that you each have this in your genes. My guess is you might be able to use it somehow. At least one of you likely can. I'm not saying you should. I'm just saying if you had been exploring this affliction, you might be able to understand how hard it is to refrain from using it. If everyone in the world had to walk to their destination and you were the only one with a car, wouldn't you use it? Even knowing you might get to the end of your life quicker if the car crashes?

I'm not looking for sympathy with this long letter I've written you. I guess I'm just trying to explain my choices. I mean, I still feel like I've lived a long life, after all. It's simply that my days were spent between the pages of time. I lived in the space between words spoken by others, taking pictures, surfing, and exploring the woods *on my own. That was my decision and mine alone. I could have filled my days pursuing a career, going to movies, waiting in lines, or hanging out with family and friends, but I didn't.*

So often, we wish for more time. Hell, even me, sitting here now, I'm tempted to use my gift, no, curse seems more appropriate, to hold each moment a little longer, even knowing what it has done to my body. But from what I can tell, when you can have that extra fifteen minutes that you pine after, it never lives up to your expectations. The wine sours. It's like the freshly baked bread that collapses the moment you slice into it. Maybe the fleeting nature of time is what makes it perfect. So how do we savor it?

The closest thing to an answer I've found was following me around in my back pocket for over a year. It wasn't until this fall that I finally understood the beauty of it. It all came to me while out on my daily walk through the downtown neighborhoods of La Crosse. Now, would things have been different if I had listened to her long ago? Maybe. Just maybe. Either way, thank you for reading this. I'm sorry we didn't walk the journey together.

———

Wells walked past the public library and continued down the sidewalk, kicking the occasional black walnut from his path and exposing the dark stains bleeding into the cement. The morning air was crisp. Since moving into his apartment, Wells had made a point to go for a walk every day, regardless of the weather.

He stopped at a busy intersection and waited for the walk signal. He checked his phone for any new messages and texted Monica asking how things were going at work. Of all his sisters, she had been the most difficult to reach since he returned. Even as children, they seemed to butt heads. Wells was hoping he would find some way to make peace with her before his time was up, but he was starting to think that was a bridge that would never be built.

The cars continued to speed through the intersection, racing to their destinations, and he looked toward the bustling coffee shop to his right. Through the window, he saw the barista pass a drink to a customer with a smile. He was tempted to enter, but the walk signal began beeping, bringing him back to his morning stroll. His limp was almost gone. His left foot was the last thing to improve since the stroke. His vision had returned first, then the control of his hand, and finally the sensation that he had a scuba flipper instead of a foot began to ease.

His walks usually lasted an hour or two, depending on the weather. Sometimes he picked up a book from one of the small free libraries along the way. They stood like literary pastors doling out written communion to the willing. He had been particularly looking forward to this walk due to the number of rummage sale signs that had popped up early in the week, indicating today, Saturday, was the day to sift through other people's treasures.

It was at the second house he happened upon, one of the older mansions in the historic neighborhood of the old logging town, where he found it. The home and carriage house had been painted pearl white, and they were accented by green shutters and a slate roof. The detached garage was open to the cool air with card tables littered with paraphernalia from a life raising children, souvenirs from distant travels, and checkout-aisle impulse buys.

Wells passed by several toys he recognized from his childhood and a World-War-II-era bamboo fishing rod from

Japan. Just past the pile of assorted jewelry, he saw something that brought him to a halt.

There, at the corner of the table with its strap dangling off the edge, sat an old polaroid camera. A pink dot was stuck to the viewfinder. Fifteen dollars. Wells picked it up and turned it over in his hands, looking for signs of wear.

"Do you have any idea if this still works?" he asked the woman who was handing a young mother her change.

"As far as I know. We bought it about thirty years ago, but you know how those things go. Cameras just got better and better. It might even still have film in it."

"I'll take it," Wells said, handing her the cash.

The woman was right; there was film inside. After refreshing the batteries, Wells took his first photo from the three shots remaining. It was a picture of his parents at the small table in his apartment. His dad was leaning in toward his mother, smiling. The film came out bleached and streaked, but behind the artifact, the wrinkled smiles of his parents burned through the image captured in the old film. "Where did you get that old thing, anyway? I didn't even know they still made them," Margaret said while looking at the picture Wells had only taken fifteen minutes earlier. His father leaned in, putting an arm around his wife.

"At a garage sale over somewhere by Cass Street. This is an old one, but I think they are making a bit of a comeback. It seems like most things seem to eventually come back in style. It's *vintage*." Wells put air quotes around the word and grinned at his parents who were now lost together in the picture.

"It really does make it feel like both a distant and recent memory, doesn't it?" Charles said.

"It's a miracle the film even worked after all this time," Wells said. Without thinking about it, he rubbed a bruise on the back of his left hand. Margaret looked over and watched her son. She noticed a pallor that hadn't been there a few months ago.

"Do they still have you on blood thinners?" she asked.

"Yeah," Wells shrugged. "I had to get one of those stupid pill boxes to keep track of all the meds they want me to take each day. You know, the ones with the days of the week written on top. I feel like a nursing home resident."

"Trust us; we know exactly what you're talking about. If I don't empty that pill box each day, I'm up all night trying to whiz."

"Charles!" Margaret elbowed her husband in the ribs.

"What? It's the truth!" He winked at Wells. Charles liked getting a rise out of his wife from time to time. Wells could appreciate the sense of humor.

"So, I've been thinking," Wells said as he got up and poured himself another cup of coffee from the old Mr. Coffee machine he picked up from the thrift store. "We need to figure out a way to tell them. I know that I could really help with that. It's not in our favor that I haven't exactly been the best brother over the years, but still, I need to try somehow. At least for their kids' sake, you know?"

"I know. We've wrestled with this forever, but you're right. Maybe we can do it together. I would say Christmas, but I know Heather and Monica are heading to their other sides for the holiday. What would you say about meeting with each of them individually?"

"I'm not so sure," Wells moaned. He sat back down and looked into his mug as if deciding whether or not to share something. "I...I have started writing something. Kind of like a memoir, I guess? I was thinking, if they could read the story first, then we might be able to talk about it. It just might be easier to process, you know? I even had the idea to somehow show them one of these." He gestured at the polaroid of his parents. "Maybe I could visit each of them and take one when I stop time or something to prove it all. I don't know. I've just messed things up so much. I'm not sure if they'd believe what I've done to myself. And you both warned me about this. About how it would be hard on my body, but I was just a kid. I... That type of medical stuff doesn't even seem real when you're young," he laughed. "But now look at me."

Wells sipped his coffee. His body was young, but his expression was of someone much more weather-worn than his parents. His aura was weighed down by regrets and missed opportunities. More than anything, he looked exhausted.

"There's still time," Margaret said. Wells couldn't tell if this was directed to herself or him. "You know Heather; she'd love you to stop in and visit. And Leslie and you have always had an understanding. She loves you dearly. Monica is just different. She takes more patience and understanding. With time, I think she'll come around."

"With time?" Wells laughed. He sighed. "Okay, I'll keep trying."

"That's all we can do," Charles said before picking up the polaroid and reliving the casual moment he had just shared with the love of his life. "All we can do is try."

———

In my little apartment, I lay in bed completely still. I am so motionless and quiet that I can feel my heart beating. I can almost feel each individual valve open and close as the blood travels from my body to my heart and then into my lungs to be refreshed with oxygen. It returns to my heart and courses up my neck and into this wrung out and failing brain.

I tried to picture this living muscle inside my chest working away minute after minute, hour after hour, day after day. This fragile little animal that's been with me since the very beginning must be so tired. Every time I stopped the world around me, my heart kept going. Recently, I've been wondering if, had I wanted, could I stop my heart, too? If I kept my mind going, but forced my heart still, would I survive? And for how long? It's such a fragile thing, and the heart is so easily forgotten, yet every second it's there, ticking away while we make the most of our lives.

I think the least we can do to honor the little bird who works feverishly inside our chest is to be sure to live these moments purposely, building bridges where they can be built, and following the paths in front of us with sincerity.

CHAPTER 33: THE APARTMENT

"Mom, it's okay. I can get the door." Heather walked out of Wells' bedroom and through the small living room. She unlocked the top latch of the door and opened it to see Leslie smiling brightly. Heather was struck by how silvery her sister's hair looked in the hallway lighting. Maybe it was the fluorescent bulbs, but Heather had a feeling her youngest sister was going gray early.

"Foods here!" Leslie said, handing over the two shrink-wrapped pizzas. "Any chance the oven is preheated? I'm starving."

"No, sorry," Heather said. "But I'm sure it won't take long to heat up. Oh, we're just tossing our coats here for now." She pointed to a kitchen chair that had been moved next to the front door. A pile of collapsed cardboard boxes and a few rolls of masking tape were stacked against the wall.

"Here," said Heather. "I'll take those." She took the pizzas from Leslie and walked over to the kitchenette to preheat the oven.

Leslie set her jacket on the chair but kept her eyes on a particular frame on the wall. It was a full-size sheet of paper with something handwritten.

"No way!" Leslie said as she recognized the poem by Charles Bukowski. "Nirvana."

The framed photo next to the poem caught her eye. She had never seen the people before, but she recognized the scene immediately. "Oh my god," Leslie said. The old waitress smiled in the dusty sunlight of the diner. A shaggy-haired man sat, cup of coffee in hand, laughing back at her. It was the diner Wells wrote about. A swell of emotion hit her unexpectedly, and she had to use all her strength to fight back the tears. She wasn't ready for proof of her brother's search for tranquility greeting her at the doorway, but there it was. The photograph glowed with the warmth of Leon's Diner. Leslie could almost see herself in the shot, exchanging dirty jokes with the old vet.

"He was such a gifted photographer, wasn't he?" said Margaret, who had just appeared at Leslie's side. She put her arms around her daughter.

"This is amazing," Leslie said, pointing to the photograph. "It's exactly like I imagined it."

"I know. This is why the newspapers always gave him so much flexibility for his freelance work. He always got the shot. If they only knew his little secret. They probably would have asked even more of him, I suppose."

"Listen, I'm not sure what you had planned, but if no one else wants these, I'd love to have this one at some point." Leslie rubbed her thumb across the smooth frame.

"Oh, sure. We'll get everything out and let you all take a peek. I'd like you all to have something that speaks to you."

"Knock, knock," Monica announced, letting herself in.

"Oh, good, you made it," Margaret said as she came to hug her oldest daughter.

"Hi, Mom. I do have to be out of here by one to catch a meeting before Jack picks up Michelle. There's a dance tonight, and I've got a few emails to finish before that. It just never stops."

"Well, the pizza is in the oven, and you can just head out whenever you need to. He didn't have a lot of stuff, to be honest, so it shouldn't take too long." Margaret noticed Monica swallow hard at the mention of the pizza and swore she saw the glow only mothers recognize, but she decided not to mention it.

"Sounds good. Are Heather and Dad here?"

"Yup, they're in Wells' room." Margaret pointed back through the kitchen toward the bedroom.

Monica walked through the apartment. There were two recliners and a coffee table. Something she couldn't quite place was odd about the way the room was arranged. Like the room was incomplete. She looked around and saw a shelf filled with books and a few picture frames. The walls had several large prints taped up like posters. There was a guitar leaning against a closet where nearly ten shoe boxes were stacked upon one another. They were labeled with dates in thick black marker. Suddenly, she realized why this room seemed off.

"Did you guys already pack up his T.V.?" Monica asked.

"I don't think he had one. Right, Mom?" Leslie asked. She was walking over to inspect the guitar.

"No, he didn't. He told us he sold it right before heading off to Virginia."

"Wow," said Monica, eyebrows raised. She didn't think she knew anyone without a television. She didn't know how she and Jack would survive without it there to calm the kids at night and whenever they needed to get anything done around the house.

"When did Wells start playing guitar?" Leslie asked. She sat in the chair and cradled her body around the guitar, sliding her hand over the neck. She plucked out a few chords that suggested the guitar was still in tune or at least close to it.

"I'm not sure, but I think he got that when he moved back here. It might have been part of his rehab for his left hand. I know he played it almost every day though. He mentioned it on the phone a lot," Margaret said. "Besides going on walks, I think he spent most of his time these last few months reading or playing guitar."

Monica perused the bookshelf. It wasn't a massive piece of furniture. She assumed it was second-hand, but despite its size, she was amazed at how many books were crammed onto it. She tilted her head to read the titles.

"'Einstein's Dreams,'" she read. "Isn't this a little above his level?" She flipped through the pages. She saw notes scribbled in the margins saying things like, "If only this was how time worked," and "What if Katelyn, or anyone we love for that matter, was the center of time, and the closer we were together, the slower it passed?" Again, another eyebrow raise from Monica. Maybe her brother was a little more insightful than she realized. She thought of herself as a person who was rarely surprised, but within five minutes of walking into Wells' apartment, it had already happened twice.

"Oh, I thought I heard you out here." Charles walked into the kitchen with Heather trailing behind him. Heather cracked the oven door to check on the pizza.

"How's it looking?" asked Leslie.

"Still a little ways to go," said Heather.

The smell of melting cheese and sizzling meats wafted through the room. When the scent hit Monica, she went pallid.

"Monica," said Heather. Her voice was cut with a slight edge of concern. "Are you okay?"

"I'm fine." Monica waved her hand and steeled herself. "Just another long shift yesterday. Still recovering, you know?"

Heather gave her a lingering look, the type that frustrates an oldest sibling, the one who is supposed to have everything under control.

"Really," Monica reassured her. "I'm fine. What all still needs packing?"

The family spent the next hour emptying Wells' dresser and closets. The clothes and towels were folded and boxed. The kitchen drawers and cupboards were cleared, though that didn't take long at all. The girls helped Charles break down the bedroom furniture and carry it into the small trailer parked in front of the apartment building. When they finished, they all sat down in the living room. They had purposely left the couch and a few chairs so they could pick at the remains of the pizza and divvy out a few of Wells' items.

Monica walked back from the bathroom and sat next to Heather on the couch. Leslie was sitting cross-legged on the floor, and Charles and Margaret were in chairs. A stack of three shoe boxes rested in front of Margaret.

"Thank you all so much for helping today. It really does mean a lot to your father and me," Margaret said.

"Of course, Mom," said Leslie. She picked up another cold piece of pizza and began tearing off portions of the crust to eat first.

"God, what I would give to be young again and have your metabolism," Monica said.

"Leslie, she's just saying that you look amazing," Heather said, jumping in to shape Monica's statement into a compliment.

"My time will come, I'm sure."

"Yeah, have a few kids and see if you can keep that body." Monica reached over and picked up the top shoebox sitting in front of her mother.

Margaret watched her oldest daughter closely. She wondered if the word "few" was an unintentional slip. Whether the children liked to admit it or not, mothers always knew their kids best, no matter how old they were.

"So these are, what, pictures Wells took?" Monica asked. She started flipping through photographs like rifling through a library catalog system. She sifted through the box quickly and passed it on to Leslie who cradled it reverently. Leslie ran her hands over the photos and picked one at random out from the middle just as Monica grabbed the second box.

"Oh my gosh," said Leslie, staring at the picture with her jaw hanging slack. Everyone turned to look at her. All her family could see was the blank white side of the photograph facing them. Leslie looked up at them. "I think this is Katelyn."

She turned the picture around and they all looked at the face of a young, athletic-looking girl holding a surfboard. She was laughing and her blazing red hair shined off her shoulders. In the background, they could see a gray, cloud-covered sky and the crashing waves of Lake Superior.

Heather reached for the photo. Margaret and Charles leaned in for a closer look.

It wasn't as if Wells had written sonnets about Katelyn, but she had clearly played a major role in his life and story. Looking into the bright eyes of the girl who likely had gotten to know their brother better than any of them was stirring. Monica looked on with vague interest.

"Do you think she knows?" asked Heather. "That Wells died. Do you think she's heard?"

No one responded for nearly a minute.

"You know," Heather continued. "I think we need to find her and tell her. Mom, did Wells say if he had gotten back in touch with her at all?"

"He didn't," Margaret responded. "But, I do know he tried. He told us he sent her a letter. It could have been his manuscript he sent her, for all I know. But, no, I don't know if she's aware."

Charles noticed Monica holding another photograph and sitting uncharacteristically quiet.

"What's that one, Monica?" Charles asked.

Monica was holding a picture of a bird with a snake-like neck stretching high into the sky. The perspective was from below the bird, but the bird must have only been a few feet above Wells' camera. The tangerine sunlight seeped through the tips of the feathers. Monica could just make out a hint of crimson on the bird's head. The picture was breathtaking. She couldn't find the words to answer her father. Even she, the rational, evidence-based eldest sister, could not escape the truth buried in the beauty of this picture. She handed it to her father who looked for a moment, wiped his eyes, and passed it on.

From then on, pictures were passed in silence, only interrupted by sniffling. Pictures of sunrises on the Appalachian Trail and one from an uninhibited view above the clouds. There were pictures of surfers riding the frigid waves of the granite-lined northern shore of Lake Superior with ice clinging to their eyebrows and beards. There were shots of children running along beaches with sunsets that seemed to echo throughout every surface of the sand and water. In the last box, every picture was of the girls. Leslie, Heather, Monica, Mary, Adrienne, Maya, Michelle, and Samantha. There were also a few pictures of Margaret and Charles, caught in a moment when they believed no one was watching. They were leaning into one another as if huddling under a blanket of what could only be love.

After the pictures were put away, the chairs and couch had been moved out, and the final round of vacuuming had been completed, the five Monasmiths stood on the hard sidewalk outside Wells' apartment. They each carried something in their arms from his life. They exchanged hugs and goodbyes. Even Monica, whose hugs were often brief and stiff, partook in the long, close embraces being passed around. It didn't seem to matter that she had stayed well past her intended time of departure.

When all the kids had driven off, Charles checked his pocket one more time to make sure he had dropped the keys in the mail slot as instructed and pulled Margaret to his side.

"I think that went alright, don't you?" Margaret asked.

"Yeah, I think Wells would have been happy with that," said Charles. "In the end, all he wanted was for us to be closer. The girls are all so different, but I think...I think it went alright." He nodded and looked up at the cloudless sky. The first stars of dusk were making their entrance above them. Their breath plumed upward and disappeared.

"Yeah, me, too." She squeezed her husband and then began walking to their car. "Maybe we could have them all over for an Easter supper."

"That'd be nice," Charles said.

"I could show the girls how to make angel food cake."

"Now you're talking."

Charles opened Margaret's car door and closed it after she sat down. He walked over to his side of the car and the two drove back across the river to their home where they would watch the evening news, eat popcorn, and play their nightly round of cards.

EPILOGUE

Monica

The pager clipped to Monica's side buzzed for two long seconds and then beeped irritatingly.

"I know. I know." She picked up the pager and read the text notifying her she had a new admission coming from the emergency department for respiratory failure. The working diagnosis was a presumed viral-related illness.

"Not another one," she said to herself. She sat in a small cove of computers designated specifically for physicians. In a few hours, it would be packed with residents who were fighting for any free computer they could get in order to finish the morning notes prior to rounding with their respective teams. Right now, in the middle of the night, it was empty. It was, dare she say, peaceful.

Monica scrolled up to the patient search tab on the hospital's electronic medical record system. She paused for a moment as her cursor hovered over the typing field. She looked around to confirm none of the nursing staff was nearby and began typing.

M-O-N-A-S-M-I-T-H

Comma

M-O-N-I-C-A

It was against hospital policy to look up family medical records, including your own. She wasn't sure if the hospital was auditing their doctors with chart searches, but she needed to check her labs. Her pregnancy had continued, and she still hadn't told Jack or her family. So many pregnancies don't end in a baby, so she felt like she didn't want to get everyone riled up before she was absolutely sure. But with this recent madness involving Wells, she had to at least know the gender.

Monica double-clicked on her name and hovered over the laboratory tab. The results were supposed to be back today. She had already checked several times but each time, the results only read "pending." Now, the word "final" was staring her back in the face.

She took a deep break. Somewhere inside in her belly, she thought she could already hear the answer speaking to her. She couldn't describe it, but she knew the way you know which direction the tide is moving as you wade in the shallows of the ocean. If you are still enough, the push and pull is obvious.

Monica clicked on the prenatal genetic testing lab and read the words that popped up.

"Trisomy twenty-one, negative," she read. Then she scrolled down. "Gender."

She stared at the screen for a long time, reading the result over and over again. She thought of her parents. Monica thought of her dad walking in on her young brother who had unknowingly tapped into a power that many would die to possess. She thought of the first time her parents had realized their young son discovered how to wield that power and eventually found themselves eulogizing that same boy. Lastly, she thought of the decision that would now lie before Jack and her. Would they tell this child's sisters? Would they try and walk through this together, or would her son be traveling down a path in secrecy like her brother had.

Something shifted inside her. Like a single snowflake landing on a mountain's edge which tips over a drift and ultimately leads to an avalanche, Monica felt a surge of emotion rise up and tumble out of her. Monica cried for the first time since childhood. Her entire body shook as she laid her forehead down on the desk. When her pager buzzed again, she remembered where she was and the importance of the task at hand. She pushed the tears back and wiped her eyes. Right now, someone in the hospital was sick. Her son would be born later. At this moment, her primary responsibilities were to her patient.

Leslie

When you're ready, think of me and imagine yourself doing backflips underwater.

Leslie read the words over and over. She sat in her apartment by an open window, tracing the letters with her fingers. She could feel the subtle depression left by the pen and could almost see the small sphere that rolled the ink onto the page. It was June, and the mid-afternoon was mixing air currents like a cocktail. The scent of lilac flowers and rain was intoxicating, hopeful.

Nearing the end of her lease, Leslie had no idea what her next steps would be. More school? New apartment? Finally meet someone? She held the photo Wells left for her and flipped it over in her hands to look at the words again.

"I'm ready," she said, as if it were as obvious to the empty room as it was to her.

Just then, an absurd thought occurred to her. It was the handwriting in which the words were written. She knew everyone in her family had similar handwriting, but, as far as she knew, she was the only one who used a cursive "l" while writing in script. The sentence written on the back of the photograph looked as if *she* had written it, which was clearly impossible.

To be sure it wasn't her brother's penmanship, she jumped up and rummaged through a drawer, searching for a few notes from her brother that had come with CDs.

"Ha," she laughed, feeling affirmed. Wells, indeed, did not use cursive for his "ls."

And if it were her mother's handwriting, she would have never switched between script and cursive. Margaret Monasmith had the most elegant cursive handwriting of anyone she knew. If she were writing you a letter in cursive, the entire document would be written that way out of principle if nothing else.

"So, if you didn't write it," she said, as if Wells were sitting there in the room, "and Mom didn't write it..."

It was strange. The more Leslie looked at the handwriting, the more certain she was that it was her own. But how could that be possible? She had absolutely no memory of the photo before it had been given to her. She knew when he had taken it, of course, but that was only because she could remember the day he visited her for the last time. She read the line again.

When you're ready, think of me and imagine yourself doing backflips underwater.

She grabbed a notebook and pencil from her bedside table that she used to capture her dreams and flipped to an open page, and she rewrote the sentence. Leslie set the photo next to the freshly written words for comparison. If this were a court of law, she'd be guilty. The handwriting was hers.

She gaped at the words staring back at her, wondering how it could be possible. The answer was simple. She shook her head. It couldn't be hers. And regardless, what the hell did it mean?

Another warm, sweet breeze rolled through the window. Leslie closed her eyes and swore it tasted like honey; thick rolling honey that tumbles off the back of a spoon and rolls out in waves across butter melting on warm toast. She imagined the words written on the picture. She could see herself wading in a warm sea with golden, shimmering waves. She willed the woman in her vision to take a deep breath and push herself under the surface. Leslie could see the bubbles swarm around her like bumblebees made of glitter. She watched this version of herself all the while holding Wells in her mind. She forced the submerged girl to arch her back and drive her head backward. Her arms beat like wings in the water around her, and she tumbled in circles.

A rumbling sound, like driving on the highway with the windows down, began to fill Leslie's ears. She felt a shove on her back and snapped her eyes open. She looked all around and instead of her warm bedroom, she found herself in a chilly quiet apartment that looked very familiar. She saw a guitar standing next to a chair, a shelf packed with books, and to her left, a framed poem by Charles Bukowski. She was in her brother's apartment. On the coffee table were several stacks of papers and a large manila envelope next to a receipt for a Jimmy John's sandwich. Leslie looked at that date on the receipt. It read January 19th, 2020. Sometime between now and the twentieth, Wells would die.

"Oh my god," she said, not sure what she was seeing. She told herself it had to be a dream, but her senses seemed too alert.

She could smell strong coffee and goosebumps rose on her arms from the air of the chilly apartment. She was in one of her father's old T-shirts and a pair of shorts. Outside the window, the blue and gray light of a snow-covered parking lot sent another shiver up her neck.

She jumped when she heard the sound of a toilet flush and a running sink.

Oh no, she thought. *I'm trespassing. I need to get out of here before someone sees me. I need to wake up.*

But before she could move, the door to the bathroom opened and a man walked out, stopping at the sight of her.

"Leslie," Wells said, shocked to see his sister in the middle of his apartment. "What are you doing here?"

"Wells?" Leslie couldn't believe what was happening. This dream had moved from confusing to frightening and now was quickly approaching tormenting.

"I didn't hear you come in. And you're wearing shorts. In January." Wells wore a quizzical expression that turned to a smirk. "Is this like a 'walk of shame' sort of thing? I mean, I don't need the details or anything, but I'm just saying. Shorts? Really?"

"Wells," Leslie said. "You're..." She stood, mouth agape, staring at her brother. Wells looked tired and thin. He had dark bags under his eyes and faded stubble on his face.

"Are you alright, Leslie? Are you high or something?" Wells was now wavering between concern and suspicion.

"You're...you're..."

"I'm...in my own apartment which you seem to have broken into?" He thought another joke might get her to come clean about her sudden appearance.

"You're alive," Leslie said and took a step closer to her brother.

"Am I not usually?" He shook his head and looked around. "Here, let me get you something warmer to wear and I'll pour you some coffee." He started walking away but was stopped abruptly by Leslie who had thrown her arms around her brother from behind, clutching her hands to his chest.

"You're alive! I know this is a dream, but it feels so real." She was crying. In her arms, Wells felt as thin as he looked. The sweatshirt he was wearing didn't add much padding to his frame. He shrugged his shoulders and shook her off.

"Okay, seriously, what is wrong with you? And how did you get in? Mom doesn't even have a key."

"You told me to come," Leslie said, now smiling and wiping away tears. "You wrote it on the back of the polaroid you took of me that was with your biography. It just took me a while to figure out how to do it."

Something about these words put a serious expression on Wells' face. He squinted and started to really see her. He saw the soft tan on her skin and the summer clothes. He looked at the coffee next to his manuscript. He only just got back home from printing the copies. He was just about to staple it all together so it would be ready to give to his parents when they came over tomorrow.

"How do you know about that? Mom told you?"

"No. It was on the photo. The one you took of me while you stopped time, like you gave to each of us. You wrote about doing backflips underwater."

"So you know about our family thing? And how I stop time?" Wells was confused. He spent the entire fall with his parents trying to work through how to tell his sisters about this condition the family carries, and the day before he is about to hand over his story, his sister shows up and says she knows all about it.

"Yeah. We all know about it." Now Leslie was the one getting confused. Her tears had stopped. This dream was the strangest thing she had ever experienced. It was surreal, yet tangible. "We got the package at Mom and Dad's the day of your funeral."

Wells, who did not think this was a dream, was stunned. This strange visit was turning from a funny pop-in to a bad prank.

"Alright, Leslie, that's enough. How do you know about my manuscript?"

"I told you," Leslie didn't think she should have to re-explain things in her own dream. She bent down to the coffee table and found the stack of polaroids. She sifted through and found hers. She flipped it over to show him his words. When she did so, she found herself looking at the blank, white backing of a square photograph.

"It hasn't been written yet?" She was confused.

"What hasn't?" His patience was wearing thin. He was tired, weak, and annoyed. His head had been pounding since the morning, and it wasn't getting any better. What he really needed was a nap and not this bizarre interruption.

"Look, Leslie, I don't know what's going on. Yes, I do want to talk with you about this condition, but I don't think now is a good time. I…I had wanted Mom and Dad to help discuss it with everyone there. Maybe once you all get this, we can walk through it together. I know it's a lot to process, but we'll get there. I'll answer everything, I promise. But, honestly, I'm kinda feeling a bit low on energy today and was hoping to rest. I was going to give these to Mom and Dad tomorrow." He pointed at the stack of papers. "I guess you can take your copy if you want, now that you've already looked at it. And you're more than welcome to hang out for a bit. I just need to lie down."

Leslie sighed. He wasn't comprehending the situation.

"No, Wells. You. Are. Dead. But it doesn't matter because this is all a dream. You put those in the mail, and then you died. We had your funeral. And Monica is pregnant again. I mean, we came here and boxed up all your stuff. You wrote on the back of that letter for me to think of you when I was ready and imagine myself doing backflips underwater. I finally did it, and there was this rumble in my ears, and I must have fallen asleep because then I wound up here." She was rambling and now short of breath.

Wells stared at her intensely.

"A rumble in your ears," he repeated. He considered this. Leslie really did seem to think this was a dream, but what if it wasn't and she was telling the truth? He had always figured she would be the sister who might have more ability to control her time than the others, but what if she could do more than just slow or stop time? What if she could move through it?

"So, I die. Tonight?" he said hesitantly.

"Yeah, or maybe tomorrow, I guess." Leslie spoke extremely casually for someone who was just delivering a death sentence. "Wells, I'm so glad I get to talk to you like this, but this dream is so weird. Honestly." She laughed.

"Leslie," He spoke slowly, as if each word was fragile. "I don't think this is a dream."

Leslie searched her brother's eyes, and her smile slowly faded. Now she looked around the apartment as if the curtains had been pulled back and the clear winter sun was finally shining through. It was exactly as she had seen it before. If this was a dream, the titles of the books on his shelf would have been gibberish, and the photographs would have looked like vague shades of color. Thirty seconds ago, she couldn't fathom how this could be happening, but the longer she stood there with her skin tingling in the poorly heated room, smelling the fresh pot of coffee, and seeing her bother with such clarity, she began to believe it was really happening. She was actually in her dead brother's apartment, speaking to him in what could be some of his last hours alive. The blood rushed out of her head, and she began to feel as if she might pass out. She summoned her strength and backed up into the couch. The last thing she wanted now was to go unconscious and lose out on the opportunity to talk with her brother one last time. Wells walked over and sat beside her.

"How is this possible?" Leslie asked.

"I don't know. I can't move through time. I just stop it. As far as I know, that's what Mom and her brothers could do, too. None of this should be possible, but who's to say what's possible when it comes to our family, right?"

Color was coming back into Leslie's cheeks. She looked at her brother with a sudden realization.

"Wells, if I'm here, maybe I can save you. You are supposed to have a stroke at some point. We could go to the E.R., like, right now, and I'm sure they could save you somehow." She spoke with an intensity that brought tears to her eyes.

Wells was silent. He was thinking hard about the idea of trying to cheat death.

"I don't want to go to the hospital, Leslie," he finally said.

"Why not? Wells, don't you get it? You are going to die. Like, really soon. We could stop it." Leslie grabbed Wells' hand as she spoke. His skin felt thin and fragile. She didn't understand why he didn't understand her. His calm demeanor was unsettling. Wells took a deep breath before he spoke.

"The truth is, Leslie, I've known this was coming. In fact, this last week or so, I've been having spells again. Pretty frequently, in fact. I guess they are just more small strokes, but I've been thinking of them like the ticking on a clock, letting me know the bell will soon toll. So, I've been preparing for this. It's okay."

"Wells, it's not okay. I've been to your funeral. We've all read your manuscript. We came here and emptied the apartment, trying to figure out what happened to you and understand what this means for us. Heather still feels awful that she couldn't save you. Monica is pregnant and acting really strange, even for her. Mom and Dad," Leslie was having a hard time speaking through the sadness and urgency, "the funeral was really hard on them. This all has been so hard without you." She was crying now. "And I miss you. I can't find any good music without you around. I thought I was doing fine and accepting it, but now that I'm seeing you…I just don't want to lose you again."

Wells leaned over and hugged his sister. He held her while she cried into his shoulder. They sat like that for several minutes. As they sat there, he thought this was one of the most special moments he had ever had with Leslie. He smiled at the irony that it would take his death for them to have their best hug.

"So, even Monica read it?" Wells asked.

Leslie laughed.

"Yeah, hard to believe, but she did. I think she has even cut back on work a little. This new pregnancy has her acting a little different. She texted me the other day, and I can't remember the last time that happened."

"So Monica is really pregnant? I heard you say that but didn't believe it."

"She is. She told us not too long ago. She's due in a couple months. Well, in my time, that is. August or something. She's having a boy."

"Wow." Wells thought about the implications his story had for his oldest sister now that she was expecting a boy. "And Heather?"

"She's holding it together. I think she's really stepping into the matriarchal role of the family, just seeing how tired Mom gets, and I know she wishes she had reached out to you more. She doesn't want the family to drift apart like we have been doing over the last couple years. She's even planning a summer cabin getaway and making sure everyone can come. I'm pretty sure she is about to email Monica's hospital administrator to make sure she has the time off."

They both laughed. Leslie was feeling a little better, just like she always did when she got to talk to her brother.

"And what about you? You said you were doing okay?"

"Ugh, I don't know. I'm still trying to figure out what I want to do with my life. My lease is up soon. I was thinking about possibly going back to grad school. I like the idea of teaching, maybe college level, but I don't know."

"You should. You'd be a phenomenal teacher. You might still be able to pick up shifts in the bookstore."

It was funny. Wells' words weren't profound, but his encouragement carried no shade of doubt. His belief in her was empowering.

"Yeah," she said. "Maybe I will." Leslie's eyes shifted to an upper corner of the room, and she seemed to drift off to a place where she could see what that future might look like. The lines around her eyes softened, hinting to Wells that she liked what she saw from her vantage point.

"So, out of curiosity," Wells said, interrupting her daydream, "how exactly did you figure out how to get here?"

It took Leslie a moment to consider what she was doing before all of this happened, retracing her steps.

"Let's see. It's June, or it was, rather. I was sitting in my apartment looking at the photo and the words written on the back when I had the strangest feeling the handwriting was mine. It just didn't quite fit yours or Mom's. I grabbed my dream diary and wrote the sentence over and then closed my eyes, thinking of the words and you. Then there was this soft roar in my ears and sort of a shove. Then I was here."

Wells picked up the picture he was planning on giving to Leslie. He hadn't planned on writing anything on the back. He flipped it over and saw it was completely blank.

"What did the words say?"

"It said, 'When you're ready, think of me and imagine yourself doing backflips underwater.' Weird, huh?"

"Not really," Wells shrugged. "When I do it...when I purchase time...I have to sort of pull myself inward through my nose. Or at least that's how I think of it. It's similar, in a way." Wells looked at the picture of Leslie he was still holding in his hands. An idea occurred to him, and he grabbed a pen off the table. He handed it to Leslie.

"Here."

She took the pen and polaroid as Wells walked off to the kitchen. Leslie looked at the picture of herself wearing a happy expression. In the picture, her happiness made her look weightless. It had been a while since she felt like that.

"What should I do?" she asked.

"Make a move," Wells said. He had returned with two cups of coffee, steam swirling up like a dancing spirit, spinning around and disappearing into the air. Beautiful, then gone. "Put the pen to paper, Sis. It sounds like I need to head to the post office to make sure these get to you by the weekend, so I need you to put your finishing touches on that."

"I've had trouble making decisions like this lately. I guess I'm just afraid to move forward when I know things can be taken away so quickly."

Wells nodded, trying to think of a response.

"What kind of person would you rather be? One willing to take steps forward, even when the path is dark? Or the person who decides to close their eyes and wait until the sun lights up the path for you?"

Wells sipped his coffee. Leslie thought about this for a moment and then flipped the photograph over. She set it on her knee and scribbled the words that had become a mantra for her these last few months, not knowing what they meant. When she was done, she smiled at what she created. It looked exactly as she remembered it the first time she read the words.

"You know," she said, handing the picture and pen back to her brother. "It's kinda cool. I can come back anytime I want and see you now. I can keep you updated on how everyone is doing and what Monica names the new baby."

Wells stared at his sister and then at the stack of papers beside them. He realized he needed to write a note as well if he was sending this off in the mail today.

"No, Leslie. I don't think you should. And you shouldn't try to stop time either."

"What? Why not?" Leslie was slightly surprised and slightly offended by his rejection. "And why shouldn't I stop time? You know, since you've been gone, all I've wanted to do is talk with you again, and now I can, so of course I should come and see you."

Wells sighed, staring into his cup. After a few seconds contemplating his answer, he looked up at his sister whose eyes were again glistening with tears. This time, it was fear.

"It's like a cup of coffee, this life." Wells lifted his cup. "The height of the pour is the length of your life, you see? And that's a hard thing to change. I tried to, believe me, thinking I could control everything. But all I did was distill it down into a myriad of lonely experiences, experiences that I wasn't able to share with anyone. For most of us, I think life is like that Norwegian egg coffee they serve at Mom and Dad's church. It's more tea than coffee, you know? You could drink that all day and your blood pressure wouldn't rise more than a millimeter. Knowing what we can do, the temptation is to stop time and turn that cup into both a taller pour and a stronger brew, but when we stop time, we walk away from so much that the cup can never really fill up. It's the challenge we face with this affliction. I used to call it pausing time, but now I know it was a purchase. There was a cost. I think it is pretty safe to assume traveling through time has the same cost as stopping it does.

"Instead of filling up your life buying more time or escaping to update me on what I already know will be amazing experiences, consider strengthening your cup of coffee by being more present in each moment. Be thoughtful about your decisions. Feel the wind. Find the complexities in the flavors of your food. Put your phone down when someone you care about talks to you. By mindfully walking through your days and making intentional choices, your time will go by fast, but you'll be in awe of all that filled your cup."

Wells stopped, realizing his rambling had got him excited and he saw a few sparkling lights dancing in his vision. Leslie sniffed and wiped her nose with the shoulder of her t-shirt.

"You sound like one of those motivational books that Dad keeps by the toilet."

They laughed.

"I think it's time you go. You've probably stayed longer than you should."

Leslie resisted a little longer, but finally conceded, and she and Wells hugged for a long time. At some point during their hug, Wells wasn't sure how long, she disappeared from his embrace and his arms closed around himself. He finished putting his stories together, pairing the photos with each stack of papers. Then he grabbed a pen and began writing a note to his parents before heading to the post office.

Mom and Dad,
I have a feeling I won't be there when you tell them…

The End

ABOUT THE AUTHOR

David Loring Nash is an author and singer-songwriter from Southeast Minnesota. His works include the novel The Man in the Pines, a re-imagination of the legendary folk figure, Paul Bunyan. He was born in Rochester, Minnesota where he spent his childhood before attending Augsburg University. After college, he traveled the country for nearly a decade ultimately settling in La Crescent, Minnesota by way of Omaha, Nebraska and Norfolk, Virginia. He spends his free time daydreaming, writing, and chasing his children (David and Anna) and the outdoors with his wife, Sara.

ABOUT THE PRESS

Unsolicited Press is based out of Portland, Oregon and focuses on the works of the unsung and underrepresented. As a womxn-owned, all-volunteer small publisher that doesn't worry about profits as much as championing exceptional literature, we have the privilege of partnering with authors skirting the fringes of the lit world. We've worked with emerging and award-winning authors such as Shann Ray, Amy Shimshon-Santo, Brook Bhagat, Kris Amos, and John W. Bateman.

Learn more at unsolicitedpress.com. Find us on twitter and instagram.